The Thief
with the
Golden Heart

STEPHEN PHILLIPS

This story is a work of fiction. Any similarities to names, people, places are purely coincidental.

Cover art by Stephen Phillips. Graphics provided by depositphotos.com

Table of Contents

ACKNOWLEDGMENTS

A thank you to everyone who helped me put together the latest story, and those who provided the feedback and support to make it happen.

Chapter 1:
Happy Times and Stories

Among the shadows of the Forge, a cloaked figure approached a small pedestal. In one hand, she held a cloth bag. She opened it to reveal a crystal sphere, its surface giving a subtle glint in the light. It had been several months since the Raven Hunters were betrayed by one of their own. All of them did their best to recover from the damage and things were returning to normal. Selese had taken on the role in finding and retrieving dangerous or troublesome artifacts. The most recent was one she took with great satisfaction. The procurement was one challenge she couldn't turn away, and she now stood in the very forge she had fantasized about stealing that item from.

As she pulled the bag away, a small metal ring appeared from inside and Selese placed it onto the pedestal. She placed the small sphere on the ring before whispering words challenging to understand for anyone other than those who knew what they were. Her activity brought another shadow that darkened the light across the pedestal as it approached. As it entered the light from above, the figure of a man stopped beside her, his partially hidden smile approving her actions.

"Do you think a simple alarm spell will be enough to let us know if this moves anywhere, Selese?" the man asked.

Selese nodded before chiding him, "Raymond, you doubt me? I'm insulted." Her tone was filled with a mix of playful sarcasm and friendly warning.

Raymond huffed, giving a smile before saying, "I forgot. Once a thief, always a thief? Or at least think like one?"

Selese shook her head before looking at the man who was part of the Sanctuary itself. "It should be secure until the new area is built." Then, she turned away. "I can't believe that's even being debated. After what happened."

Raymond chuckled, remembering the breach of the Forge not so long ago. "That is what the Circle can be like." He looked at her. "And I think probably why you haven't joined their ranks. Forgiving your other previous transgressions, of course."

Selese cocked her head, an annoyed stare aimed toward him, "Really, Ray?"

Raymond smiled, "I know you have a good heart, Selese. Regardless of the past, you've endured. The rescue of this item itself is proof of that."

Selese nodded, "the Sphere of Lieben. I'm happy the other two were destroyed. Now, no one can be harmed by them."

Raymond could see her eyes looking out into the darkness across the Forge walls. He knew she was thinking of the man who saved her, Aiden Hoff. The old geomage had rescued her from the leader of the Broken Feather, Jeffrey Britlan.

Raymond, who ran the Sanctuary, remembered Britlan, one of the few remaining wraith mages. The mage had tricked Selese, promising to remove the magic she had inside her so she would no longer be hunted. The wraith mage had one of the three Spheres created for a single purpose: removing the essence from a living being. In doing so, its owner could use the husk left over for whatever purpose the desired. The rest of her family all suffered that fate because of superstition and greed. Britlan, instead, had removed Selese's heart, hoping to use her body as a vessel for the power hidden in the Effigy of Tarnus, the icon he had stolen. Aiden saved her, and destroyed the sphere Britlan held, but that never stopped the wraith mage from continuing his art.

In his bid to save Selese, Aiden quickly fashioned a heart made of gold for her while enduring an attack from the same man who tricked Selese. However, Aiden's endeavor took a heavy toll—his resolve the only thing saving her. But he used most of his energy to defend them. In the end, Aiden was so weak he had resorted to strangling Britlan with his bare hands to save her. Aiden was weakened and eventually lost his life.

2

Raymond sighed. Even though he didn't need air, his actions were still those of a man. He placed his hand on Selese's shoulder, telling her, "You were never truly a thief, not in a selfish way, Selese. I know others have seen you like that, but in my time as caretaker and as a warrior, I have seen very few who truly struggle to find their place." He watched Selese look at him with those dark eyes of hers. "Selese, you are not just a thief. You are an exceptional thief."

Selese gave a smile and a quiet laugh. She seemed to understand Raymond's joke.

"I know others still see you as what you were. As do I," Raymond said, watching Selese's expression turn to one of disappointed anger. But Raymond still smiled at her.

She knew not to be angry toward him. He had been conscious for several hundred years and didn't always say things in a clear, understandable fashion.

"I hope you meant that in a good way, Ray," Selese said.

The man nodded, "Of course. I see you as an exceptional thief, one who has survived what most could not, and of course, I believe that you've always had a heart of gold." He paused, "even before getting the one you have now. Your actions have proven that many times already."

Selese felt a warmth in her chest, where her heart used to be, the gold metal that now beat there feeling comforted. She looked up at him and smiled.

Raymond gave a humorous huff, "that is, of course, when you're staying out of trouble."

Selese laughed.

When the Forge quieted, she looked to the door. "We should probably make some place deeper than where this is now. Just in case something happens, like before."

Raymond nodded, understanding the reference to when their best hunter and trusted ally betrayed everyone, revealing himself to be in league with the Broken Feather.

"That is the plan. But we have other issues regarding the relics we are holding for the other sanctuaries. We cannot move quickly while they are entrusted to us."

Selese looked at him again, "I have a great design. Even I'd have trouble getting in. I can show you…."

She quieted, seeing Raymond raise his hand, "I do not believe you have time for that."

Selese looked around. There was no one in the Forge, so she turned to look at him, confused.

Raymond nodded, "You've grown a lot since you arrived, including gaining new friends. Which I believe is where you should be."

Selese thought for a moment and remembered, "Oh my gosh, it's the seventeenth." She smiled, asking, "What time is it?" She answered her own question by looking at her phone, the reminder for Amanda's birthday visible on the screen. "I have to get going. We'll talk later, Ray. I have to go get my gift."

Her voice faded as she ran out of the Forge. Raymond laughed as he closed the door behind her with a solid thud.

* * *

Amanda stared out the window as she sat at the large table. She was daydreaming. The last few years at school had been more challenging than any in her life. Nevertheless, she had done well with her classes, with only a semester or two left before graduating. She continued to work alongside the Raven Hunters, unofficially, of course.

Her concentration was interrupted as she spied Colleen port into the room from the shadow of the stairs. The long blonde hair of her friend hid the pointed ears beneath as she met with Selese, who had only arrived moments before. They both waved to Amanda. She looked around to see the room filled with friends and family as they wished her a happy birthday.

There was also the unmistakable smell of flowers, the forest, and food filling the air. And, after a bright flash, the atmosphere filled with birthday wishes within the noise of laughter and celebration.

Amanda smiled as the large cake decked out in an almost outrageous display was brought in. It was tall enough to block her from seeing the other end of the room. The light from above caused a shadow across the table beneath. There were many around wishing her the best for her birthday, as Luke stood beside her. Then, wrestling the crowd, he leaned down to say something to her.

"I don't think I had this many people at the party when I turned twenty-two," Luke said, giving her a well-aimed kiss on her lips before sitting next to her. "I don't think I had this many people in all my birthdays." Luke grabbed the drink he had placed on the table earlier.

Amanda looked around, a wide smile on her face at seeing everyone. Humans, elves, fairies, and an array of others, magic and non-magic, stirred about. It was magical in more ways than one. Amanda leaned into Luke as he pulled her close, her eyes again taking in all those who came to wish her well. She spied Linda bringing in some more candles. As her friend held them out, several fairies scooped them from her hands, placing them on the cake before Amanda. Linda snapped her fingers, and the candles all lit at once.

"Where did you learn that?" Amanda asked with excited curiosity.

Linda smiled before telling her, "Scotland, enchanted candles. They light with a snap." She again snapped her fingers, and the flames that danced on their wicks grew. Their new light brightened the table before Amanda. Her wonder was only broken by the ringing of a phone, and Amanda felt the familiar sensation of her valued communication device in her pocket. She removed it and her eyes went wide with panic.

"It's my parents," she said her voice frenzied.

Linda motioned, yelling for everyone to quiet, but the celebration continued. She looked to Ron, who put his fingers to his lips and gave a loud whistle. Its sound bounced from the walls all around.

"Okay, everyone, quiet!" Ron yelled.

As the room fell silent, Amanda answered the call, the video of her parents appearing on the small, cracked screen. "Hi, Sweetie, Happy Birthday!" her mother said excitedly, Amanda looking embarrassed.

Her father waved, saying, "Sorry we couldn't be there. We're both stuck at the terminal at O'Hare."

Amanda had already known they wouldn't make it to the party. For the last couple of years, she had gone home for her birthday but decided to stay at school for this one. Her parents had given up the house in New York and headed out west. Both of their jobs brought them work around the world. She missed them but knew they loved her. But Amanda still hid the knowledge of what else was at the school. As she spoke with her parents, a fairy floated behind Amanda's head, and Ron raised his brows as the small, winged wonder moved to the side. *How did they not see that?* Ron thought, looking at Linda. His wife, seeing his questioning stare, whispered to him, "Roween enchanted her phone. It only shows humans."

Ron whispered back, "Too bad she can't enchant it not to break. She's been through, what, eight phones since she started here?"

Ron's words made Linda laugh before she held up a small, colorfully wrapped box, and she replied, "What do you think this is for?"

There was a confused look from Amanda's parents on the small screen as the girl's mother watched Ron and Linda. "Is she behaving herself?" she asked in a humorous but motherly tone.

Ron looked around as if not acknowledging her question before smiling and nodding. "Oh, you want me to answer?" Ron mocked before telling her parents, "Yeah, she's been boring. We've seen her doing nothing dangerous since we got here a few weeks ago. It's been quiet since Linda started the seminar for literary businesses." His statement prompting a confused look from his wife.

Amanda turned to look at Ron for clarification. Her friends had come up at the request of the Raven Hunters and Selese to work on some theories about recent thefts of artifacts nearby. But, seeing his glare which expressed, *get back to the call*, Amanda understood he was improvising. A minute passed as she spoke with her family, and Linda could see the large flames from the candles starting to melt the icing on the cake.

"I hate to interrupt, but the candles are melting the cake," Linda said, and Amanda interrupted her parents. Within moments, the room filled with a fumbled rendition of "Happy Birthday," and Amanda blew out the candles.

Everyone cheered, and as she started talking to her parents, Ron heard her mother say, "No drinking, you're still too young." He jokingly turned, holding a bottle of rum behind Amanda, pointing to it. He then pointed to Amanda, holding the bottle as if guzzling from it. Seeing the look of complete disbelief from her father, Ron unscrewed the top and grabbed a glass; he tipped the bottle, and nothing happened. So Ron mockingly tried again and looked into the open top of the bottle. But when he shook it, it looked genuine.

Amanda then heard her father say, "It's one of those trick bottles. It's magic or something, right?" Making Amanda turn around in horror to see Ron smiling back.

She grabbed the bottle and shook it without the cap, and nothing happened. Finally, she turned to see her parents laughing. Ron took the bottle from her, placing the top back on. "Don't worry, trick bottle. We'll keep an eye on her." Ron stepped away to help Linda with the cake as Amanda finished her call with her parents.

He could hear, "We love you. Happy birthday sweetie."

Amanda hung up and turned to see Luke examining the bottle. He unscrewed the cap and started to pour it into the small glass. He was startled as the fluid inside started to escape. Then, in a panicked jerk, he tipped the bottle up, spilling some.

"Easy kid, that's the expensive stuff," Ron said as he handed the small shot glass to Linda. Before pouring himself another.

Luke looked on in awe. "Magic rum bottle? Where did you pick that up?"

Ron smiled back, "Barbados, got a case of them from an adept down there. Brilliant man, these only work for the people you trust, who are old enough, or when you want it to pour."

"I'll have to start hanging out with you two more often." Luke's words brought a frosty stare from Amanda. His survival instincts kicked in as he turned to her to say, "along with you, of course." His eyes stared into Amanda's.

Linda walked by, putting her hand on Luke's shoulder, whispering, "Smooth save," causing Amanda to burst out laughing before Linda handed her a piece of cake.

The night went on, and Amanda enjoyed the feeling of everyone around her wishing her well. It had been a few hours, and guests had already left. Only a few remained. Linda sat in the chair, giving a subtle groan as she relaxed.

"That was a lot of work." She looked over to see Ron slowly sliding comfortably into his chair, a look of exhaustion showing on his face.

Ron looked over to her, "You know, we've had some fun times, but I don't remember them being this tiring."

Linda nodded as she took a small present from the table and tossed it to Amanda, "You missed one."

Amanda almost missed catching the small package, causing it to bounce into the air a few times before grasping it firmly. When she read who it was from, she looked up. "You guys didn't have to get me anything."

Linda smiled, "Oh, I think we had to get you this. It even has something special attached to it."

Amanda opened the small package to find a new phone case, but it seemed different. It was soft, not like the hard cases she had purchased before. She looked at Linda as she held the floppy case in her hand. Linda, however, smiled, seeing her confusion.

"It's a case. It'll protect your phone," Linda told her as she sipped her drink.

Amanda looked uncertain, and Ron huffed, "Maybe we should show her."

Linda nodded and asked Amanda to hand over her phone while Ron left for a moment. When he returned, Amanda gave him a strange look, seeing him wearing a full-face shield, and carrying a sledgehammer and a dustpan. Linda removed the girl's old case and slipped on the new one. As it seated, the case snugged against the phone, becoming solid.

Linda looked at Ron as she placed the phone on the floor, "You two may want to hold on for this."

Both Amanda and Luke stared, confused, as Ron pulled back the sledgehammer with a full swing and brought it down on the phone. Then, the world stopped, and Amanda felt her heart skip as the head of the hammer reached the fragile glass screen.

Suddenly there was a shower of metal dust and wooden splinters as the head of the hammer fractured and the handle split. The phone, however, sustained no damage. Ron picked it up, shaking off the remnants of the tool he once held, and brushed off the metal shards, handing it to Amanda. She hurriedly whisked it from his hand to inspect it. But, again, there was no damage whatsoever. She looked to Linda to see her friend giggling as Ron swept up what remained of the hammer.

Amanda heard Ron say, "It'll handle just about anything you can throw at it. Roween helped with it. She enchanted the sleeve to protect your phone." Ron turned to place the dust in the trash before continuing, "You can use it on any phone. So, when you upgrade, you won't have to get another."

Luke gently pulled Amanda's phone from her hand as she silently looked toward Ron. He shook his head, "Too bad you only made one. This could be useful."

Linda chuckled, "Oh, she's the last to get that. Ron and I have had something like that for a while now. We talked about it when we came back from the Keep. We both had to get new phones after that magic magnetic doorway pulled them away from us."

Ron laughed as his wife continued, "The doorway attracted all items that produce light, especially if made of metal. It drains the light leaving the item worthless."

Amanda looked between the two friends, "Wait, I don't remember that. When did we have that adventure?"

Linda looked at Amanda, "You were in school. That doesn't mean we haven't been busy. The Hunters aren't the only people helping protect magic artifacts." Linda seemed to think for a moment. "Although, it would have been nice to have some backup on that trip." She leaned in toward Amanda. "We both were stuck in a bog for an hour. We took a wrong turn trying to evade the local authorities."

Hearing the last statement, Selese joined the others in listening to the story. She whispered a happy birthday to Amanda, handing her a small package.

"That's from me. It's not much, but, hey," Selese said as Amanda unwrapped the package. She opened the box to see three bandanas in different colors. Amanda looked at her friend.

Selese smiled, "Remember that place we went to about seven months ago?"

Amanda nodded, saying, "You're not talking about that children's ball pit thing, are you?"

Selese nodded, giving a devilish smile, "You looked so embarrassed when you realized those people were watching us."

Amanda did remember. It caused her to snicker. "I felt so stupid reaching down into those gross old plastic balls. I wanted to hide my face." She pointed to Selese and muttered, "And it was dusty. Could have used a mask."

Selese nodded, "Well, now you have something that can be both." She chuckled. "And you can look like a bandit doing it." She then patted

Amanda on the shoulder before looking at Ron and remarking, "I want to hear the rest of that story. It sounds like you two were getting into trouble."

Ron gave a smile along with a snort.

Luke said, "You mean you were almost caught doing something illegal?"

Linda smiled, "Not illegal, but we weren't authorized to be there either."

The young man nodded, "Right, not like the Raven Hunters have been in a spot like that before."

Ron and Linda agreed, smiling at his innuendo.

"The good news is that the spell is powerful enough that you can even use your phone as a shield. I found that out by accident," Linda said.

Amanda looked to her friend, seeking more information and feeling a little left out that they had been on adventures without her. Instead, she listened as Linda spun her story.

"We were in a circular room. The walls lined with suits of armor. We realized we were in trouble when we made it toward the center."

Luke sat forward, "What happened?"

Linda continued, "Well, we were asked to investigate a missing enchanted spear. No one told us that the spear was part of an entire room of enchanted armor. I was looking for a map on my phone when I turned to see a blade coming toward me. I held my phone up to protect myself and discovered it could be used as a shield."

Amanda looked horrified at the thought that her friend had been in mortal danger with nothing but a phone to protect her. Luke also showed concern but asked, "If the room was full of armor, then how did you escape? Besides, I've read that no one enchants armor anymore. It hasn't been done for ages."

Ron answered this time, "Whoever set the trap wasn't really thinking about it. At least in my opinion. So, the entire group of armor moved in unison and kept in a circle. If you push one down into the armor next to it, they fall like dominos." Ron took a drink, "We only found out later from our contact that the armor didn't attack all at once because we weren't carrying weapons. It turns out it's been a deterrent for accidental visitors for over four centuries."

Luke and Amanda looked at Ron in disbelief.

Ron smiled, "But if I had been holding the spear, we probably wouldn't be speaking right now."

Although it seemed he was making a joke, Amanda knew otherwise. Ron tried keeping things safe for everyone, including himself, and that adventure almost cost them their lives. He told them that they hadn't gone on many adventures since. At least not without help from others.

Luke became curious, "What others? The Hunters?"

Ron bowed his head, "The Raven Hunters aren't the only game out there. It turns out there are organizations not quite as large. A bunch of smaller ones too. Personally, neither of us is really a team player, but we've made friends around the world with others like us."

"So, do you have a name?" Selese asked.

Her question caused Ron to drag his hand down his face, "No, Selese. There is no team. Look, Amanda, we've been keeping some of our adventures secret from you for a good reason."

Amanda felt hurt but turned to see the caring concern in Linda's eyes. She looked back to Ron as he spoke.

"I mentioned that there are other groups out there. And not all of them are understanding. Some, we found out the hard way, are fine with working alongside groups like the Broken Feather."

"What?" Selese yelled, startling Shrive, who was devouring a burger and was now by her side.

She asked, "What'd I miss?"

Ron laughed, "Look, this is a party. None of you should be worrying about any of this. It would be best if you were enjoying yourselves. All I'm saying is that there are others out there like the Raven Hunters. Just be on the lookout for them."

Ron stood and looked around the room to see only a few people remaining, "Now come on. It looks like the party's winding down." He pointed to Shrive and Selese, "You and you can help us clean up."

Amanda watched as the others started cleaning up. Luke stayed with her. She looked into his brown eyes and said, "I can't believe they told us that story."

Luke moved closer, "They're just being protective. And it probably has something to do with that overseas agent meeting tomorrow."

"What meeting?" Amanda asked him.

Luke bowed his head, "They've come over to ask for a consultation with Selese. She's doing the job for free. Can you believe it?"

"Why didn't she tell me?" Amanda seemed hurt by his reveal, but Luke moved closer.

"Amanda, she doesn't even know what it's about yet," Luke told her.

"So, how did you find out?" Amanda asked.

Luke smiled and said, just before he kissed Amanda, "I overheard it. Only top hunters are in the loop. Besides, you're not a Raven Hunter."

As his lips pulled back from the kiss, Amanda whispered, "You're right. I'm not a hunter, at least not yet."

Linda smiled, seeing the two of them together. She waved Ron over before saying, "Maybe she can have somewhat of a normal life."

Ron nodded, then replied, "That's if she is lucky. She always seems to find a way to get into some kind of trouble."

Chapter 2:
Witch's Endeavor

At the estate of Temperance Hastings, a woman stood staring at an old oil portrait while two lawyers sat at the desk behind her. The picture was of the matron from over two hundred years ago. The estate lawyer looked up, seeing her viewing the painting, and could see the familial resemblance, "You are the spitting image of her. It's remarkable."

Allison smiled, responding, "Yes, Mr. Donnelly, it's quite a resemblance."

She then turned to finish signing the papers.

Mr. Donnelly noticed that she hesitated when picking up the pen before switching to her other hand. But as she signed the papers, he took more interest in the fact that she did not contest the articles or the fees he was charging.

"Too bad no one's seen Temperance Hastings for the last several years," the lawyer said. "And to think she found you all on her own. It is truly amazing; we hadn't even known she was looking for an heir," Donnelly said.

The bastard probably thought the money would go to his firm so they could divide it up. I'm still waiting for them to contest the will, Allison thought as she signed the last page. "I didn't even know she was alive. I'm thankful I had Mr. Mitchell here to help guide me through all this."

Her lawyer inspected the pages, ensuring everything was accurate, before handing them to Mr. Donnelly. The man viewed the paperwork and made some notes before placing them into his portfolio. He passed a card to the woman, "As of now, you, Mrs. Allison Thomson, are the full and legal heir of Mrs. Hasting's holdings and estate." He looked to the woman and her lawyer before saying, "Mrs. Thompson, it has been a pleasure handling your, ahem, great aunt's estate. I hope we may continue to do business in the future."

Allison gave a smile. It was well practiced and hid her disdain toward the man before her. The woman's lawyer, sensing the tension, immediately stepped in. He rose, holding out his hand, saying, "Thank you, Sean. I'm sure Mrs. Thompson would be happy to discuss future dealings at another time."

The other lawyer stood and paused before walking around the desk. Mitchell spoke, "I'm sure she is devastated in learning that her great aunt has passed. And as her current representative, I'm sure there will be another time to discuss things." The man not-so-gently pushed the other lawyer toward the door as he closed his case. Allison stood, her face suddenly sullen as if in reflection.

The lawyer looked at her and nodded, "Of course. Please let me know if my firm or I can be of any future assistance."

Mr. Mitchell followed the man and led him to his vehicle, returning less than a minute later. He entered the room to see Allison again staring at the picture before walking to the window to watch Donnelly drive away.

"That is a good likeness. I forget, where did you have that painted?" Mr. Mitchell asked.

Allison sighed, "Lomazy. I believe it was around 1860. Mariusz was quite an artist." She paused, giving a sensual grin, "In more ways than one. Mack, remind me to have a new one commissioned. That canvas is looking a bit ratty," Allison said as she sat in the chair behind her desk. Her hand was resting on the small packet of papers. "You know it is becoming difficult to continue doing business in this fashion. I fear technology is catching up with us," she said as she motioned for the man to sit.

Allison placed her chin on her interlaced hands as she leaned forward on the desk before giving another small sigh as she looked to the empty spot on the shelf to her right. "How long have you been in my employ, Mack?"

The man raised his head in thought, "About seventy-four years. You're not planning on replacing me, are you?"

Allison shook her head, "No, of course not. I was thinking about how to be ready for our next changeover." She leaned back. "You know how I like to be prepared." Allison sighed again, her eyes showing concern, "It is getting difficult to stay anonymous. I may have to change bodies this time."

Mack looked toward the door, his voice straining to sound practical, "You have the girl. Why not do it now?"

The woman looked despondent, saying, "Humph, her energy is still young. She's too strong to make the switch. She would fight too hard. Unless I had help, of course."

Her lawyer looked back at her, "So? Break her like you did the others you told me about."

Allison huffed, "Even if I were up to it, the sphere of Lieben would still be needed to make the transfer."

Mack responded, "Why not make another?"

Allison sounded almost defeated as she spoke, "I would need to find an alchemist I trust. Besides, the loss of 3,000 people would stand out. In the old days, it was so much easier to sacrifice peasants."

Mack had a grin of practicality as he spoke, "Then you plan on stealing it back?"

He had been in her employ, as well as having been her confidant, for some time. He had also gained a lot of wealth from their exploits. Mack knew that his employer needed to work through her plans. She would always have a way out of a situation; he knew her true nature. She was a cold, calculating witch with powers he didn't understand. But that didn't matter to him. He accepted everything she was as long as she allowed him to share in some of her power.

Mack's attention was drawn to the gold chain around his wrist, the metal still gleaming as if it was made yesterday, along with himself. By wearing it, he had been given eternal youth, enhanced strength and mental prowess, fast healing, and of course, magic. *Who cares if the price was some unimportant person having to die to give me this long life.* To him, it was a winning combination, the bracelet that gave him vitality and magic he used to win many court cases, making him highly successful. The only thing he had to do to receive such a gift was to offer his undying loyalty to the woman who now called herself Allison Thompson.

The woman rose to walk around the room, her eyes taking in every memory she had of the artifacts. She removed a book and held it before her. As she opened it, a small spirit appeared, its mist-like shadow emanating from the pages. Allison whispered a few words, and the small spirit nodded and dissipated as its essence moved in all directions. Seconds later, the windows glowed as the shadow touched the glass. Mack looked around, hearing no sound from outside. He looked back at her as she spoke.

"You never know who may be listening," Allison said as she tapped the book cover, its old wording glowing at each touch, the word *lietonis* clearly visible. "That ought to make some ears bleed." She knew magic well. Her long time on the planet had taught her many wonderous and sinister things. Yet, her thoughts were not even focused on the small spirit she released. She knew full well the book she handled and the essence of the howling spirit that now served her whims.

She looked over her shoulder toward Mack, "Did we ever hear from the Feather on the acquisition of the *tianqiu*?"

Mack nodded, "The essence contained was able to be extracted. Although I don't know how you would use it. It was only the spirit of a feudal warrior. The coven couldn't even control it. The vial and *tianqiu* should be here in a few days."

Allison snorted, "Useless amateurs. We're fortunate they were able to contain it at least."

The man nodded, making Allison smile.

"I'll deal with my new toy when it arrives." She gave a lascivious smile toward Mack. "Warriors are so much fun to dominate and so useful."

She placed the book back on the shelf and touched the edge of the frame, making the case move to expose a hidden door behind. The dull metal of the entry covered in thousands of engraved symbols; Mack could swear that some of them were changing as he stared. When Allison touched the metal, there was a loud clunk, and light exploded from around its edges.

"What's next?" Mack asked as Allison again turned to look at the empty shelf. Allison took a moment to answer. Then, she turned and slowly headed toward the empty shelf.

"Did you find out which one of those cursed hunters took it?" Allison said with a slight growl before stroking her earring.

"The *sphere of Lieben*?" Mr. Mitchell nodded. His mistress referred to the item now recently missing. "We know the hunter was a shape-shifter. They have a few in the Sanctuary, but not many who could get through your protection spells. However, it may be difficult to try and steal it back. The entire town, including that school, are surrounded by those accursed light towers."

"Taking a life was much easier when I had the sphere." Allison stroked her earring before looking perplexed and annoyed. "Hmm. Mack, where is she? She's not responding."

The woman continued to hold onto her earring and spoke several words. Within seconds, a howl of pain from a young woman emanated from the rear of the mansion. Allison turned to Mack. "Go find my doll, would you? And tell her to come." Allison's stare became heartless, "We have some business to discuss."

The man jumped from his chair, "Of course, mistress. I can finalize the paperwork later."

Allison nodded as Mack exited the room before she looked in the mirror on the wall, creases now showing around her eyes. She watched as her wrinkled skin again became smooth and supple. She returned to her desk, and within seconds a young woman, seeming to shiver from pain, was shoved into the room by Mack. Allison gave a single wave and he closed the door, remaining outside. The young woman stood, seeming conflicted, almost as if trying to run but unable as Allison stared at her.

"My dear Gina, if you persist in fighting me, you will outlive your usefulness," Allison said coldly.

The young woman looked away before Allison pointed to the chair. The young woman obeyed and sat, making the witch smile, "Now, Gina, I have a job for you." Gina raised her eyes, a hint of fear poking through the glasslike stare she displayed. The thoughts behind them were of flight, but as the older woman again stroked her earring, any semblance of mutiny disappeared from Gina's eyes.

"Now, my pretty little doll, I have good news for you." Behind the young woman, the large metal door from earlier could be heard creaking open.

Allison smiled as she looked toward Gina, "I'm sending you back to school. Come, we have some preparation to do."

* * *

In the Sanctuary, Selese shivered, making Shrive ask if she was cold. Selese joked, "No, probably someone thinking about me."

Shrive smiled, "That happens more than you know."

Selese smiled before realizing what her friend had said, "Wait, what?"

Shrive laughed and, shaking her head, said, "I can't believe you're doing this job without getting paid."

Selese leaned back, "They were having too much trouble trying to find the items. But, when I overheard, it sounded like a good challenge." Then she looked down, "Besides, Li Xiu is the daughter of the current Regent Zu. And he was a friend of Aiden Hoff."

Shrive looked suspiciously at Selese, "Does she realize you know who she is?"

Selese shook her head.

Shrive's eyes softened as she looked at her friend. Of course, Selese wasn't always this way, but helping out the daughter of a friend of the man that made her gold heart did seem fitting.

It was a short while later and in one of the offices of the Raven Hunters that the representative of the Sanctuary in China, Li Xiu, stood reserved but attentive as the three of them worked through the information about the recent theft of a *tianqiu* on loan from the Chinese facility. Xiling Snow Mountain had been its previous location. It had taken years for the museum in England to convince them it would be safe. Although it never made it to the museum. Instead, it disappeared within the archive back in its homeland. The Sanctuary had been called in because those guarding it were turned into clay dolls. It was something they hadn't seen before.

"Any ideas on how they broke in?" Shrive asked before looking toward Li Xiu, who remained emotionless.

Selese stared into space. She couldn't see any sign of easy entry, let alone an exit. The local version of the Sanctuary in the United States had protected its archives some time ago. It would have taken a master sorcerer to even attempt to get in. She was perplexed and turned to see Shrive staring at her.

"What?" Selese asked.

Shrive shrugged, "Nothing?"

Selese became annoyed and swiped the file toward her friend, gently tapping her square on the nose. As Selese stomped away, flopping in the chair nearby, Shrive mockingly rubbed her nose.

"It's not like I can just magically snap my fingers and reveal how they did it," she huffed at Shrive, who picked up the papers from the floor. Selese then looked to Li Xiu, and a curious expression filled her eyes. "Is this all the information from the theft?"

Li Xiu straightened but said nothing.

Selese smiled, "So the answer is no."

Li Xiu looked insulted at the insinuation and was about to respond when Selese suddenly stood before her, making her step back. The small metal coins Li Xiu carried for their magic and protection jingled on their string as Selese leaned close. Selese lifted her hand and lightly waved in front of her before pointing to Li Xiu.

"I'm not accusing you of holding information from us." Selese paused, then looked repentant as if to concede, "Actually, I am. Sorry. But the more information we have, the better we can help."

Li Xiu straightened again, "You are the thief. Not me."

Selese nodded, "Right. And you asked for this thief's help."

The frustration and suspicion from everyone in the room would have melted a glacier, but the stalemate was broken when Shrive asked, "Can we make copies of these?"

Li Xiu nodded and Shrive spoke a few words. Within seconds, another stack of papers separated from the original, and a duplicate file appeared on the desk. She handed the originals back to Li Xiu and held on to the others. Selese looked toward Li Xiu and could see she was wrestling with something; *she isn't telling us everything.* There was a minute while Selese paced around the room. Li Xiu fought back a yawn while looking at the clock, which already read 1 a.m.

"Perhaps we should continue this in the morning," Li Xiu said.

Selese looked at her, fighting back another yawn, and apologized, "If you're tired, we'll continue this in the morning. I don't sleep much."

Li Xiu again looked insulted and became more resolved. She looked at Shrive, who only spoke, pointing to Selese, saying, "I like to sleep. I Just don't get too much when she's around." Li Xiu fought back a smile.

Selese looked annoyed and motioned for the files Shrive held, and she again looked through them. She flipped through the pages and stared at the copy before her. Selese's gaze became transfixed before her eyes and mouth went wide. Li Xiu could see the hint of a smile appear as Selese cocked her head toward her. Selese muttered, "Secured building, nothing can be ported out. All items would have been found when exiting due to searches." Selese slammed the file shut, shaking it before her. She looked toward Li Xiu and smiled.

"Not everything on the case is here, that's for certain," Selese said. Li Xiu again appeared insulted.

Selese chuckled as she walked up to Li Xiu, "I understand that you don't trust me. But the more information I have, the better I can help. It's not like I'm asking for any money here." She pulled a paper from the file and held it up to Li Xiu. "You didn't mention a piece of paper was left in its place."

Li Xiu seemed stunned. *How did she know that?*

Selese watched as Li Xiu fought to contain her amazement. She then shook the paper again. "The person who took the item was the investigator. They probably didn't even know they did all the work for the thief."

With disbelief, Li Xiu shook her head and said, "You mean a transmutation spell was used?"

Selese nodded, "Simple, early-user spell. Well, as long as you don't fold the paper in half. Then, all you'd have to do would be to change it back."

A look of disgusted disbelief fell over Li Xiu's face. Like many other investigators, she had wondered why the investigation files were rifled through at the ministry. However, nothing seemed to be missing, though there were a few pages out of sequence. She mentioned that fact to Selese.

Selese smiled, "All they'd have had to do was make a photocopy, put the original in their file, and walk out with it."

Li Xiu could feel the awkwardness of overlooking the simple explanation. She looked to Selese and could see her staring back with eyes of concern. She didn't have to ask, as Selese offered some consolation.

"I had thought about using that same trick before when planning a job." Selese seemed to be disheartened as she continued. "I was always afraid I'd be caught that way. I like being direct when it comes to stealing. Too many people blame you for everything if they think it's you but don't know for sure."

Selese smiled apologetically, "Making a copy is fine, but transforming it back should have allowed a simple finding spell to locate it." Li Xiu nodded, making Selese say, "My guess is it's probably been destroyed. I'm sorry."

A practiced smile appeared on Li Xiu's face, "That would explain our inability to locate it." Then, she paused briefly. "I'll inform my superiors of what you've surmised."

Selese smiled, "Wait 'til morning. You look tired. Maybe get some sleep first."

Li Xiu tilted her head, looking at Selese. "Why would you care? You're a thief."

Shrive stepped forward but stopped when Selese held her hand up, giving Shrive a friendly, "Easy there, cat girl, I can handle this myself."

Selese sighed, "I am a thief, or was, and a damn good one. But that was before. I'm not the same person now." She looked to Shrive. "I've had some friends show me I'm much more than just a thief."

The woman looked back to Selese, "Perhaps you're right. Informing them after I am rested would be best."

Selese smiled, nodding in agreement before saying. "Good. And when you're rested, maybe we can show you around town if you like. I understand it's your first time on an assignment outside your homeland."

Li Xiu nodded. She had been ordered to work with the Raven Hunters and those in the Sanctuary but was told not to trust them. Li Xiu began to understand why her superiors insisted they reach out to the Sanctuary, and especially to this former thief for help. Selese had gained a reputation. Even without much information, she had already solved several thefts, including this one. And for each one she had asked for little or no compensation. Li Xiu had already known that a finding spell didn't work. If the object had been transmuted and returned to its original state, the *tianqiu* would have been located. The conclusion that it was probably destroyed was now a viable answer.

The agent yawned, no longer hiding the fact that she was exhausted. She looked to see Shrive fighting back sleep as she stood behind the padded chair on her right. Li Xiu looked to see Selese still looking over the paperwork. Her sense of duty was now being challenged, but as she went to step forward, her feet snagged the shallow carpet. Li Xiu felt herself tumbling toward the ground and was surprised to find a soft landing as the padded chair slid to break her fall.

Selese looked up from the desk, "You both look exhausted. You should get some sleep."

Shrive agreed as Li Xiu positioned herself in the chair, "I'm fine. If you can keep going, then I can."

Selese smiled, "It's night, and you're not me. I'm part darkling. We don't sleep much." Selese's manner changed to a more caring tone, "This isn't a competition. This can wait till morning." She then stretched and placed the papers in the top drawer. "Li Xiu, we can finish this up tomorrow. Besides, it'll give us a chance to show you around." Selese said as she walked around the desk. "We're not as bad as your people may think. When protecting magic and humans, we're all the same."

Li Xiu nodded, saying, "Tomorrow then?"

Shrive joined them, "Tomorrow. Let's not make it too early. I want to get some good sleep in." Li Xiu watched Shrive push Selese, making the thief smile as she placed her hands on the desk mockingly to support herself.

The agent nodded and, seemingly unsure, said, "Tomorrow, about 10 a.m.?"

Selese nodded, "Fine with me. Shrive?"

Shrive nodded, "We'll meet here and then head out. You can update your people first if you like."

Li Xiu nodded, and she walked toward the shadow of the large bookshelf, disappearing with a wave. Shrive looked at Selese, saying, "She doesn't trust us."

Selese nodded, "It's alright. I'm sure she'll understand we're all on the same side."

She then walked toward the shadow and said, "Turn the lights off when you leave. I'm going out to have some fun."

Shrive suddenly found herself alone and shook her head. "Try not to get into too much trouble." She then walked to the door and turned the light off; a catlike human figure appeared for a split second in the moonlight before disappearing into the remaining shadows.

Chapter 3:
A Thief's Mind

It was almost 2 o'clock when Li Xiu entered the same office she had left during the early morning. Selese was sitting in the chair, nearly motionless, reading the paperwork from yesterday. The entire file was now strewn across the desktop. As Li Xiu approached, she was startled when Selese, not even looking up, asked, "How'd you sleep?"

The woman paused for a moment before answering, "Very well. Thank you." She moved closer, "Have you been up all night looking over the case?"

Selese nodded, saying, "I came back early. I'm looking for an answer. Something in here is bothering me."

Li Xiu stared at the papers across the desk. They seemed to be in no particular order. But when she went to take one, Selese yelled, "Stop! You'll mess up my train of thought. Just wait a minute. I'm almost done."

The woman continued taking the paper from the desk, making Selese smile. "Hmm, not afraid of me, are you?"

Li Xiu cleared her throat before she spoke, "No. I have no need. I'm trained to defend myself from even the most adept assassins." The woman was startled as Shrive suddenly appeared behind her as she faced off with Selese. Her eyes were drawn from the one she knew as a thief now facing the blueish-green eyes of a predator. Li Xiu didn't stop Shrive as she tugged the paper from her grip.

Shrive looked at the paper, her words ringing with a warning as she spoke, "How many times have you faced someone who actually tried to kill you?"

Li Xiu looked back with annoyance, "I've never had to. My training has kept them away."

Shrive smiled, "You're lucky. That's good. I hope it stays that way." Then, Shrive looked at Selese and said, "Sorry, I'm late. I slept a bit longer than I anticipated. So, what'd I miss?"

Li Xiu looked sternly toward her feline-themed host, "We've been looking over the files. Did you come up with anything about why they may have taken the *tianqiu*?"

Shrive looked at the page. She shook her head before apologizing for being late again.

"No need. She got here just before you. You're fashionably late. We can work on this all together now," Selese said, bringing a stern glare from Li Xiu.

Selese slid from her chair to the two looking at the page Shrive held. She showed them the page she was examining. And the mention of the traces of gold and iron found smudged on the paper left at the security office.

"Traces of gold, silver, and iron on the paper, but no magic was found. What does that tell you?" Selese asked.

Shrive shrugged as Li Xiu stared at the page, her mind working as fast as possible. She didn't understand what Selese was getting at and looked up to see the woman staring back. The look in Selese's dark eyes was one of inspiration.

"Gold is a mutable element. Silver is used in human magic, but the iron…. that I don't know," Li Xiu said

Her actions brought an elated huff from Selese, "You're good. You know your magic. I've been thinking this through, and I can only think of one thing that might have happened." She paused, "or at least one thing I would have done."

Li Xiu looked to Selese to explain.

Selese smiled as she spoke, "They changed the relic to a picture. Then they took their time to extract what was inside that at the security station. Probably in the lab while they were testing. With all of the spells and devices working, no one would be able to tell what they were doing."

Li Xiu looked down before returning to Selese, and an air of insult showed in her stare, "You mean you think one of my people did this?"

Selese nodded.

"I do not believe you. What makes you so sure that the essence of what was contained in it was transferred?" Li Xiu responded.

"Let's say I'm very familiar with what's needed to transfer essences," Selese replied.

Selese's voice was filled with frustration and anger, Shrive noticed as she watched her friend's hand hover toward her chest. Shrive's eyes followed as Selese took a breath to calm herself as she walked toward the window. Selese held the paper up as she stared out into the sunlight.

"It was an inside job. Someone in your facility is working for the Broken Feather or someone else, or they are just being paid," Selese said as she crossed her arms, still turned away.

"That is an insult. Why would I believe the words of a thief?" Li Xiu yelled.

Shrive gently placed her hand on Li Xiu's shoulder, "She's not accusing anyone. It's just a theory. Besides, you came to us, remember?"

Li Xiu looked to see the predator's frightening but caring blue-green eyes. But, her thoughts now calmed as she said, "You of all people should know how security works."

Shrive nodded as she heard Selese say, "Yeah, Miss Goody here has never stolen anything." Selese turned with a smile, "She's a better person than me."

Li Xiu looked confused as Selese handed the paper to her as she walked back to the desk. Selese's words followed her as she spoke, "You mentioned that none of your investigations showed anything. That leads me to conclude that someone or something is not working on your side." The chair squeaked as Selese sat hard. "I'm sorry, it looks like it was probably an inside job. And whoever did it is probably still working there."

Li Xiu showed a split second of anger but then thought about what Selese said. She ran the facts through her mind and eventually came to the same conclusion. She looked to Selese to see her smiling.

"If someone in the facility, did it, then who do I tell?" Li Xiu asked.

Shrive looked to Selese, her eyes open in curiosity at Li Xiu's question.

Who would you tell?

Selese shrugged, "I don't know. But, to be honest, whoever it was has probably hidden or destroyed the evidence. Even if you knew, you wouldn't be able to prove it." Selese leaned back in the chair, "It's happened here a few times. But we survived."

Li Xiu looked concerned, "It's happened here. How many times?"

Selese chuckled, "Too many. You may have heard about the most recent that happened a couple of years ago."

Li Xiu nodded, "The Forge? I understand that all of the Raven Hunters were even shut out from there as well."

Shrive looked insulted before Selese laughed.

Selese then confirmed, "That all happened. And it was someone everyone trusted. Someone high up on the council. No one knew they were part of the Broken Feather until it was too late."

Li Xiu looked beaten, "I understand that only one hunter and a human, along with yourself, tried to subdue the thieves. But they were able to get away."

The woman expected to see Selese insulted but saw the determination in the former thief's eyes as she spoke. "They got away; they took the icon. But we're pretty sure they don't have it now, or they would have used it to attack us already."

Li Xiu nodded, "That would make sense. But I don't know who I could tell if it was someone inside our facility. I mean, it could be the very person who committed the act."

Selese moved to stand before Li Xiu, smiling at her, "Then don't tell anyone. Just let your people know that the evidence points to an inside job, but there is no hard information. Then let it go." Selese huffed, "It may keep a target off your back."

Li Xiu thought about being hunted by the perpetrator before she smiled, touching the coins she wore, each carrying an element of power and protection, "Maybe you're right. It's much stricter where I work. We don't allow anyone who's not a scroll witch or hunter within the facility." Li Xiu then looked around, searching for someone, "I'm surprised your other friend isn't here."

Selese smiled, "Well, she's got her own problems to deal with. She is supposed to be graduating next semester, so she has been focusing on her schoolwork. Besides, she not a Raven Hunter."

Shrive spoke up, "Technically, neither are you."

"Shrive's right. I'm not a Raven Hunter." Selese watched Li Xiu smile before telling her, "They have this dumb rule about not having a criminal past. They seem to be stuck on that for some reason."

Shrive burst out laughing, and Li Xiu joined her. The Chinese representative then looked at the papers strewn across the desk and sighed, "Too bad she can't help us this time."

Selese looked to the desk, then snapped her fingers. They all watched as the papers slid together in order. Including the one that she held, making Li Xiu look on in awe as she asked, "You enchanted the pages?"

Selese nodded, "Yep, it was Amanda's idea. She came up with it some time ago. That way, if a page were missing, they would stack separately. It made sense to me. Now all of the paperwork here is done the same way. So, if someone takes something, we'll know."

At that moment, the growling of Shrive's stomach was loud enough to get the attention of everyone in the room. She looked down before apologizing, "Sorry, didn't get anything to eat yet. I came right over when I realized I overslept."

Li Xiu smiled, "I have not eaten yet either. I wanted to get to work on this case again." She looked to see Selese leaning against the edge of the desk. "It's good to see that you have help from other sources. That's why they sent me here."

Selese nodded before seeming to think for a moment before pointing to Li Xiu, "Yeah. Maybe we can introduce her. I'm sure Amanda would like to meet someone from another Sanctuary."

Li Xiu nodded in agreement, "Besides, I've never met an FOF before."

"What? you have something against a friend of fairies?" Shrive yelled.

Seeing Shrive take offense at the woman's statement, Selese stepped in, "Easy, Shrive, don't ruffle that mane of yours. Amanda doesn't mind being called an FOF, remember? Besides, how many people do you know that can simply ask some of the most powerful magical beings on the planet for help, and they'll do it?"

Shrive turned to Li Xiu, "Actually, many of those in the Sanctuary still don't like her being here. They think all non-magic humans should be forbidden from entering. But that girl always finds a way in. Usually, someone or something just walks her in."

"That and she's really good at figuring things out," Selese added.

Li Xiu looked to the two in the room, "You almost sound jealous of her."

Shrive's stomach growled again just before she answered, "Sometimes, but she's been a bit jealous of us at times as well. She can't shadow walk like us or change appearance like Selese. I can't even do that. I can only change to my feline form."

Li Xiu laughed before turning to Selese, "I've been meaning to ask. Most elves, darklings included, cannot change appearance. At least not without an element. I've heard you can change appearance quickly and at will. Would you be able to show me?"

Selese stood, facing Li Xiu, and changed into an exact copy of the woman. Li Xiu touched her own face saying, "You look like a mirror."

Selese smiled, "Yeah, I'm pretty good at it."

Li Xiu grabbed Selese's hand, inspecting her arm. "I understand it's complicated and can take much to change form. Can I see the element you use to transform?"

Selese firmly but gently pulled her arm back, shaking her head. Then, Shrive, feeling a bit of the emptiness in Selese's actions, spoke, "Well, she has something most people don't have."

Li Xiu looked to Shrive, "What is that?"

Shrive was about to tell her when Selese interrupted, "Hey Shrive, you two must be starving. Maybe we should get something to eat. And then come back to all of this."

Shrive looked to Selese, her intense stare clearly communicating that she wanted Shrive to keep that knowledge to herself. Shrive understood, so she smiled, changing the subject, "Maybe we should get something to eat. Hey, if we stop by that Italian place, maybe Amanda will be there. She's probably done with her classes for the day."

Li Xiu heard her own stomach growl and looked to Shrive, "Perhaps we should. I can see the element later. It'd be useful to know how you do it so quickly."

Selese nodded. "Well, it's sort of my thing. It's useful for me. But, on the other hand, I'm not sure I want many people to know how I do it. Aside from those who already know."

Li Xiu said, "Perhaps it is better. I recall my question." She looked to Shrive, "I have not had much Italian food. I would be grateful if you are willing."

Shrive smiled, seeing Li Xiu in her uniform, and looked to Selese, "You would probably be less conspicuous in regular clothes. Do you have any?"

Li Xiu nodded. "I have to remain in uniform while at the facility back home, force of habit. I can go change. What time would you like to go?"

Selese chimed in, "About 4:30. We can usually get a good table just before it gets busy."

Li Xiu nodded, "I'll see you both at 4:30 then." The woman walked to the nearest shadow and disappeared.

Shrive looked to Selese, "You didn't want her to know about your…" She pointed to her heart.

Selese shook her head, "No. Too many people know about that already. It just seems to bring a lot of trouble for me sometimes."

"I can understand, sorry."

Selese smiled, saying, "Thanks for catching the hint. You know, you're alright as a friend for a straight-as-an-arrow cat girl."

Shrive nodded as her stomach growled again, making Selese say, "I don't know, hearing that stomach of yours growling, we may have to get you some food sooner. You might try to eat me."

Their laughter was muffled by the door as Li Xiu listened. She smiled, hearing them, and turned, thinking, *I have been to several facilities all over the world. Normal people and those like us always seem to never see each other. Who would have thought that a thief and a hunter could be close friends. No one will believe my report on this Sanctuary when I return.*

Chapter 4:
A Witch's Plan

Gina was admiring herself in the mirror, the new dress drawing a subtle smile of remembrance across her lips. However, any happiness quickly turned to a scowl before changing again back to a smile. This alternated for more than a minute as she stared into her reflection, her mind trying to find memories. Finally, the woman's eyes brightened as she noticed the spot of sun on the floor from the window. She turned, reaching for the open pane, only to feel the painful shock from the earrings she wore. It caused her to fall to the floor as Allison walked into the room.

"My dear, you know very well that you have not been excused. Besides, you have work to do." Allison looked over the young woman, "That is a pretty dress. But I think too formal for where I'm sending you."

Allison searched through the pile of clothes laid out on the bed. There were at least three cases already packed. She had chosen clothes for the girl to send along with her to the art school in New York. Of course her goal was not to enrich Gina's mind, but to have her find her missing Sphere. Allison knew well about the Sanctuary; she had been there near the time it opened. The school itself had not existed until several decades later. She also knew of the Forge and its accursed magic. The fires were lit and maintained by magic. The hunters used it to infuse its metal to guard everything within the circle of lights around the school and Sanctuary, protecting them from all dangerous magical creatures that had roamed the forest.

Mrs. Thompson knew about the creatures as well. She had created many of them long ago during her search for immortality. Her early days in the Sanctuary and the Great Hall were still within the frame of her memories. She also knew the secrets that the iron and metal held. When she was forced from the Sanctuary, without its resources, she could no longer continue her research. So, in her desperation, she created the creatures that walked the forests around the very same.

Temperance had found and succeeded in restoring some of her youth, but she was still looking to extend it for much longer. She had hoped to find her way back into the graces of the Circle but, even after centuries, was unable. So many Raven Hunters died the night they discovered her plot and subsequentially expelled her from the Great Hall and her research. But the Circle knew of her obsession to become immortal. And in their efforts to save the lives of many future hunters, they made a pact with the woman now calling herself Allison Thompson.

Gina appeared in a new dress, less formal and more contemporary. Allison smiled, seeing the woman looking at herself in the mirror. "Yes, my dear, I think that will do quite nicely." Gina looked to the woman as she touched her shoulder. "My little doll, I have given you precise instructions. First, you will find the Sphere and the shapeshifter who stole from me and bring them to me. And to further your educational enrollment, you will perform your little trick for them when questioned."

Gina nodded, saying nothing, but held her hand up and snapped her fingers. Within seconds, water from around the room collected above her hand into a small ball of liquid. Seconds later, she closed her hand, and it fell to the floor.

Allison looked into the mirror as she touched her earring. "Good, good. Now, I don't want you to get any ideas about running. I'll be able to find you no matter where you go." The older woman pressed the earring she wore, and an expression of pain came over Gina's face. Allison closed her eyes, and when she opened them, she could see through the girl's eyes, the mirror image showing Gina's skin wrinkled and falling from her bones. The image then quickly turned to what Gina's eyes could see now displayed in the mirror before her. She moved her head as the image changed to show what her eyes viewed. Allison leaned close, whispering, "You agreed to my terms, my dear. All of this may be yours when I'm gone. All it will cost you is a little of your youth."

Mrs. Thompson moved away, "Now, my dear, I think it's time for you to head out. I'll have Mack take your things to the car."

It was only a few minutes before Allison stood outside near the car. Mack was loading the girl's belongings into the back and could see Gina sitting in the rear seat. Mack looked up, motioning to Gina.

"It is almost mid-semester. How do you propose they will allow her in?" Mack asked.

Allison nodded, handing him a letter from someone he didn't recognize. Finally, his mistress told him, "Mack, that should convince that witch, Brentwood, to allow the girl in. Make sure she gets it, will you?"

Mack nodded, asking, "Is she going to do what you ask?"

"She'll behave. She's aware of the consequences of her refusal." Allison sighed, "It's not that she can't be replaced. But she knows no matter where she is, I'll find her. So truthfully, even if she stays within the Sanctuary boundary, she'll have to leave sometime."

Mack nodded, "I'm surprised you're not coming along. I'd think you would be 'happy' to visit your old haunt."

Allison scowled toward the man, "I cannot go there. I can't even get past that damn boundary line. So, it'll have to only be you and the girl." The older woman sighed heavily, "it's part of the bargain. I cannot set foot in the sanctuary to retrieve my research, and no Raven Hunter or member of the Circle can set foot in my domain."

Allison snapped her fingers, and a ring of mist appeared. Electricity jumped within the roses far above and down to the ground around them. The glowing circle around the estate was now visible, illuminated by her actions. Allison smiled. "That boundary has been protecting this estate and me for over four hundred years—since I was forced from the Great Hall."

Mack looked around, "So they can't do anything while it's there?"

Allison smiled, "Actually, it's around me, not just the estate. But, yes, that is its purpose. When the Circle made the original pact exiling and blocking me from the Sanctuary, I scoffed, knowing that the Raven Hunters thought my punishment would be a curse. The joke was on them, however, when I added that they could not interfere with me in any way." She spun around, laughing as she looked back to her ally, "No Raven Hunter can ever come near me. Unless I allow them, of course."

"Except that thief, apparently. I must ask, how are you threatening the girl to obey you? You can't do that without the Sphere of Lieben?" Mack could see the fire burning behind his mistress's eyes before she answered.

"Thank you for reminding me of that, Malcolm Mitchell, Esquire." The growl in her tone made several birds fly off suddenly.

Mack could feel his legs readying themselves to move on their own; he had seen this woman angry before with others, but most of them could no longer voice their opinions in any fashion. He stepped back, "Right, sorry, won't happen again. I'll just take your, uh, heir to her new place then, shall I?"

Allison nodded slowly, "That would be prudent, Mr. Mitchell. And please do hurry back, we have some other business to attend to. You may find the encounter most agreeable."

Mack smiled, closing the door as Allison looked back to see Gina staring forward with a glass-like expression. "You all ready to go, miss?"

Gina nodded once.

"You seem awfully quiet. Are you all right?" Mack asked.

The girl nodded, "Yes, Mr. Mitchell, I am only following mistress's commands. I am to remain silent until we reach the sanctuary border, then I am to make friends with some of the others to find the shapeshifter and Sphere. And then I will contact you to bring them here once they are subdued."

Mack looked into the mirror, "So, no conversation?" Gina said nothing, and the glass-like expression again filled her face.

The man sighed, "it's going to be a long three hours."

* * *

Mack opened the door, and Gina stepped out from the back. She smiled like any other young woman who was going somewhere for the first time. She entered the administration building, and Mack followed closely behind. Gina tapped on her phone, and as she hit send, she froze mid-step for a moment before walking up the steps again.

"Are you all right, miss?" Mack asked.

The girl turned a familiar smile, "Yes, Mack, just making sure my doll is doing as she is told." He could see the glass-like stare in Gina's eyes. It was there for a moment before life returned to Gina's gaze, and she appeared frightened before her expression quickly turned to one of confidence.

"Miss?" Mack asked.

"Thank you, Malcolm. I'm fine. Mistress only wanted to see where we were." Gina answered. She was returning to herself again.

Mack nodded, "Of course. I have the paperwork you need. However, since classes have already begun, I don't know if they will allow you this semester. They have strict rules. I've been going over them. I don't know how Allison expects you to be accepted this time of year."

Gina looked up at him with a smile. "I have a trick I can show them that may change their minds. But I don't think it would be appropriate to show it to them quite yet."

Mack placed his hand against her shoulder, "We'll come to that when we get there. Let's get you processed in."

As Mack waited for the clerk to finish processing the paperwork for Gina, he looked around the small room, its wooden decor warm and familiar. *This looks like my office at the mansion.* He absentmindedly fiddled with the gold chain around his wrist. Then, he was startled to hear someone yell for his attention.

"Mr. Mitchell, the paperwork is in order, but I'm afraid Gina cannot start classes, since we are in the middle of the semester. She will have to wait until the next semester," the woman behind the counter told him.

Mack gave a triumphant grin as he produced the letter his employer had given to him. He handed it to the clerk, saying, "Please reach out to Dr. Brentwood and tell her there is a student that needs to see her about enrollment. When she reads the letter, she will understand."

The clerk went to open the letter, but Mack pulled it from her grip. "That is for Dr. Brentwood's eyes, not yours, miss, uh?"

The clerk smiled, "I did not say my name, Mr. Mitchell. But one moment while I contact Dr. Brentwood."

Mack heard the clerk speaking and was surprised to listen to her arguing with Brentwood on the phone. The call ended, and a very practiced smile appeared on the clerk's face. She told Mr. Mitchell and Gina, "Dr. Brentwood will see you to discuss your enrollment. Please head to the building next door."

Mack felt his confidence rise as he looked over the woman behind the counter. He gave a cordial "thank you" and motioned to Gina. Then, they both headed outside to speak with the doctor about Gina's enrollment.

Walking into the building, they noticed the silver-haired woman sitting at the reception desk. She looked up, motioning for the two to approach.

As they neared, she spoke, "Mr. Mitchel, Gina Ellsworth, Dr. Brentwood is expecting you. This way, please."

The woman pointed to the elevator instead of the surrounding rooms.

Mack nodded and guided Gina toward the elevator saying. "Thank you... Uh?"

The silver-haired woman smiled, "Please head up. Dr. Brentwood is waiting for you."

As they walked toward the elevator, it opened. Mack looked at the desk, hearing the woman say, "Floor five is the one you want to press."

Mack did so, and as the doors closed, he felt very uneasy seeing several crystals flicking around the metal box of the elevator as it moved.

When the elevator stopped, the doors opened to display an ornate hall. Mack took notice of the furnishings and realized they might probably be older than he was. Finally, they reached Dr. Brentwood's office and entered. Within only a few steps, Mack and Gina felt their feet dragging against the carpet, almost as if it was grabbing against their shoes. Gina screamed as the rug fibers wrapped themselves around her legs. Mack had the same problem, but his reaction was much different.

"What's the meaning of this?" Mack yelled, only to see Colleen in a fighting stance as the door behind them closed securely.

Colleen looked toward them, her eyes with the stare of a seasoned hunter. Mack was readying to attack her with a lightning spell when he heard someone say, "That would not be wise, Mr. Mitchell."

Mack turned to see Dr. Brentwood standing inside the doorway of her office. He lurched, trying to free himself from the hold of the enchanted floor. Dr. Brentwood stayed behind the threshold of her office door as she glared toward them.

It seems our intelligence on the Raven Hunters is lacking some updates, Mitchell thought.

Mack was seasoned and knew when to negotiate.

"Dr. Brentwood, I presume," Mack said, sounding again like his professional self.

The doctor looked back at him, her words warning as she spoke, "Who are you?"

Mack smiled, his litigatory mind full and practiced, "I apologize for any misunderstanding, doctor, but I am only here to enroll my employer's charge."

Dr. Brentwood looked to Colleen, "Colleen, Mr. Mitchell has a letter for me. Would you please bring it over?"

Mitchell politely handed the letter to the woman, and she gave it to the doctor. Dr. Brentwood opened it, her eyes softening as she read. The wording was from Amilee Dobson, a good friend of hers. Amilee ran one of the smaller safe houses in Beddgelert. However, Claire realized that she hadn't heard from Ami for some time. However, it was common for them to be out of touch for months. Not much happened in Beddgelert when it came to magic.

Dr. Brentwood finished reading and looked at the two still snared in the carpet. Both were still struggling to release themselves. Then, finally, the man looked at Claire, and she held the letter before her, "Mr. Mitchell, this letter is not from your employer."

Mack being the schemer he had always been, agreed, "No, it is not. I work for Allison Thompson. She is heir to Temperance Hastings. I was given to understand that you would know what it was about. My employer has not explained what was within. I was only told that it would convince you." There was no way he would repeat what his mistress had said about the letter and Brentwood.

Claire thought for a moment. *Temperance, why is that name familiar?* She nodded, "My dear, it says that you can prove what this letter says."

Gina looked to Mack, who shrugged. But the girl understood and snapped her fingers, creating a small ball of water above her palm. Mack looked on in amazement. Until this moment, he didn't know the girl had any magic. *Did Allison give those powers to you?*

Colleen stepped back, still defensive as Dr. Brentwood watched. Mack looked around, his new knowledge added to the vast files in his mind. Being an attorney, he knew how to read people, and he could see Dr. Brentwood now had a different opinion of them both.

With a wave of her hand, the carpet retracted, releasing them. Mack fixed his tie and faced Brentwood. "My apologies, doctor. I did not know we would have to prove such a feat to enroll."

Dr. Brentwood, curious, smiled and said, "You didn't. However, you don't seem fazed by the event you have seen."

Mack nodded in agreement before saying, "Doctor, I have been in the employ of my client for some time, and I have, shall I say, seen some things."

The doctor asked him to elaborate.

Mack did his best, even including his so-called employer's past. Mentioning that she has worked with another sanctuary in the past, the one mentioned in the letter. The doctor nodded; "I know Allison's exploits with the Sanctuary in Wales." She then motioned for them to enter. "I apologize for the security; past encounters have warranted the increase. Please, come in. We can discuss your charge's situation."

Mack nodded in agreement, "That is understandable, Dr. Brentwood. It would be most disagreeable if one of your enemies were able to infiltrate and harm anyone."

Chapter 5:
She's Not One of Us.

Li Xiu sat in the passenger seat while Selese drove to the restaurant. In the back, Shrive tapped away on her phone.

"Selese, Amanda's there already. She'll grab us a table," Shrive yelled over the loud music playing.

Selese nodded, turning down the radio, "Sorry, I love that song. Hope it wasn't too loud."

Li Xiu shook her head, saying, "I listen to all music when I can back home." She glanced back at Shrive. "I'm surprised we didn't shadow walk to this place. It would have been much easier."

Selese snickered, "There's no shadow walking outside the campus or the Sanctuary unless authorized." She glanced over at Li Xiu. "Even I follow the rules, sometimes. Besides, it makes it easier to get home if needed. And, driving makes you look like everyone else around here."

Li Xiu nodded in agreement as she turned forward.

It was only a short while before they arrived. The parking lot was almost full. And their guest looked around at all the vehicles as they walked inside. The sounds of laughter and people enjoying a good meal and good time filled her ears as Li Xiu stood next to Selese. Within seconds, a hostess pounced on them.

"It's good to see regulars here again. Your friend has a table already reserved. Follow me."

Shrive gently grabbed Li Xiu's arm, guiding her along as Selese led the way. But, she graciously told Shrive, "It's hectic tonight."

Her feline counterpart smiled, "Pizza fry night. Probably one of the worst foods you'll ever eat, but worth every bite."

Shrive spotted Amanda and pointed to her, pulling Li Xiu along. Amanda was talking to someone on her phone, and they could hear her say "love you" before hanging up. Selese rushed over as Amanda reached out, "Thought you guys weren't going to make it. I didn't think traffic was that bad."

"Finally able to get lover boy to call you back?" Selese chided. Amanda looked at her before laughing, "that wasn't Luke, my parents called. I sent them some money from my last commission. They were telling me that they didn't need it."

Selese looked back at Shrive, "Doesn't she always say love you all the time when she's with Luke?"

Amanda hit Selese with a friendly tap, before throwing her hands up and then pointing at the table. "I do not say love you to Luke all the time."

"Maybe next time I'll record it." She looked over at Shrive, "I'll probably have a lot of opportunities."

"It really was my parents, not Luke, uh…" Amanda seemed embarrassed, and stammered, before sitting and motioning to the table, "c'mon, you guys are playing rough today."

Selese told her she was only joking as she sat.

Li Xiu watched Amanda smile before she looked around, the noise of all the talking and others making the friends yell to hear each other. A server came over and asked for their orders right away, handing them menus. He asked Li Xiu first, but she didn't know what to order. She peered around looking for advice. Amanda told her, "Anything you want. I'm buying."

Shrive looked surprised, "Wait. You're treating?"

Amanda nodded, "I got paid. The artwork for Ron's latest book came in, and I was paid for the three commissions I did last month. So, tonight's on me." She then said to the server, "Steak tips, side of spiced rice, unsweetened iced tea."

She pointed at Selese, who responded, "Same."

Amanda pointed to Shrive, "Porterhouse and pizza fries, beer." When the server asked how she wanted it cooked, Amanda swore her cat teeth were showing as Shrive answered, "Rare."

She then pointed to Li Xiu, telling her, "Anything you want, on the menu, of course."

Li Xiu read through; she had to follow a strict diet back home. All hunters in her group required it. She spied something she had always wanted to try, and her eyes lit. She then told the server. "The big house burger, with onion rings and chili on the side. And a large soda."

Amanda smiled, looking at the server, "You heard the girl." The man hurriedly wrote down their order and headed back, allowing the group to talk again.

"Where's Luke?" Selese asked.

Amanda seemed to have difficulty hearing her as the band started playing. Finally, she moved in, and Selese held up her hand before placing her finger down on the table to draw a circle with a vertical line through it. Her tracing left a faint glowing line, and the room became much quieter as she put her hand over it.

Li Xiu looked around, "Everyone's quiet now. What's happening?"

Selese leaned over, telling her, "Localized sound veil, all the tables here have them. It makes it easier to talk and also not be heard."

Amanda smiled, "I wish I could do that."

Selese looked at her, "When you make up your mind about joining."

Amanda nodded, "I've still got a few things I want to do. Besides, I prefer a smaller team." Amanda referenced Ron and Linda and their recent exploits outside the Raven Hunters.

Shrive laughed before asking the same question as Selese, "Where's Luke? I'd expect him to be here tonight."

Amanda nodded, "Me too. But he's working. Something about a museum robbery in the city. He hasn't gotten back to tell me the details."

Selese told her, "He's probably out working on that Statuette of Ferron theft. The Sanctuary had lent it to them after making sure all spells were removed. It is an intricate piece of carved marble. You could probably make a fortune finding the right buyer."

The other three looked at Selese and watched her smile, saying, "Hey! I like to keep up on things. You never know when falling back on a previous career might come in handy."

Amanda laughed; she could tell Selese was joking. Shrive shook her head. "You're a terrible influence. Do you know that? If Gabs heard you, she might think…" Shrive paused, looking around, "Where is Gabs? She's usually interrupted one of us by now."

Amanda looked at Shrive, "She's taking some time to, uh…." Amanda pointed to Li Xiu. "Does she know about, you know, things around here?"

Shrive looked to Li Xiu and nodded, "Yeah, Li Xiu is one of us. Different location. They go by *Yín yā lièrén*."

Amanda looked puzzled, "Yin Yow, Leer ren?

Lin Xiu sat tall, "I'm impressed. You almost said that correctly. It means silver raven hunter." She then looked to Shrive before asking, "Are we allowed to speak about this outside the Sanctuary?"

Shrive shook her head, "Not usually, but Amanda is still sort of one of us, but also not one of us."

Li Xiu looked at Amanda, "That doesn't make any sense. She is one of us but not one of us?"

Amanda nodded, "Things aren't always meant to be understood. Sometimes you just go with it."

Li Xiu looked surprised, saying, "Those are wise words."

Selese raised her brow, looking at Amanda, "I think you've been hanging around my mother too much recently."

It was Li Xiu's turn to be puzzled, and she asked, "Your mother?"

Selese nodded, "Yes, my mother, you met her when you arrived. She's the one whose office you sat in giving your report of that theft."

Li Xiu looked surprised, "Dr. Brentwood is your mother?"

Selese nodded.

Confusion now filled Li Xiu's eyes, "If you know about the Sanctuary, the Forge, and the Raven Hunters, how are you not one of them?"

Selese gave her a glare causing Li Xiu to realize she had said something wrong. She looked back apologetically before saying, "Is this one of those complicated things?" causing Selese to nod slowly and Li Xiu to retract her question.

Shrive asked again why Gabs wasn't there, and Amanda was happy to answer.

"She had so many commissions come in she needed some down time. But instead of heading home, she's at the grove."

Selese spoke up, "It is nice there, very relaxing. Lots of fairies flying around doing fairy things. And it feels sort of homey."

Li Xiu smiled, "I've never been to the grove before. I understand that no matter where you are on the planet, it's at the same place."

At that moment, their conversation was cut short as their food arrived. Selese passed Shrive's order down as Amanda grabbed hers from the server. Then she handed Li Xiu her plate, and Amanda watched as Xi Liu looked at the large platter, her eyes happy as she craned her neck. And as Amanda watched Xi Liu's reaction, she could see the tattoo on her neck on the left side just above her shoulder. The symbol, Chinese in nature, looked familiar. She put it to memory as she dove into her meal.

A short time passed, and everyone was enjoying themselves. When they finished, they stayed at the table talking and catching up. It was only a short while, and the clock read half-past eight when things started to wind down in the restaurant. Amanda watched as the symbol again appeared on Li Xiu's neck as she turned to speak with Selese.

Amanda took a moment before politely asking Li Xiu if the symbol meant something. The woman's response was unexpected.

"There's no tattoo on my neck, see?" She held her collar down, and neither Selese nor Shrive could see anything.

Amanda gave a stoic look back, her annoyance hidden within.

Li Xiu laughed, "If you see something, then describe it." Li Xiu was now concerned, but she hid it well. She did have a mark; it was meant for her protection. All members of the *Yín yā lièrén* had one similar, each personalized. It allowed their people to find each other if something went wrong. It was hidden by several masters using concealment magic. And they were so successful that no other Raven Hunters could see the markings.

Amanda knew what she saw and said, "I might do better drawing it."

Li Xiu scoffed, trying to hide her concern. She looked Amanda in the eyes, saying, "Draw it then. I want to see what you think you see."

Selese looked to Amanda, then to Li Xiu, asking, "Are you sure you want her to do that? Amanda is good at remembering symbols."

Li Xiu nodded—she didn't believe Amanda could see the mark she wore. She also knew about Amanda from their files on her back home. They had a lot of information on her adventures with Ron and Linda. She stared back at Amanda, clearly certain she didn't know anything. Amanda pulled out a pen and started drawing on a napkin. She drew a circle first and then started on the symbol. Li Xiu's eyes went wide before she pulled the napkin from the table. Xi Liu's grip tightly crushing the thin paper as her eyes, now unsure, scanned the three people around her. Amanda felt terrible seeing her reaction, and feeling sorry, told her she didn't mean any harm.

Li Xiu shot back, angrily whispering, "How can you see it? Seven masters used concealment spells. Even they can't."

Shrive looked at Li Xiu's neck, "I still don't see anything."

Before tugging on her silver chain, Amanda thought for a moment, revealing the small wooden ring beneath her shirt. Li Xiu could see the small, plain object, and her eyes filled with surprise.

A fairy ring? She does have a fairy ring?

Li Xiu looked on as Amanda said, "Figured I'd show you my secret since I can see yours. It's only fair."

Li Xiu asked if she could see the ring, and Amanda agreed. She held the chain to the ring as Li Xiu inspected the small wooden circle. But, when she pulled it away from Amanda to get a better look, the ring became intangible and drifted through her fingers. It now swung in the air on the chain from Amanda's hand before she put it back over her head.

"Ooo, that's a new trick. When did you get that put on?" Selese asked.

Amanda smiled before replying, "Last year. Roween thought someone might try and take this from me." Amanda held up the wooden ring. "So, it only stays tangible when it and I are safe, or if I don't want someone to take it."

Li Xiu interrupted, "I wasn't going to take it. I just wanted a better look."

Amanda could see her friends now looked at Li Xiu with suspicion and hurried to reassure everyone. "I know. It would have let me know if you were a danger. It's all right. This sometimes has a mind of its own anyway." That statement sated any concerns her friends had about their fellow hunters. She gave a smile, and they all started talking again.

* * *

It was late as Mack was heading back. He mused about the files Brentwood had shown him during their meeting. Gina had been accepted and, instead of starting classes, would have instruction on using her powers from others in the Sanctuary. Brentwood also showed him a picture of Allison from her files, which was different from what he had seen. *It looks like you're slipping, Allison. You missed a few things.*

Mack turned into the long driveway and parked inside the garage. He had been on the road for several hours already and was not feeling tired. He again tapped the gold chain he wore, giving a smile. He had also stopped by the museum earlier, remembering that another *tianqiu* was in the branch in Albany. He used magic to bypass the security. But after returning to the car, he realized that the item was fake. Forgetting the hour, he entered Allison's office to find her trying to tame the warrior the Feather had procured for her. As he entered the chamber behind the bookcase, her amusement was boisterous and filled with challenge.

"Ah, Mack, you're missing all of the fun. These feudal warriors are so entertaining when they try and disobey me." Mack could hear the howling of the spirit as Allison used her magic against it.

"You know it's late. How long have you been attempting to tame that thing?" Mack asked, knowing full well that the woman he knew as Allison didn't care about the spirit.

She looked to the clock, "My, how time flies. Perhaps I will give this spirit some time to consider the offer I've presented." She winked at Mack before saying a few words of a spell and watched as the spirit retreated into its bottle. "I'll play with that later. I hope all went well with my little doll?"

Mack smiled, "It did. She was enrolled and now has access to the Sanctuary."

Allison barely contained her happiness, kissing Mack on the lips.

"Good, I can't wait to find the sphere. And the thief who took it from me."

Mack informed her that Brentwood had several files on Amilee Dobson, telling her, "The pictures look nothing like you. By the way, when did you give Gina water abilities?"

Allison laughed, "My dear Malcolm, I gave her nothing. That is her power, which is why she has lasted longer than the others, Gina is part water sprite.

Chapter 6:
A Doll's First Day

Gina sat in her room, her eyes opening to stare into the sunny spot on the floor by the window. She was ordered to remain in her room until summoned by Allison's command or to attend training, as per her previous instructions. She had stayed awake most of the night, waiting as per her orders. Finally, however, sleep did catch up with her.

About a minute later, her fingers started to move, and her eyes shifted to look around in the shadows created by the morning sun. She lifted her hand, and an expression of freedom trickled into her eyes.

She stood slowly, her mind a murmur becoming full of words she had almost forgotten. She turned to see her face in the large mirror, the dim light illuminating half of it. She reached out to touch the image only to have the other half fill with the image of the woman who sent her to this place.

"Ah, you're awake, my dear. I sometimes forget that you are, after all, human, well mostly anyway." Gina watched as the image spoke but said nothing in return.

Her eyes, however, spoke thousands of words as the fear pierced through them—her will allowing her to start to turn away.

"Oh, Gina, my sweet little doll. Are you having thoughts of being free again?" Then, the woman's face filled with a sinister grin, "Let me do something about that."

Gina heard her thoughts quiet, and she moved normally, almost in sync with the woman in the mirror.

"That's much better. Now, my dear, report what has happened so far." Allison's image ordered.

Gina told Allison that she had not found the shapeshifter after entering the Sanctuary. "I think they said I was kelpie?" She sounded almost elated when mentioning that she could create more than a small ball of water from the air.

Allison muted her excitement by giving her an order, "Do not show them your full abilities." Gina nodded in understanding.

"Are you to report to the Sanctuary today?" Allison asked.

Gina nodded before replying, "Around 3 p.m. I am to learn to control a small container of water. I… I….am looking forward to it."

At her mansion, Allison peered into the mirror she used to see through Gina's eyes. Her annoyance held in check, she reached out to grab a cup of tea from her desk. She murmured to herself, too quiet for her doll to hear, "My dear Gina, or whatever your name is, I still don't remember what you told me. You still think you are going to be free of my spell?" The woman looked around her office, "You just can't train good servants anymore."

Allison returned to the mirror. Her smile showed an unnatural shape. "Gina, you are ordered to complete your training with minimum control. Do you understand?"

In the mirror, the girl hesitated but nodded.

"Good, I want you in the Sanctuary as much as possible. Get them to pity you for neglecting your understanding of your powers. I want them to gain trust and sympathy for you." Allison seemed to think for a moment, "I will give you more freedom if you complete this task. It might even fulfill our contract."

Gina shifted on her feet, an air of excitement as she nodded.

"Good, remember that you are bound to me for this. So, when I give you some freedom, it is to be used to fulfill our contract, nothing more."

Gina nodded again in understanding.

"Excellent. Now, it's early. Take some time. Do what most people do in the morning, bathe, get some breakfast. But be ready. Later today, I will be checking in on you."

The image faded from the mirror, and Gina blinked her eyes. While Allison used her to see, she could not close them. The dry air caused them to sting before she could moisten them as she closed her eyes.

"I'm hungry, thirsty," Gina muttered before turning on the faucet, cupping her hands beneath to catch the water. She brought them up to drink. The cool water was refreshing, and she felt it invigorate her.

"Water, so good."

Gina drank again before standing straight. She felt the water infuse her with strength. She turned to the sun again, "I am hungry. I think I'll get something to eat." Allison heard the girl's words as she watched her walk toward the door. The witch smiled, "Well, my dear. Let's see where you go." She looked to her desk, seeing the stack of papers from the estate transfer. "But only for a short while. I do have some important things to do today."

In the campus cafeteria, Selese was sipping on her coffee, reading a copy of one of the reports from some recent thefts. After taking another sip, she placed her cup down, muttering, "Amateurs, you took a wood idol in the middle of the forest. I don't know why you think no one saw you. It's made of trees." She placed her cup on the table without a sound.

She looked up to see Amanda and Luke walking in together. *Well, at least someone knows how to keep them around.* Selese thought about how Cayden accepted the transfer to the west coast for an extended assignment. Luke, however, remained, but only under protest by the Council. Selese waved to get their attention, and Amanda quickly spoke with Luke before heading to see her.

As Amanda neared, Selese asked, "Just coming back from a run?"

Amanda sat, saying, "Yeah, I'm still faster than him," which made Selese laugh.

"Work?" Amanda asked, motioning to the papers strewn across Selese's side of the table, causing Selese to nod as she looked around.

"Listen, I want to go check something out. You doing anything later today?" Selese asked.

Amanda thought for a moment, it was Tuesday, and she had only one morning class. Her mid-terms were over with, and she was looking for something else to do other than studying. What Selese was offering was just the thing.

"A short adventure and a little mystery, huh?" Amanda said just as Luke placed a cup of coffee down before her.

Luke sat, looking at Selese. "It didn't even take long for her to think about it."

Selese smiled, almost laughing as Luke picked up one of the papers from the table. "Selese, these are not supposed to be removed from the Sanctuary. So how did you get them out?"

Selese remained silent, and Luke was going to ask again when Amanda grabbed his arm. "She's not going to tell you."

Amanda looked at Selese, "Plausible deniability?"

Luke chuckled, "So in other words.... I don't want to know."

Selese chimed in, "It's probably best that you don't. That knowledge might corrupt you."

They all gave a quiet laugh.

As Gina entered the cafeteria, she could hear laughter from one of the tables. She ordered food and took it to a nearby table while Allison watched through her eyes.

"So long ago, things have changed," Allison muttered while Mack flipped through the paperwork to ensure everything was complete.

He looked up briefly, "Time will do that." Mack then looked at the mirror. "It hasn't changed that much. It looks like most things did back when I went to law school."

Allison glanced at him before returning to the mirror, "Things have changed a lot. In fact, I don't even remember places like this when I was young. The closest I remember is the local tavern."

Mack looked quizzically toward her, "How old are you?"

Allison sighed, saying, "Mack, you never ask a woman her age. It's impolite."

Back at the cafeteria, Gina placed her tray on the table, including a large water bottle. She opened it, taking several gulps before turning to her food. She almost attacked her meal, the food tasting wonderful. But instead, she gulped down each bite, not noticing the stares now aimed toward her. Luke included.

"That looks like the new girl. They asked us to stand guard while testing her powers," Luke said.

Amanda turned to see the woman devouring her meal, "It's like she hasn't eaten in days." Amanda's assessment was correct. It had been almost two days since Gina had actual food. That was something Allison seemed to neglect before sending her on her mission. Amanda stood, "We should ask her to come over. We all know what it's like being someplace new, don't we?"

Selese nodded, but Luke didn't. Instead, he looked at Selese, "What? I grew up in the area. Your father brought me in because I was causing trouble around town." Amanda shook her head and headed over to talk with the woman.

Amanda stood at the table a few seconds before Gina even noticed her. Then, when she did look up, Amanda introduced herself.

"Hi, are you new?" Amanda asked, watching Gina nod after a moment. "I'm Amanda. Did you want to join us? It's better than sitting here alone."

Gina gulped down her food and sat silent for a moment before responding. "Uh, sure. Okay."

Amanda waited as the woman placed the large water bottle on her tray and picked it up before asking, "What's your name?"

Again, the woman hesitated, "Uh, Gina."

Amanda pulled out the chair. Gina looked unsure as she placed her tray on the table. She sat across from Selese, next to Luke. Amanda stood beside her, "Everyone, this is Gina."

They all introduced themselves, and Gina smiled, looking away from Luke. Selese left the papers on the table as she asked Gina where she was from.

Gina told her she was from Maine but didn't give more detail. Instead, she looked around and reached for her bottle of water, accidentally knocking it over to spill across the papers Selese had on the table. Instinctively Gina reached out, holding her hand over the water, pulling it toward her hand away from the table. What was soaked into the papers now floated above them. In shock, everyone at the table watched before Amanda stood, leaning over to block the view from people behind her. She hurriedly reached over, pulling Luke to a standing position. Selese understood why they stood, and she pulled the papers from the table, whispering to Gina, "Stop," before she pushed Gina's hand to the table allowing the water to splash all over everyone.

Selese was hit with the brunt of the deluge while Amanda brushed herself off. Gina looked horrified and went to stand. But Amanda grabbed her shoulder, pushing her down gently. "Easy, everyone's okay. Not like we haven't spilled anything before." Selese shook her head in annoyance. She was soaked. Gina said she was sorry as she put the top back on her water. Luke rolled his sleeves up as he grabbed a handful of paper towels.

Through the mirror, Allison watched as Luke dried the table. She could still see through Gina's eyes. And as he wiped the table, Gina focused on the tattoos on his arm. She could see the words *happy time* showing as one. Gina cracked a smile as a clouded memory of her life before and the vague image of an old television show rushed into her thoughts.

Not thinking, she pointed to his arm and, with surprise, said, "I remember that TV show."

Luke looked at his arm and smiled before singing a small part of the show's song, making Amanda laugh, and Selese held her phone out, saying, "Do that again. I'm posting it."

Luke shook his head, "Nope, not singing that again."

They laughed as Allison watched. She turned to Mack, "Stupid girl can't even read. Those aren't words. It looks like a symbol of some kind, and it looks familiar," She touched her earring, and Gina reached out, grabbing Luke's arm to pull it closer to get a better look. Her actions almost pulling Luke across the table. Causing Amanda to look defensively toward her. She released his arm, saying, "I don't know why I grabbed your arm, sorry."

Allison examined the symbol and released her earring. "That's not a symbol. That's a protective element. He's a Raven Hunter."

Allison brought her hands to her face covering her mouth, concerned, saying, "No, no, no you stupid little doll. That is not a place for you to be right now."

Mack stood behind Allison, "What's wrong?"

Allison spoke, "That young man is a hunter. My mirror filters concealment magic. So, she can't see the symbol. And with those people is not a place for her to be right now."

Mack being the more practical person at the moment, told her, "You probably don't want to control her right now. It may not be a good idea."

Allison looked at him. She became concerned and turned back to him, "What did the other girl say her name was?"

Mack thought. "The one on the right said her name was Amanda. I didn't catch the other's name."

Allison hunched forward in thought, "Amanda? Why is that name familiar?"

She then looked to the shelf to see a small metal and glass cage. "Terrell. That girl helped put Terrell in the Circle's dungeon."

Allison rose from her chair, walking toward the bookcase that concealed her workshop. She turned to look concerned and, with a hint of anger, said, "You stupid doll. That is not a place you should be." But after a moment, Allison seemed to change her mind as she looked through Gina's eyes.

Mack looked at it from a less practical standpoint, "She could ruin everything."

Allison looked to the mirror, "No, this could work to our advantage. If she befriends these hunters, then she may gain access to someplace more vital."

Mack looked at his employer, "What will you have her do?"

Allison leaned against her desk. "Nothing, I'll have her do nothing until she is close enough for me to take back the sphere. For now, I believe we will let my little doll play on her own."

The witch sat at her desk, her concern turning to tempered optimism. "Mack, I'll allow her some freedom at least while those damn hunters are around. I'll check in on her when needed. They may even bring her close to where the sphere might be."

Mack nodded, "Maybe have her search around in a disguise?"

Allison looked back to her assistant, her eyes bright as she smiled, "you know Mack, that's not a bad idea."

She then opened her workshop and pulled a fabric bat from the shelf. Allison ran her hand beneath some of the material, then said a few words. The cloth disappeared, along with her hand. Her arm truncated where the material started.

"Mack, that is an excellent idea. I believe we will have to make a present for my little doll."

There is more power in this world than can be dreamt of.
To harness it is not enough. It must be mine.

- Adrijana Dervishi (Aka. Allison Thompson)

Chapter 7:
A Thief's Job

As the alarm sounded, Amanda drowsily fumbled for her phone. It took some doing before she was able to finally silence it. "Shouldn't have broken the clock," she mumbled looking down at the cracked screen now cradled in her hands. It was Saturday, and she had spent most of the night with Luke after dinner but came home after he was called in by the hunters. Her friend Shrive was called in as well. Amada's plan to take Shrive and Selese to investigate the recent theft had fallen through. Selese was also called in to meet with Li Xiu's superiors via video conference about her deduction that the *tianqiu* was probably destroyed. So, although things at the Sanctuary had been routine until recently, things still did go wrong.

Amanda took a minute before standing. She looked around the room to see the sun coming in through a crack in the drapes, her mind turning to when they were in the restaurant. She still felt terrible about her meeting with Li Xiu.

"Don't think about it," Amanda muttered. She was upset that Li Xiu left soon after the meal, taking the napkin with the element Amanda drew, and decided not to join them last night after the incident. She gave an excuse that she needed to report in. It wasn't the first time Amanda had accidentally alienated someone, and she was sure it would happen again.

This whole, magic, and non-magic thing is really confusing. And a lot of work, she thought.

But something else was bothering her. She had met Gina yesterday, and something seemed different about the woman. Amanda had met water sprites before. And she knew a thing or three about elementals. Roween and Linda made sure to educate her. *Elementals heal using their element and enjoy being near them. And, if the girl was part elemental, why didn't she desire to be closer to her element?*

Amanda shook her head as she stared at her desk. Her eyes hung drowsily as she turned on the light. Her hand almost missing as she grabbed a pencil and her sketch pad. But this wasn't her regular sketch pad. This was the one she kept aside for when she was with Ron and Linda. This book contained things she found, including a log of creatures and symbols she kept for reference. And recently, when needed, she asked Luke if Dr. Brentwood could help identify something. However, Brentwood seemed intrigued that she kept a log of such things.

She opened a page filled with several symbols. One she remembered from when she went with Luke to Japan. She smiled, seeing "Hidama" scribbled near a character for one on the page. She also noticed the small scorch mark on the corner from when Gabriella stared at the symbol too long. It created a small bird that lit fire to the paper before she slapped her hand down to put it out.

Amanda felt a chill and wished she had on something warmer before she looked down at the page again.

I could magic one of those up and maybe make it a little warmer. I guess it's a good thing I don't have magic. Amanda thought. *Well, at least not yet.*

She then opened an empty page and started sketching the symbol from the other night. As she finished, she remembered not to complete the circle around it. It was something Luke and the other scroll witches warned her about. If you wanted to ensure it wouldn't accidentally cause the element to activate, you left it open.

Amanda sat quietly, her eyes half-closed as she stared into the tiny shadow of the pencil she held. Her mind was again caressing the same question she was asked when she arrived. *Do you really want to join them?*

She shook her head and placed the pencil down. Her eyes turning again to the tiny sliver of light from the drapes. Amanda stood, walking over to open the drapes.

"Might as well let some light in and get ready for my morning run," Amanda mumbled as she pulled the drapes open.

But as her eyes adjusted to the bright light, she became startled by someone standing on her small balcony. But instead of moving to flee, Amanda stood to fight before noticing who it was.

"Gabs! What are you doing?" Amanda yelled, recognizing her best friend with her feet on the railing as if ready to jump to the next one.

Gabriella stood silent for a few seconds before saying, "I was trying to get back into my apartment. I locked myself out again." Gabriella looked sheepishly toward Amanda. "And I didn't want to wake you up. I know you like to sleep in on Saturdays." Her friend gave a look of amused accusation before saying, "At least when you're here."

Amanda could swear she felt herself blush when Gabriella said that, and she cracked a smile. "Let me get your spare key. Hold on." She then unlocked the large window. It was common to use it to access the small balcony on the buildings. Almost everyone had one, but most people used it for storage. Amanda's, however, had several plants growing on it instead. Just in case a particular miniature guest dropped by.

Gabriella climbed in as Amanda turned to hand a key to her.

"Gabs, I want that back right after you get in. You do have a key still, right?" Amanda asked.

Gabriella nodded, "Yeah, just left my keys on the table, again." She sounded annoyed.

Amanda nodded and noticed Gabriella staring, making her ask, "What?"

Gabriella hesitated, "Um, why were you opening the drapes? You know you're pretty much naked, right?"

Amanda looked down to see herself and rushed to grab the sheets of her bed to cover herself, complaining, "I wasn't expecting someone to be standing on my balcony, alright?"

Gabriella laughed as Amanda rushed to cover herself before saying, "Mandy, It's all right. Not like you haven't been in a situation like this before. Remember those enchanted clothes back in Milan?"

Amanda's face turned beet red as she remembered, "That sleazy, uh, woman. Yeah, I remember." Amanda paused briefly, "I remember you were in the same situation."

Gabriella started laughing as she faked covering herself and reminisced. She had gone with Luke and Amanda, along with several hunters, to investigate claims of a sorceress enchanting clothes. Gabriella had always wanted to see the artwork in Italy, and she figured that if Amanda was going, maybe she could also. She remembered that the designer was so focused on making money that if you didn't pay her a continued sum, she would make the clothes literally disappear, usually while you were wearing them in public.

Both she and Amanda had gone shopping and were wearing some of the very same designs when they met up with the woman. The designer/sorceress didn't like the local Hunters cutting into her profits. She had made an example of several who had already attempted to do so previously. That's why the Raven Hunters were sent to investigate. And, when Cale insisted that she would expose the world unnecessarily to magic, she acted against those wearing the clothes she enchanted. And having been wearing mostly those same designs at the time, Amanda and Gabriella were standing pretty much naked when the designer snapped her fingers.

Amanda chuckled, remembering the other hunters who still had clothes trying to help cover them and the others who had also bought something while there. If it weren't for Shrive, the designer would have gotten away, at least for a while. She looked at her friend seeing her wipe sweat from her face. Amanda asked, "I'm going out for a run. You coming?"

Gabriella thought for a moment and then huffed, "Normally I would. But I'm exhausted."

Amanda looked at her. "Why not? You usually want to."

Gabriella sighed, sounding tired, "I'm beat. I've been jumping from balcony to balcony all morning. And climbing over all the stuff everyone has on them." Gabriella leaned closer. "There's some weird stuff out there, Mandy. I mean some really filthy and weird things. And climbing over them was really tiring."

She held up the key, "I'll go with you tomorrow. But, first, I want to take a shower."

Amanda followed her friend to the door and peered around the frame as she unlocked her door. Gabriella turned, tossing the spare key to her as she waved. "See you later, Mandy."

Amanda closed the door and leaned against it. She shook her head, "I guess climbing a building would be tiring. Never thought about trying it."

She then pulled the covers she was wearing off, tossing them to the bed before heading in to get dressed. As she opened the closet to get her exercise outfit, she mumbled, "I wonder if normal people with normal lives go through this stuff too."

Gina opened her eyes to find herself still in her bed. The covers were warm, and she pulled them close, not wanting to move.

It's been so long since I've woken up in my own bed. That witch keeps taking my body out for a run. Always has me sitting in a chair like some toy.

Gina pulled the covers back over her head.

The sun warmed the covers as Gina woke again. The morning was already dwindling, and she had not moved. She had forgotten what it was like to sleep in like an average person. But as she lay not moving, her hand started twitching, her arm, and finally her shoulder. They all conspired to push her out of bed.

Gina felt control of her body wane as the disturbingly familiar haze filled her mind. She found herself standing before the large mirror in her room, her image replaced by Allison's.

"My dear, you look rested." Allison turned to look at her desk, taking the cup of tea from it. "Perhaps I should allow you to sleep in more often."

Gina was about to speak, but she knew the consequences of disobeying Allison.

"Well, my little doll, you have not forgotten your manners, I see," Allison said. Before taking a sip from her cup. She held it properly on her lap before motioning to Mack nearby. She then looked into the mirror, "I have a gift for you."

Mack held the cloak made of dark material, which had a shimmer of silver all along its surface. The patterns were similar to many she had seen while at the mansion. She could see the long cloak and Allison smiling.

"My dear, touch the mirror," Allison spoke.

Gina, however, didn't react so quickly. And Allison noticed. The witch lightly held her earring, and Gina felt her arm move toward the glass. She tried pulling away, but Allison's control was much too powerful. As her hand rested on the cold glass, Mack held the cloak to the surface, and after hearing a few magic words from her master, she felt the fabric in her grasp. Instinctively Gina tried pulling away, but Allison still had control.

"Now, my dear. That is an extraordinary cloak. Any thief would kill to possess it," Allison said before she took another sip of tea.

Gina held the cloak, its fabric soft, and she felt her hands and limbs again. She looked to the mirror seeing the cloth reflected. After Allison said a few magic words, everything the cloth covered disappeared. In a panic, Gina threw the cloak to the floor.

"Now, now, my dear, don't be ungrateful. Pick it up." The last sentence Allison gave sounded like an order.

Hesitantly Gina picked up the cloth and held it before her. She could see through the thin fabric, but as she did, she watched herself disappear. She moved the cloak several times over her head but stopped when she looked up to see the smile on Allison's face.

Allison chuckled. "It seems you like my little gift. I know you will appreciate it. It took me hours to enchant."

Gina stood feeling complete control of her body and placed the cloak over herself. She stood here, most of her image disappearing with the exception of her neck and head—the only thing she could see was her master. She smiled before pulling the hood over her face. The rest of her faded from the reflection, leaving only Allison.

The witch handed her tea to Mack, who happily took it from her as Allison stood. "Now, my dear, I'll instruct you how to use this gift."

Gina lifted the hood away. "What am I supposed to do with this? What if someone pulls the hood off?"

Allison chuckled, "I made it so that it magically latches when it's over your head. Only someone with strong protection magic can remove it by force. And I doubt you'll find anyone like that outside the Sanctuary. Now listen, here is how it works."

Gina listened as her master explained how the cloak worked and that she would use it to spy on any hunters she felt might get her close to the forge. Now uncertain as to why her master was giving her this, Gina asked, "What am I supposed to do with this?"

Allison stood, an expression of mastery toward the girl, "My dear little doll, have you forgotten already why you were there?"

Gina shook her head before answering. "To find where they have the sphere you lost."

Allison smiled. "Not just that, my dear, you will steal it back for me. You will be my thief."

Gina shook her head; she had just started learning about her powers with water, and her master was telling her that she was to betray those helping her. Gina felt a conflict she had never experienced before. She went to release the cloak and let it fall to the floor. She had started to say "no" when she felt all control of her body fade, and Gina watched as her body stood at attention.

"Oh, my dear little doll, you don't have a choice in this matter," Allison said as she willed Gina to sit tall in the chair. "You will do as I command. And you will bring back the Sphere of Lieben."

Allison watched as Gina's head nodded in silence. Allison then looked to Mack, saying, "I almost forgot. Mack, fetch the box from my worktable."

Mack nodded and headed into her workshop before quickly returning with a shoebox-sized cardboard box. Allison walked toward the mirror, and Gina stood mimicking her actions.

They both touched the glass, and Gina felt the box in her hands as she pulled it through.

Allison smiled, "Those work with the cloak, my dear. Shoes and gloves. They will allow you to be silent and not leave fingerprints or footprints behind." The witch smiled. "They will also allow you to climb walls without falling."

The witch sat again, "I'll allow you your movement again, my dear. But be warned that these outbursts are becoming tiresome. You may become less than useful."

Gina felt a tingle up her spine when Allison spoke. She could feel her threat.

Allison motioned for her cup, and Mack handed it to her. The witch took a sip, "Now, my dear, I want you to learn about your powers and keep your eyes open."

Gina hesitantly nodded, and Allison's image faded from the mirror.

"I could have used something like that long before I took up law. They would have come in handy," Mack told her.

Allison smiled at him.

Mack sat in the chair nearby, asking, "Aren't you wasting those on the girl?"

Allison politely looked at him before saying, "They sent one of their best thieves to steal from me. But, of course, I'm just enhancing what she already is, a thief. After all, that is how I acquired her in the first place."

Mack smiled, "Oh, I remember, you had her when I returned from, uh…." Mack paused, "persuading one of your critics."

"They stole from me. So, now I'll steal from them." Allison said before looking at Mack, "Whatever happened with that client you persuaded?"

Mack smiled, looking at his hands as he pulled some dirt from his nail. "Well, let's say if they really want to find them, they are going to have to dig a really deep hole."

Chapter 8:
Suspicion

Amanda was leaning against the wall, her eyes focused as she watched Gina attempting to use her powers. All the while, Amanda was wondering why she had never tried using them before. *Why didn't she desire to be closer to her element, water?* That thought was still bouncing around in her head. Amanda watched, looking for something to prove that the woman she knew as Gina was possibly hiding something. "Do I really think she's faking it?" Amanda muttered as she watched the woman hesitate and struggle to manipulate the water in the small pool before her.

Luke approached and leaned on the wall next to Amanda. "She's really having trouble manipulating the water," Luke said, making Amanda turn toward him. She could see the concern in his eyes, like maybe he wasn't telling her something.

"You think she's faking it?" Amanda asked.

Luke sighed, "If she is, she's good. But I don't think I've seen any elemental having this much difficulty. It's like something is preventing her from using her powers correctly." Luke chuckled, "I'm surprised she let you stay and watch. She seems pretty shy about using her powers around others consciously."

Amanda smiled, saying, "Guess she doesn't mind me being around."

Luke leaned in, "I know I don't mind."

But, as he leaned in closer, they both heard, "If you two kiss, again, I'm insisting you get a room."

Luke turned to see Raymond Cranston standing next to him. The man, or what was left of him, ran the Sanctuary. Seeing him pop up unannounced could be awkward to those new to the facility. Amanda, at first, wondered why anyone would choose to be bound magically to a building.

That was until Raymond told her why he decided to do so. His story was one that she found fascinating. She discovered that Raymond wasn't bonded to the building but to the crystal used to light the Forge. She still couldn't believe that Raymond was over six hundred years old. His consciousness resided within the Forge's fire and the crystal it used for energy. Raymond was a Celtic warrior. In his previous life, he vowed to keep the world safe from evil magic and those who wielded it.

Amanda smiled, shaking her head, saying, "How many people do you freak out when you just show up, Raymond?"

The old warrior replied, "Oh, a lot."

Amanda watched him chuckle.

"I'm here to inform you that Selese will be finished shortly. And that she's scheduled a portal using the Shadowed Hall for your short trip." Raymond said, causing Luke to look at Amanda for clarification.

But Amanda looked at Raymond, asking, "Did she say where?"

Luke stared at her, hoping to get an answer, and heard Raymond say, "The museum where another *tianqiu* was stolen. It's near, upstate, not in China, by the way."

Amanda huffed, saying, "Good, I didn't bring my passport." Then, hearing a loud splash and complaining, Amanda again watched Gina trying to use her powers with little control. She started to feel bad for her; Amanda had met many magical creatures, and all had some control of what they could naturally do. But Gina seemed different.

Raymond then said, "Oh, and your friends are already there. Lord Cale insisted that they investigate as well."

Amanda turned to thank Raymond for the information only to see Luke staring back at her, his eyes filled with a suspicious glint, and heard him say, "You know, for someone who isn't sure about being a Raven Hunter, you certainly do a lot of work like we do."

Amanda focused on Luke as if saying, *What are you going to do about it?*

Raymond noticed the interaction and laughed before he vanished from their sight. Amanda told Luke, "You know, if I hadn't been used to magic, that would have freaked me out."

Luke said, "So, your group's together again?"

Amanda nodded. "Unofficially. They still don't want me going to any dangerous places."

"Neither do I."

"Oh, it's so nice that you care." Amanda smiled, giving Luke a gentle kiss. "Selese asked me to come to the Sanctuary to discuss the snooping she proposed earlier. Before she was called back in."

Amanda looked into his eyes. She liked it when Luke smiled. She knew he was concerned about her, but she also knew he didn't mind her being involved with the hunters. Unfortunately, the moment was interrupted as they heard a loud splash and several people yelling, with Gina repeating, "I'm sorry, I didn't know I could do that."

The two looked over. "What'd we miss?"

Amanda smiled, "Guess we'll find out eventually." Amanda seemed to think for a moment. She had copied the symbol, and during Luke's report, Dr. Brentwood had asked her to stop by with a drawing of what she had seen.

"Damn, I forgot to bring something for your boss," Amanda said.

"I'm sure Lord Cale won't mind getting it when you get back," Luke told her.

Amanda shook her head. "No, your other boss, and not me."

Luke thought for a moment and watched Amanda mouth the name Brentwood. Then, before she sketched out the symbol on the pad she carried, she started out of the room, saying, "I'll be back. Hopefully, I won't keep Selese waiting too long."

About an hour later, Selese was waiting for Amanda at the Shadowed Hall. She had already cleared the short trip and, given the recent requests from their fellow hunters across the other end of the world, Li Xiu was also joining them. Li Xiu stood nearby, examining the columns that held the ceiling above. She even took a rubbing of some of the symbols. As she finished, she walked back to stand next to Selese.

Selese didn't look up from her phone as Li Xiu stood quietly beside her. "They're not going to let you keep that."

Li Xiu looked at Selese, smiling, "Keep what?" She then showed her pocket and hands empty.

Selese moved closer, pretending to remove a small piece of dust, diverting Li Xiu's attention, and then moved back to show her the paper rubbing of the column Li Xiu had placed in her pocket only a moment ago. "This. They won't let you keep this."

"Wait, how did you get that? I've used that to secure items before," Li Xiu asked.

Selese smiled. She turned the paper to dust using the graphite from the pencil and her powers as a geomage. "Any good thief knows about a hidden pocket spell. It comes in handy. Also, they're easy to steal from if you know how they work."

Li Xiu started to show anger before one of the guards that protected the hall appeared behind her.

"Stealing elements is forbidden. Even given your status as a hunter, we would have to either imprison you or send you back." The guard's words were filled with finality.

The woman looked up to see the man towering over her, and she stepped back. Her following action was to strike at the man delivering a blow to his midsection. She was surprised to feel the force of her impact push back against her arm. The recoil blunted only by the man grabbing her forearm, holding her fast. She tried to pull away, but it was like trying to pull her arm out of solid stone.

Selese looked up, her expression annoyed, "Even I'm not crazy enough to mess with Shadow guards." She looked up at the man. "Dent, could you release her, please? I'm already trying not to make this a Hunter—not to mention an international—incident."

The guard tilted his head as he looked at Selese, "She's your responsibility?"

Selese nodded. "Yeah, I'm not happy about it either. But, it seems they need our help."

As Selese finished her sentence, Amanda appeared from the door that led into the hall, "Sorry, had to stop by and get something to Dr. Brentwood." She looked at Li Xiu nursing her injured arm and asked, "Did I miss something?"

Selese nodded, "Li Xiu tried knocking down Dent."

Seeing the woman in mild pain, Amanda held back a smile before asking, "You alright?"

Li Xiu nodded, "I forgot that shadow guards wore enchanted armor. They have it back home as well."

Selese tapped her on the shoulder with a friendly punch, "Good to know. Come on, let's get going."

* * *

They arrived at the museum, appearing in the shadows of the display room. They could hear Ron speaking with one of the guards about the theft. Selese split away, leaving Amanda and Li Xiu together. The two looked at each other, and Amanda said, "Maybe we should find the others first." Nodding in agreement, Li Xiu followed Amanda as she walked toward the sound of Ron's voice.

As they turned the corner, appearing from around the column, they heard the guard yell, "Hey, what are you two doing in here?"

Ron turned to see Amanda and an unknown woman standing next to her before Amanda held her hands up. "Just taking notes. They asked us along for the investigation."

As the guard started toward the two, Ron placed his hand on the man's shoulder and spoke a few words causing the guard to freeze mid-step. Then, he pointed to Amanda and the other woman, "You're late. And who's this?"

Amanda looked amazed at seeing the man standing balanced on one foot, frozen mid-step. "Where did you learn how to down that?"

Ron paused, "Uh, Budapest. Weren't you told you had to come in through the front entrance? They have to log everyone in and out of here."

Just as Ron finished his sentence, a police officer inspected the frozen guard. Amanda tapped Ron's arm, alerting him to the situation. However, Ron's reaction was not what she expected. "Sorry, Chuck, had to freeze him. These two showed up out of nowhere."

The officer walked over. "They with you?"

Ron nodded.

Officer Chuck looked at the two women, "You were supposed to come in through the front entrance." The officer looked back. "Now I have to adjust his memory."

Li Xiu looked confused and asked the officer, "Are you with them?"

The officer was about to answer when Selese appeared from around the corner, "I've got us logged. . . uh. . . in. . ." she paused, seeing the guard frozen and the officer standing next to Ron. As she walked over, she heard the officer say, "Hi, Selese. You did tell these two that you had to check in out front, right?"

Selese took a moment before recognizing the man's voice, "Officer Charles? Is that you?"

The officer smiled at Selese, "Wow, the last time I saw you was almost ten years ago." He seemed to reminisce for a moment, "I caught you trying to steal a spear from some antique shop." Then, he turned to Ron, saying, "I had a hell of a time keeping her in a cell."

Seeing Selese smile as she walked over didn't affect Li Xiu, who again asked if the officer was with them.

The officer nodded, showing his forearm and placing his hand over it, causing the raven symbol to appear. "Yes, I'm one of them."

Ron scoffed, joking, "Technically, you are, but us, well. . . "

Selese chuckled, "If we're being strict, technically, Li Xiu is the only other Raven Hunter here."

Chuck looked to Selese, "I don't remember seeing her when I last reported in. Is she new?"

Selese shook her head. "Well, she's from another Sanctuary. The one in China."

Ron looked toward Linda as she walked into view, saying, "She's part of the *Yín yā lièrén*, then."

"Probably." Ron said, then looked to Amanda. "We try to stay out of their hair. They play pretty rough."

Ron glanced toward Linda, "We're better off here than having to deal with what Brentwood is facing back at the Sanctuary."

Li Xiu began to wonder what he was speaking about before she looked at Linda, as a question entered her mind. "Wait, how do you know of us if you're not hunters?"

"The Circle has files on your people, as I'm sure they have some on the members here and the Circle," Ron said, stepping forward. "But, between us, I hope you don't have to go back to your superiors with this. We have a few friends over there as well. Couldn't have helped out Zhang if we didn't."

"Zhang who?" Li Xiu asked. Ron smiled, saying nothing.

Linda said, "Your people have their network, as do we. And truthfully, if they had given us the information up front, we might have been able to have stopped several people being turned to stone in Chaozhou."

Li Xiu thought for a moment—she had heard recent rumors of a warlock who had escaped by turning the guards to stone. She remembered that the master of the local Sanctuary had thanked some foreigners for apprehending the offender.

"That huoguo he sent us as a thank you has come in handy," Linda said, coming to stand next to Ron. "It does make good food when you ask."

Li Xiu looked to Amanda, now realizing that Ron and Linda were probably responsible for apprehending the warlock back in Chaozhou. Then, she turned to Amanda accusingly, "You told me you never went to China?"

Amanda defended herself, her voice filled with a hint of anger, "I haven't. They don't take me on all of their adventures."

Ron looked at Li Xiu. "She's right; we didn't take her. Like I said before, your people play rough. It was too dangerous."

Li Xiu watched as Amanda shook her head. "Look, let's stop all of this. Didn't we come here to work together on a job?"

Selese smiled, "that's why I'm here. I don't know about the rest of you."

Amanda agreed, "Well, what are we hanging around arguing for. Let's get this thing solved."

Ron nodded. As he and Linda turned, walking toward the storage room, they all heard him say, "Well, sounds like Amanda's back."

As Selese was walking away, the officer looked at the frozen guard, and she asked, "You want me to make an adjustment?"

The officer shook his head. "Nah, I've got this. Had to do it a lot around here lately. You head on with them, see what you can find."

As Selese disappeared into the shadows, the officer said, "Now, let's see, he saw a ghost? Nah, he thought he saw the thief and was chasing them. Nah." The officer thought for a moment and then said, "Thought he saw a giant doughnut. Yeah, that always makes fun reading in reports."

Chapter 9:
Something Seems Off

Dr. Brentwood looked at the symbol Amanda handed her, only to recognize the element as a protective beacon. The doctor then looked around her office before muttering, "Dennon used something similar against us. I hope they don't make the same mistake." She placed the drawing into a folder before putting it into the top drawer of her desk. The doctor then turned to her computer—the screen displayed the report from Ron about the recent trip they made to China. The two had decided to share the information in good faith with the Circle since they and the China Sanctuary had asked them to be involved.

Snow Mountain had sent along one of their leading hunters, Hou Chung. Since the theft of the icon of Tarnus almost two years ago, the safety of many items had been brought into question. To prevent an incident she had to agree to give full reign and aid to the regent until all of the artifacts were either secured or taken back to the Snow Mountain Sanctuary. However, security was a concern and her mind returned to one fact, *something seemed to be blocking all of the hunters from finding out who was committing these recent thefts.*

The doctor typed away before looking to the door, yelling, "Colleen. Are you available?"

Colleen seemed to magically appear from the doorway, "Yes, doctor, what do you need?"

Dr. Brentwood finished typing, "Do we have an update on the new student yet? Anything on her progress?"

Colleen thought for a moment before moving quickly and returning with a folder. "Nothing yet. According to the reports, she has little to no control of her abilities." Colleen looked closely at the paper, making Dr. Brentwood take notice.

"Something unusual, Colleen?" Dr. Brentwood asked.

Colleen nodded, "She seems to have times when her powers appear to wane. I don't know if that's usual for a water elemental."

The doctor sat back, "It's irregular. I have never heard of anything such as that happening." She then motioned to Colleen for the file. Dr. Brentwood read through the report, and what she saw didn't make sense. Her mind began to ponder recent events. *These events started when Malcolm Mitchell showed up with her.* She knew the man listed as her ward had magic; it was detected as soon as he arrived. The lawyer freely admitted that he had a gold charm that allowed him to persuade people using facts. Although unethical, he seemed to cause no harm and did appear to do some good with his chosen profession.

Dr. Brentwood looked to see Colleen patiently waiting for her to say something. Then, as the doctor closed the file, she said, "Have them test that girl Gina again. If she has difficulty with her powers, there may be a conflict within her."

Colleen nodded, "I'll alert the crystal team. Are we looking for anything specific?"

Dr. Brentwood seemed in thought, "I'm not sure."

Colleen nodded and rushed away, leaving the doctor alone, and one thing came to mind: *why would things seem off since she arrived?*

* * *

It was before lunch, and Shrive was watching alongside Luke. He had been assigned to follow Gina since she arrived. Something that he didn't seem to mind. Gina seemed to stay on campus and, for that matter, mostly in her room. That fact he discussed with Shrive as they stood away from the training team.

"I don't have much to report. She seems to stay put most of the time. I've only seen her go out and get food, mostly."

His fellow hunter nodded, "Amanda seems to think she's holding back for some reason. And I've seen the same look in her eyes when she thinks something is up."

Luke nodded. He agreed that most elementals he had seen develop a natural affinity for their element. But this woman seemed to lack any control. He thought for a moment, thinking about Amanda before asking, "Where is she anyway?"

Shrive huffed before telling him, "With Selese and Li Xiu. They went to investigate that attempted museum theft. The one in Massachusetts."

Luke leaned against the wall with more force than usual. "She told me she would stay out of Circle business."

Shrive replied, "I'm not sure it is just Circle business anymore. Their small group seems to be getting some notoriety recently. Someone in the *Yín yā lièrén* requested for them to investigate?"

Luke gave an interested glance before returning to watch Gina splash some of the trainers again.

"They don't trust the Raven hunters?"

Shrive shook her head. "This was outside even their ranks. Maybe it was something Ron and Linda found while they were away. Who knows? Honestly, I don't think Li Xiu knows they were asked. But they did ask Ron and Linda to bring the *tianqiu* back to the Forge when finished. It apparently has something special in it."

Luke stared at Shrive with disbelief. "It almost sounds like you're a bit jealous?"

Shrive looked forward, saying nothing.

"Shrive, what's up? This isn't like you," Luke said.

"She's trying to be some perfect investigator. That and she knows more than she's telling us. I'm beginning to think she doesn't trust us." The cat girl bowed her head. "I don't know. It's like Li Xiu thinks she's better than all of us."

Luke continued to stare at her, not believing what she said. He had known Shrive for years and had never seen her like this. He was about to say something but was interrupted when Gina approached.

"Hey, nice to see you again. You've been hanging around a lot. Are you following me?" Gina asked, the playful tone not lost on either hunter.

Luke nodded. "I was assigned to watch over you while you're here. It's part of my job."

Gina moved closer. She tapped his chin gently, "Well, thanks for watching over me. I couldn't ask for someone as special." She then walked toward the door, giving Luke one last look before disappearing.

Shrive chuckled, "She seems to be taking a liking to you. I hope Amanda doesn't mind."

Luke responded, "Me too. I handle enough trouble already." They both laughed as they followed her.

Luke appeared in the hall near Gina's room. He kept his distance as per protocol and Amanda's request. Not that she minded him being on watch, but something in her gut was telling her that Gina wasn't what she claimed. Luke leaned against the wall, "Looks like I'll be here for a while. Might as well set up a detection spell. I almost fell asleep last time I was stuck here."

He gave a wave, tapping one of the elements on his arm, and a translucent wall filled the hallway on both sides. This spell was something new he had acquired, something from the archives to replace the element he removed. He had to find something to replace the one that Dennon used against everyone else almost two years ago. The shadowmark he created allowed him to travel but still tied him to the Shadowed Hall. So unlike Ron and Linda, the Circle could still track him if needed. Luke had been keeping watch for some time, almost two days straight, with little sleep. As he waited nearby, his eyes felt heavy, and within minutes of the silence, he drifted off, sliding to the floor gently.

* * *

Allison watched through the girl's eyes as Gina held the cloak while telling Gina what to do and how to use the symbols it contained.

"Gina, my doll, did you have any more news on the sphere?"

Gina shook her head and again held the cloak over her head. She could see the cloak, but the mirror reflected nothing. Allison shook her head, "You're playing with this as if it is a toy, my dear. Please pay attention and listen."

Allison's glare met Gina as she looked up, seeing the glare from Allison, and placed the cloak across her lap. "That's a good dear. Now, if you'll look at the left sleeve."

In the mirror, Allison watched as Gina held the sleeve. "Now, my dear, that will allow you to port using any shadow. And not with that accursed Shadowed Hall. Although it will only be a short distance."

She watched Gina look up, hearing her ask, "Will it get me into the Forge?"

Allison shook her head. "There is too much light there. Unless, of course, you can fool one of the guards into making a shadow for you." Allison sighed. "Although I do want that sphere, I would like you to test the cloak first, my dear. Preferably on something less valuable."

Mack handed Allison another cup of tea, and she playfully thanked him for the service. Then, she looked at Gina again. "The *tianqiu* that Mack acquired is a fake, my dear. I understand that there is another nearby being studied. However, I want you to steal that first."

Gina looked at the mirror. "Can I use it to get home?"

Allison shook her head. "It's a short hop only, my dear. I just told you that."

Gina looked disheartened.

Mack handed her a note, the blank paper only showing words as Allison touched it. She read the letter and scoffed, "Vikander is recruiting. He may be forming the Trimaxica once he acquires the additional icons. Then he'll create a tribunal to cement their authority." She turned her eyes toward her servant, "That letter is his way of asking for me to join. He and the others always hoped to rule this world. "

Mack looked interested. "It would be an honor to rule the world. You're not thinking of turning him down, are you?"

Allison looked at him, "The Broken Feather was created long ago. I am old enough to remember the creation of the Hunters." She paused. "I'll have to consider things. I do prefer my autonomy. It makes things much easier than having to discipline peasants. But, on the other hand, I do miss imposing my will on so many."

Allison seemed lost in thought before she spoke, looking back into the mirror, "You can use the cloak to evade others if you need my little doll. Other than that, I fear you may need to find transportation to where I'm sending you next." Allison turned to Mack, "Have you heard from any of our other informants at the Museum?"

Mack shook his head, "No. However, most employees have been sent home until they are done investigating. Therefore, we may not hear anything." The man paused to look at the window, motioning to ask if they needed to protect them as she had done days earlier. Allison shook her head, telling him that her little toy would work till it was extinguished or recalled. Then, with Mack's question, she looked at him, asking, "Do you have something you wish to share?"

Mack sat straight "Well, yes. I had heard before our contact left that the artifact was to be moved at the end of the investigation."

Allison seemed annoyed, asking, "To where?"

Mack sounded defeated, knowing the following words were those his mistress would not want to hear, "To the Forge."

Allison's teeth gave a silent snarl before she sipped her tea. Her mind was now plotting an alternative to the reacquisition of the additional *tianqiu*. Her eyes narrowed as a smile rippled across her lips. She looked in the mirror. "My dear, I will send you a location. You may acquire the *tianqiu* when I'm ready." She then waved her hand and politely placed the cup on her desk before standing and moving to the bookshelf. She ran her finger across several books and pulled one from the row.

Mack watched as she flipped through the pages and gave an evil smile as she stopped. "Well, hunters, since I cannot set foot on your grounds, perhaps a little taste of your own medicine would be appropriate."

Allison placed the open book on her desk, reached over to the magic dust she had procured, and started sprinkling it around the page. She could see the School and Sanctuary in the images displayed, and she drew a line with her finger, her touch surrounding the image with a glowing streak. She then pulled the line to a point and tapped that.

"Dust of power, travel, and rhyme. Heed my note."

"No one may pass who carries a *tianqiu*."

Mack watched curiously and went to touch the page, causing Allison to slap his hand away. "The spell will only last a few hours, do not touch this book till that line stops glowing."

Mack looked to Allison, "What is the spell?"

Allison took a sip of her tea before replying, "I am forbidding any *tianqiu* from going near the Sanctuary. Anyone who has one would be driven to that point. It's crude but effective."

Mack smiled at her. "Simple, but clever as always."

Allison chuckled. She snapped her fingers, and her chair rolled around as she sat gently down. "Oh Mack, we have known each other for so long." She looked up to stare at him with a practiced gaze. "I can't give you all of my secrets."

She then motioned for him to move away, and he obeyed. Allison looked to her mirror. "We'll have to wait. Whoever has that artifact will need help. We need only watch the hunters and see who they send."

Mack sat in the chair across from her desk. "Let the peons do our work for us?"

Allison nodded. *Once I have seven of the tianqiu, I'll be able to enclose an area where my will is law. So even if Vikander is asking for a triad, it doesn't fit my plans.*

A home is where it is warm and safe, whether it be roof, tree, or darkened cave, where life thrives is home.

- Brownie saying.

Chapter 10:
Invisibility can be Fun

It was late in the day and Gina was in her room. She sprayed on some perfume she bought the day earlier. She swore it reminded her of the ocean. Her hands felt the fabric of the cloak Allison had provided. Her mistress had yet to provide any more instructions, so Gina was waiting. Before long she turned on the television, her attention elsewhere, her eyes focusing above it into the distance. Her thoughts drifting into clouded memories.

Then she heard Allison's voice in her mind, and her previous instructions; within moments, she was back to normal. Gina huffed in frustration before putting on the cloak and walking out of her room. She paused, seeing what looked like a field of energy glistening around her body as she walked down the hall. It stopped as she neared the small area holding the vending machines. She stepped back, holding her arm up to examine the phenomenon.

Is this the cloak? She asked herself.

She stepped forward into the light. She could see no shadow from her body. Gina had to move out of the way as another student almost walked into her. *No one can see me.* Gina smiled and followed after the student. She entered the elevator and stood next to him. She had a mischievous glint in her eyes as she gently tapped the top of his ear. She watched as the man flinched, looking around before gently grabbing his ear.

Gina then did the same thing as before and watched the man spin around. His eyes searched for something that wasn't there. She was surprised as he reached out both hands, searching for something. Gina was agile enough to avoid him touching her, and she stayed behind him as the doors to the elevator opened. She heard him say, "There's more weird stuff going on again. I think the elevator's haunted this time."

The other student looked at the empty car of the elevator and smiled, saying, "Whatever," as he stepped inside. Gina exited the door and stood against the wall. She started laughing. In front of her, the man stopped. He looked around before asking, "Who's laughing?"

Gina froze, covering her mouth, *Guess this cloak isn't as stealthy as I thought.*

She crept as she passed the man only to stop abruptly, her eyes again staring into the distance. She could hear Allison's voice in her mind, "That's quite enough, my little doll. It was amusing. But we have work to do." Gina felt no control of her body as Allison took over.

It was only minutes before Gina was outside the utility building. Unfortunately, it also happened to be near the Sanctuary's main entrance. Allison recognized Shrive as one of the hunters, and watched as the one she knew as Luke grabbed her arm, telling her something.

Damn, we're too far away to hear. Have to get closer, Gina heard in her mind before she headed inside.

Gina's body moved quickly. Truthfully Allison didn't care if she exhausted her toy. She needed information on the *tianqiu* that was heading back to the Forge.

She caught up with the two hunters and followed them. She watched as the one she knew as Shrive walked away. Allison overheard her, saying, "I'm getting something to eat." She then watched as the woman sniffed the air as if looking for something.

Nothing's happening yet. I guess I'll wait here a while. Gina heard and felt the coldness of the stone column as Allison hid her behind one.

* * *

"That actually has the essence of someone's energy inside?" Amanda asked as she held the small sphere.

Selese nodded, "Yep, just like the remaining icons we have safely put away." However, Selese seemed less than enthusiastic about touching the artifact. That was something Linda took notice of. She tapped Ron's arm, asking, "Did you find anything?"

Ron shook his head, answering, "Whoever it was used magic I haven't seen before, or nothing at all."

Selese looked at him, saying, "I couldn't find anything either."

Her statement made both her and Ron stare at each other. Both could tell what the other was thinking. *But magic or not, there would still be evidence. Someone tampered with everything here.*

"Chuck! You still here?" Ron yelled, breaking the silence, hoping he wasn't interrupting the Raven Hunter from adjusting the guard's memory.

But instead, he was relieved to hear Chuck yell back, "You find something?"

All turned to see the officer enter the door of the storage room. Ron shook his head, "Nothing, absolutely nothing." Ron looked to the officer. "So, in essence, we found something. We just don't know what it is yet."

The officer looked at Linda and heard her say, "Don't look at me. He sometimes talks in riddles when he finds something." He turned to see Amanda smiling and nodding as well.

"Well, what didn't you find?" Chuck asked.

"Nothing. And that's the problem. We found absolutely nothing. We're pretty sure the scene's been mopped up," Ron answered, then pointed to Selese.

The officer looked around, "You sure?"

Ron nodded.

Everyone heard the heavy sigh from the officer. He looked at the *tianqiu* Li Xiu held.

"I had word from the Circle while you were back here. They told me they asked you to bring the item in for protection."

Ron moved to stand before Li Xiu and asked for the *tianqiu*. She reluctantly handed it to him without saying a word, but didn't know why. She just felt she could trust him. Amanda stood nearby, saying, "Someone really wants it, don't they?"

Ron mashed his lips together, nodding as he looked around, causing Linda to say, "Then we should probably leave."

Linda looked at the officer. "We'll see you Thursday for breakfast? Coffee? Same shop as last time."

Chuck nodded. "You can fill me in if I don't hear anything when I check in. I get the feeling they're not telling me everything."

Selese laughed, replying, "Oh, I'm sure they aren't."

Ron pointed to Amanda. "You go with them. Let them know we're coming." He looked to the officer. "Last time we popped in, we startled the shadow guards. We were halfway to the council room before they caught up with us."

The officer looked puzzled. "That's impossible."

Linda smiled. "We don't have tot use the Shadowed Hall. It's just convenient to arrive there."

"Then how do you travel?" Chuck asked.

Ron held up the crystal artifact. "Later, let's get this someplace more secure."

The officer nodded. "You three get going. Make sure they know these two are coming. I'll keep them safe until they leave."

Amanda protested but seeing the green of Linda's eyes staring at her with a seriousness she wasn't used to seeing made her change her mind. She and the others headed back to the Sanctuary. Ron and Linda tapped their bracelets. Within moments they faded before the officer's eyes. Chuck stood alone. "I don't know how I'm going to write that in my report."

Upon arriving, they informed the shadow guards that Ron and Linda were right behind them with an artifact that needed to be protected. Within a minute, the Shadowed Hall had several Raven Hunters inside. Amanda was happy to see Luke was among them.

"What, no babysitting today?" Amanda chided Luke, who only shook his head in disbelief. His shift watching Gina had ended, and he was coming in for a good rest.

Amanda turned, hearing Selese laughing before saying, "I'm sure they'll be along in a minute."

Ron and Linda watched as the far opening of the purple-hued tunnel approached quickly. Linda felt her body snap around as Ron was quickly left behind. She rolled as she materialized in the hall between the shadow columns—crying from pain as she sat up quickly, holding her arm, alerting everyone.

"Linda! Are you alright?" Amanda asked, rushing to pick her up from the floor.

Linda's red hair tossed as she looked around for her husband. "Where's Ron? Something separated us." Everyone looked around, but there was no sign of him.

Allison turned Gina's head and could see a group of hunters gathered by a woman with red hair as she rolled across the floor. She quickly and carefully approached to hear them.

Oh, and an amethyst gate. Another witch, perhaps? Allison thought. *I'll just deal with her like the others if she gets in my way.*

She then heard the red-haired woman say, "He still has the *tianqiu*. We have to find out what happened."

"This is wonderful. She was traveling along with the person who had the artifact. My spell worked." The witch then thought, *when you find him, I'll use my toy to tag along.* She then waited for her chance.

Linda looked behind her. She held out her arm revealing her bracelet, the silver and purple stone glowing ethereally.

"Is that an amethyst gate?" Selese asked, very interested.

Selese came over, inspecting it intently before looking to see if Linda was injured. Linda nodded, confirming what Selese had surmised.

Amanda looked at Luke. "You know what that is?" She watched Luke shake his head.

Selese turned. "You can port using the stone. Some geomages use them." She looked at Linda, "Tell me where you got this one. How much did it cost?"

Linda looked sternly at Selese and was about to speak when she heard Li Xiu say, "Wait aren't amethysts fairy stones? Humans can't use them, only fairies."

Linda and Selese looked with surprise toward the hunter only to see Amanda nearby holding her hands up, a wave of growing anger and frustration showing on her face. Linda shook her head. Her voice was filled with conviction. "Not a word, Amanda."

Amanda's brown hair covered her face as she snapped her eyes toward Linda to see her friend staring back, her eyes filled with a fire of certainty. Amanda remembered discovering that her friends were part fairy some time ago, and she felt her anger subside. Amanda knew Linda was right. No more than the few who knew already should have that information.

Amanda realized she did not need to be jealous, these were her friends, and they had their own lives. Amanda looked to Luke. "Find Shrive. We may need her to track Ron."

The Raven hunter could see Linda staring back, impatience in her eyes now as she said, "I can track him with this. I just hope he's not in trouble."

Chapter 11:
A Little Travel Trouble

Ron felt the ground hit him hard, rolling as he exited the portal. He quickly found himself in what looked like a remote wooded area. He rose to his feet, trying to get his bearings. The surroundings were unfamiliar.

Ron called out, "Linda? Where are you?"

He heard no reply.

"Amanda? Selese?"

He remained still for a moment listening, hearing no sounds of footsteps, or branches breaking, only the light wind among the leaves above.

"Seems like it's just me." His pause was warranted. "Okay, I'm thinking this is a good place to get attacked." Ron was cautious, moving closer to one of the trees. Although it was night, he could still see in the spotted moonlight. The spring leaves were just coming out, their presence creating patterns on the forest floor. He looked around again for any sign of a possible enemy but found no one—the stillness of his fairy ring, which usually alerted him to danger, became a concern.

"Whoever it was, they were strong enough to break me out of the portal. Amethyst gates are notoriously stable," Ron muttered, looking around. "I probably shouldn't wait around."

Ron looked up to see the moon for a few seconds, then pointed in a direction and started walking. He reached into his pocket, pulled out his phone, and dialed Linda. He heard her pick up and told her he was somewhere in the middle of a forest.

"It seems pretty remote from what I can tell." Ron looked to his phone, opening the map program, which still hadn't locked onto his location. "I'm still waiting for the satellites to sync. Did you make it back?"

She told him that they all had, except for him. Ron snickered as the map location showed on his phone. "You won't believe this, but I'm just outside the school. About a mile or so."

He heard Linda sigh in relief. Ron then looked at the screen and pointed in a direction before jogging toward where he knew the road was. Ron turned, heading toward the lights he could see through the forest but stopped abruptly, nearly jogging off a small cliff near the trail. The undersized wire across the trees was the only thing stopping him from making that tall step to the rock-studded bank of the stream below.

"Just found a stream. I almost walked off a ledge doing so," Ron admitted, making Linda tell him to be careful.

"I'll be roadside in a few minutes. I think I'm close to that diner out by the gas station." Ron said.

He could hear Linda tell him, "Go ahead and see if you can get inside."

Ron looked at the screen. "It's almost three in the morning. I don't think they'd like me breaking in. I don't even know if they are op. . .uf. . ."

Linda could hear rustling as Ron's phone hit and tumbled across the ground.

Ron let out a string of expletives as he rolled to sit up. His eyes were tearing as he wiped above his lip. His hand showed a decent amount of blood across it.

Ron grunted, "Dammit, I think I broke my nose. Probably ran into a branch." He looked up and all around to see nothing but the clear sky above the path he was running. He looked forward seeing the screen of his phone glowing a short distance away. Ron wrestled himself to his feet and walked to pick up his phone, only to feel something solid hit his face again. He held up his hand, pressed against something solid, but there was clearly nothing.

"Okay, this is new," Ron said and stepped back. He started waving his arms and found nothing behind him. As he walked forward again about the same spot, he again felt the solid invisible presence. Ron could see his phone down the trail and yelled, "I think I have a problem. How soon can you get here?"

Linda heard Ron's voice faint as if it was in the distance. She called his name but looked at her phone. She could not hear a reply. Linda tapped the two hematite stones on the sides of the purple crystal until it glowed with a swirling light. "Got him." She seemed concerned before saying, "I can't pull him back."

She looked to the others, "Everyone who's coming, get over here. We're going. Now!" Luke and Amanda were by her instantly, Selese and Shrive joining them, along with Li Xiu.

Linda looked at everyone. "Okay, we're doing this the hard way. So everyone who wants to go, hold on to me, and I'll take us there."

Hearing Linda yell, Allison smiled, which also appeared on Gina's face. "Seems like my spell worked. He's not able to return. I better get over there. I don't want to miss my chance to claim my prize." Allison placed her doll's hand onto Linda's arm next to Shrive. The proximity making the hunter sniff the air as a sweet smell arrived.

Shrive said, "Who's wearing perfume? It smells nice."

The confused looks from her friends were replaced by amazement as they entered the purple portal. They all arrived behind Ron and watched as he turned to look at them, his hand pressing hard against an invisible force.

Linda spoke, half concerned, "You know I couldn't pull you back. It's like something's holding you here." She then rushed over, suddenly seeing the blood along his face. She stopped, reaching up to touch his nose, gently squeezing it, making him wince away.

"Broken?" Linda asked.

Ron nodded, "I think so." She watched him brush off the pain of the injury. Linda walked forward, and passed the area where Ron was standing.

She stepped back, looking puzzled. "I think it's just you."

Ron handed Linda the *tianqiu* and raised his hand but felt nothing but air. He walked forward, surprised. "Guess you broke the spell that was holding me. We could head to the diner or somewhere where there's light. This would be one hell of a spot for an ambush."

Linda smiled, giving a nod, and walked forward. Ron watched as she ran face-first into the same energy that held him moments ago. He moved quickly to see her holding her nose as well. Linda dropped the tianqiu as she said, "Whatever it is, it's solid. I can vouch for that."

Amanda moved to see if her friends were alright. No one noticed the leaves on the ground crumbled by invisible footsteps. Li Xiu sniffed the air and could smell the strong scent of perfume, and she looked toward the others, saying, "Whoever has that perfume, let me know where you got it. It smells delightful. I want to pick some up."

The *tianqiu* remained on the ground as everyone looked around. Finally, Linda broke the silence, saying, "that's the second time someone's asked that question. Who is wearing perfume here?"

They all looked at each other, and the silence allowed Shrive to hear leaves crunching nearby.

"Shhh," Shrive said, looking around. She looked to Selese before morphing into a more feline form, her ears prominent and twitching.

Seeing this through Gina's eyes, the witch said quietly, "A shapeshifter?" She looked closely, keeping Gina still, and could hear an animal diverting Shrive's attention in the forest. The witch quickly moved her doll to grab the *tianqiu* and hide it inside her cloak. Shrive watched the artifact disappear and jumped forward. The sounds of the hunter were the only indication that she was fighting an invisible opponent. Allison used Gina to punch the now-feline woman right in the nose. The sound of a growling hiss escaped as Shrive rolled to the side as Gina hoisted her off.

The witch moved Gina, only to have Li Xiu in front of her. The witch reached out to the book across her desk and swiped across the glowing lines she had drawn. They faded quickly. The hunter felt the faint push of a hand before Shrive passed by, chasing something. She followed after the catgirl. The others were more cautious and looked for the *tianqiu* nearby while the others followed what seemed like a wisp. Shrive's eyes were bearing on the ground seeing the footsteps in the forest leaves.

They watched as a nearby tree, leaves, and wire sprang back and forth, the sound of a thud following as a large patch of leaves shifted. Then, as they seemed to move again, the tianqiu appeared from nowhere. Allison willed her servant to move, but the impact of the safety wire stunned Gina.

"Useless doll," Allison muttered as she concentrated intently.

Li Xiu picked up the artifact and held it close. She heard something behind her, but when she checked, there was no one on the ground. Gina remained still before Allison moved her slowly beside the now-transformed Shrive.

Allison smiled, looking at the woman holding the *tianqiu*, "Well, a shapeshifting Raven Hunter and a Silver Raven in the same place." Allison rubbed her hands together. "My dear little doll, it looks like you've brought me a bonus. The Silver Ravens could also use a bit of payback for denying me these items."

Under Allison's control, Gina grabbed Shrive's arm and pulled her toward Li Xiu. The surprised look on Shrive's face was mirrored by her fellow hunters as Li Xiu felt her arm twisted backward, the Silver hunter crying out at the impact of her arm being slammed against a tree. She felt the snapping of the bones, causing her to release the artifact. Allison then used Gina to push Shrive's arm forward.

"You stole from me. Now I think I'll ruin your life a bit. Until I find my Sphere, that is." Allison said, willing Gina to push Shrive into Li Xiu, causing the Silver Hunter to fall backward. In a reflex, Li Xiu reached out as she spun around, her hand grasping onto something that wasn't there. By instinct, Gina's hand clamped down on the hunter's injured arm to remain steady. Li Xiu felt that and the pull of fabric as it shifted. She glanced up to see glass-like blue eyes now uncovered as she started to tumble off the cliff. Moments later, Li Xiu felt hands wrapping around her injured arm. Li Xiu looked up to see Amanda holding tightly as she struggled to pull her up from her precarious location. The hunter looked over toward Shrive, who seemed to be struggling with something invisible before coming to help. The others soon joined them.

Li Xiu felt her feet steady on the ground, Amanda still holding onto her arm as Linda asked if everyone was all right.

Li Xiu looked around, "Where is it? The *tianqiu*?"

All eyes searched around, but no one saw it anywhere. Linda looked at Li Xiu, "We'll find it. Are you alright?"

The hunter shook her head, "I think my arm's broken." Linda watched as the woman suddenly looked defeated. "I lost the *tianqiu*. But, I thought I saw something."

Ron sighed audibly. "Technically, it was in our care, so it was our responsibility, not yours."

Li Xiu looked to Ron. She watched him look at Linda. "Make the call and tell them we lost it. We'll give them the full details."

Linda looked to Ron. "Zhang first? Or their people?"

Ron thought for a moment looking at Li Xiu. "She's injured. Call them first, then Zhang." He looked at Linda, saying, "I don't think anyone else is going to believe us about an invisible thief."

Amanda took a breath as she calmed from the exertion. Her nose caught the faint scent of perfume lingering as she walked alongside Li Xiu and the others. She turned her head to look into the forest, searching for the source, but couldn't see anything.

Allison moved her doll as fast as she could toward the lights, only pausing at the edge of the woods. Allison and her doll were nearly exhausted. She had held onto control of Gina for other adventures, but this time, Gina seemed to be resisting. She paused to give control back to her doll to save her own strength. Within seconds, the girl started breathing heavily, her heart pounding almost out of her chest. She had been aware of everything as Allison forced her to attack the hunters and steal the item they carried. Guilt started to fill her before it faded, and her mistress's voice again in her mind, "You're not done yet, my dear."

Chapter 12:
A Good Hunter Gone Bad?

The sun was rising as Gina walked into her apartment. Her heart was still pounding since Allison released control of her. Gina found herself looking into the mirror and could see her keeper's reflection smiling back.

"You did well, my little doll. Even if I had to do most of the driving." Allison stood, motioning for her to hold up the artifact before giving a triumphant smile and saying, "That is such a beautiful sight, my dear."

Gina only stared at her keeper with angry, questioning eyes. Allison must have felt the woman's gaze and looked up from the artifact, annoyed, asking, "What is it?"

It took a moment before Gina responded, "You made me almost kill that woman."

Allison sat, an unconcerned smile appearing. "She is not worth a thought, my dear. She's not even that important."

"You almost killed her. That was at least a fifty-foot drop onto rocks," Gina refuted.

Allison huffed, "If she had died, then I wouldn't have to send you back to finish the job."

"What?" Gina responded.

The witch smiled, "My dear, you know you don't have a choice in the matter now, do you?"

Gina watched as the witch held her earring, and Gina felt her mind drift. Finally, Allison released her before saying, "I have to send you in because that shapeshifter was the one trying to apprehend you. It will be easier to steal the sphere if she's in a cell under suspicion."

Gina removed the cloak hood and headed into the small kitchen, causing Allison to retake control. "Where do you think you're going?"

Allison willed the woman to sit in the chair like a doll. Gina struggled to speak and could only do so once Allison allowed her. Finally, Gina took a breath, still winded from the chase, and forcibly responded, "I need something to drink! You had me running for over four miles. I'm not some animal."

The witch sat back, stunned by her toy's reply of disobedience, and was about to reprimand her when her assistant, Mack interrupted, "Mistress, she is only human. You did have her running for more than an hour. Giving her a few minutes would be advisable."

The witch turned to glare at Mack, but he returned the same stare he used during trials. The witch felt anger but realized the wisdom in his words. *Damn. He's right. If I kill her now, finding another willing doll may take me a while. And I still don't have the sphere.* The witch thought for a moment. She knew when to be practical. "Go, my dear. Get something to drink and eat. It might make you feel a bit better. But I will still need you to do something, later." The witch paused, looking at the small sphere. "Before you go, my dear, please pass that prize through the mirror?"

Gina looked at the *tianqiu* and then at Allison as she held it before the reflective surface. Allison spoke in whispers as the small crystal touched the glass, instead of the sound of the crystal hitting glass, it started to pass through. Mack was standing, ready to retrieve it as soon as it pierced the mirror's surface.

"This is a handy object to have," Mack stated.

Allison nodded, telling him, "Yes, too bad it doesn't work for alchemic items."

Mack looked puzzled but was interrupted as Allison said, "My dear Gina, get something to eat, drink. Rest." She turned to Mack, "I sometimes forget that my doll is not just a doll." She turned to look at Gina, "I'll give you an hour. But then I'll need you to get into the Sanctuary again. I have some unfinished business."

About an hour later, Gina, rested, found her way back to the Sanctuary. The cloak she wore was immune to the detection of the sentries and cameras. After promising Allison that she would follow the other hunters, Gina had been given control. Her mistress wanted to discover what was happening to the shapeshifter she incriminated.

Gina entered the building and was wondering how she would find where they took Shrive. Gina didn't have to look hard; she could hear the berating voice of a man speaking a mix of Chinese and English. She found a spot near the wall, away from the people but close enough for her doll to hear. Gina felt her mind drift as Allison took over, viewing the events through her eyes.

"Lord Cale, this is pure ineptitude. You claim to have the best security in the world. Yet, you have lost a precious artifact."

Allison could see Lord Cale and Dr. Brentwood sitting without emotion as the Regent continued to raise his voice.

Well, well, the Circle let you two stay together. Or did you make them? Either way, Good for you, Allison thought. The witch enjoyed the idea that some still stood up to the Circle and the hunters. Going against their own rules even if they were now head of the organization.

She spied Shrive sitting alone just before the council table. The woman's position and the way she was sitting gave the witch joy. *I almost feel sorry for you. Too bad I'm not done with you yet, my dear.*

Linda and Amanda sat with Selese. Luke was behind them. His expression was something less than joyous. He was ordered to watch the two and would probably have to face discipline later, per Lord Cale. But whether he meant it or not, it was convincing enough to quiet the Regent's anger somewhat.

Allison watched the Regent turn and approached Linda and the others. His hand pointed accusingly. "You had no right to remove that artifact and bring it here. It was to be in the security of the Museum until we retrieved it," Chung yelled.

Linda spoke with certainty, "We were requested to retrieve it and bring it here."

Chung took a breath to yell but spoke normally, "I did not instruct you to do so."

Linda nodded. "That is correct, Regent. You did not. Xiling Snow Mountain did."

Chung looked puzzled; he was the Regent for that facility. He turned accusingly toward the council. "You were trying to steal it. You are using this as a ruse to discredit the theft."

Linda spoke up, "No, Regent Chung. Acting Regent Zu asked us to bring it here before sending it back to your country."

Chung turned. "You are lying. I would have been informed."

"You were not in the loop, Regent. I would ask you to check with your people. They will confirm that Ron and I were to bring the *tianqiu* there once we were able. Along with our findings," Linda answered.

"So you and your husband were given separate orders? By the way, where is he?" Chung looked to see Li Xiu holding her arm, having been rushed from the infirmary by her own people. The medical team was not allowed to treat her injuries fully. He looked condescendingly toward Linda. "He was probably minorly injured and needed treatment. My people are all here."

Lord Cale stood. "Regent, your person still needs treatment. As for Mr. Wilt, I would also like to know where he is."

Linda was about to speak when the Regent interrupted her. The man turned to Shrive, pointing. "You are correct. Li Xiu needs treatment, but she understands duty. As for this one, this thing, she should be caged like the animal she is."

The room erupted in a murmur, and Amanda stood. "You're an ass, you know that?"

Regent Chung turned, looking right at Amanda. "The FOF speaks. I am surprised her voice isn't melodically sweet, like those she prefers to be with."

Amanda started toward him, but Linda grabbed her, as did Luke. Her head snapped toward both as they held her back. Then, she heard Linda say, "Easy. He's doing this to make a scene."

The Regent smiled. "Am I? You cannot tell me where your husband is. This one attacked our people." He pointed to Shrive. "And that..." Chung pointed to Amanda, "that one doesn't know her place. She shouldn't even be here. I want her removed."

There was protest from Selese and the others, but Linda looking at Luke and Amanda, said, "Go, get out of here. I'll fill you in later."

Amanda yelled, pulling against Luke's grip, forcing him to wrap his arms around her and lift her from the floor. The Regent seemed to smile seeing Amanda treated like she was. Selese watched before looking at Linda, only to hear her whisper, "I'll fill you in as soon as I can." She looked to Selese, "We'll do what we can for Shrive."

Selese walked along with Luke, who was still fighting to remove Amanda from the council room. She stopped Luke, grabbing Amanda by the shoulders, quietly telling her, "Amanda, stop. I don't like this either. We can find a way to help her. Fighting now won't help. Trust me on this."

Amanda still fought against Luke's grip and looked back. She felt sorry for Shrive and wanted to help. She turned to see the look in Selese's eyes. And could see that mind of hers working. Amanda nodded and calmed. She followed along with Luke as he held her arm. But just as they were at the doorway, Amanda paused, noticing a scent in the air that seemed very familiar.

* * *

In China, Ron appeared in a large, bright room. He held his hands up as several of the Silver Hunters approached. He was relieved to see Zhang along with them.

"Regent Deng, I trust you got my message," Ron said as the hunters surrounded him.

The acting Regent stood silent for a moment before waving off the others. Then, he greeted Ron formally and led him toward the far door.

"The report on the original theft was something we had not considered. In fact, we've recovered one of the previous missing artifacts," Zhang told him.

Ron looked at the man, "How?"

The acting Regent huffed, smiling, "They took the copied page by mistake. We merely reconstituted the item once we realized it was the original." The Regent paused. "It seems your thief was very clever to figure it out." They continued to walk until they reached a large door. "That's not why you are here, is it?"

Ron shook his head, "this whole thing is beginning to look like several players are involved. And, I'm pretty sure the Feather is, in some fashion. I just don't know what their next move is."

Zhang motioned for Ron to be silent as he opened the door. They walked through before either said another word.

"This room is secure. Anyone listening would probably go deaf trying," Zhang told him.

Ron looked around, "I never understood why you kept your office so sparse. You'd think a man of your knowledge and talent would show his accomplishments."

Zhang sat, offering Ron a chair as he spoke, "I try not to. It makes people want more from you."

Ron nodded. "Good point."

Zhang pointed at Ron's arm. "I see the portal stones we gave you still work."

Ron held up his wrist to display the silver and Jade travel bracelets before responding, "Beats being tracked using the shadow paths. Your geomage friend seems to be quite a genius, having made these."

Zhang smiled. "Hua was quite a character. Too bad he's hiding from the hunters for stealing almost half a ton of gold and platinum."

"What would he need it for?" Ron asked.

Zhang chuckled. "He has a theory that he can make a gate to another world with it. Personally, I think he has been away from people for too long. But I wouldn't worry about him. He'll come to his senses." Zhang leaned forward, telling Ron, "He has a very short attention span. He'll probably forget about the gateway and why he stole the metals."

The Regent then sat back, "you're worried about something Chung would do?"

Ron nodded, "as diplomatic as ever, Zhang. Honestly, there is a lot wrong with what's been going on. You read our report on the other thefts?"

Zhang nodded, "the one about the Forge thefts as well. I'm surprised they allowed you to provide it."

Ron said nothing, looking at his friend with a raised brow.

"Ah, I see." Zhang understood now that Ron and Linda's report wasn't on the record with the Sanctuary. The Regent then said. "Well, anyway, your insight into the fact that all of them have been of the same type was interesting..."

Ron nodded.

"That did seem odd," Zhang noted.

Ron leaned forward. "Is there any way to use them to do something bigger?"

Zhang shrugged. "Not that we are aware. But you know how magic is. You can't know everything." He pointed to Ron, "I'd ask that little friend of yours, she may know."

Ron shook his head, "We asked. She didn't. None of the others we asked knew of any other uses for the *tianqiu*, either."

Zhang looked across his desk. "Then why are you here?"

Ron looked the man in the eyes, "It's Regent Chung. I'm afraid he might harm Shrive. Or maybe he has other plans. I'm not sure yet."

Zhang looked sternly back, "You suspect he is working for someone? That could be a dangerous accusation."

Ron nodded. "That's why I'm here. We're sure that the person who stole the *tianqiu* was invisible. And used Shrive to attack Li Xiu. We just have no way of proving it." Ron hesitated, "do you have any informants within the Broken Feather?"

Seeing the angry stare coming from their friend, Ron said, "Forget I asked. It was a long shot." He looked up at the ceiling as he spoke. "Linda can handle herself against the Circle and Chung too. Although it might become an international incident."

Zhang snickered.

Ron huffed, "I'm sure there is someone other than the Feather in play here. It's the thefts of the same type of items that are bothering me. Maybe we should focus on those." Ron looked at Zhang. "You know anyone who might know something about how to use them?"

Zhang seemed to think before pointing to his wrist, making Ron look at his own as Zhang said, "I might just know someone. The problem is finding him."

Fire, Air, Water, and Earth are the elements of magic. All in themselves powerful, but will and the spirit to wield them is true power.

- Author unknown.

(Translated from Archives of the Circle)

Chapter 13:
A Hunter Guilty Before Trial

Linda watched as Chung continued to denigrate Shrive. His words less than noble as he described her to be more animal than human. She could see Shrive holding back tears, trying to show little weakness as the Regent continued to attack her and her honor. Linda took mental notes as Chung asked Shrive a question.

"Did you or did you not push our agent over the edge of the cliff?" Chung asked with a certain manner of certainty.

Shrive shook her head, telling him only, "No."

"Are you suggesting that our agent was careless?" Chung accused.

Shrive defended herself. "No, something or someone else was there. It grabbed my arm and I felt it push me forward."

The Regent looked around the room, the disbelief evident in his eyes. He looked toward Dr. Brentwood. "An invisible assailant, how convenient." His eyes narrowed in accusation at the doctor as he huffed.

"There is no evidence of any others there except for what you and these others have claimed," Chung said, pointing to Linda.

Linda merely looked calmly toward the Regent but remained silent.

Chung was confused by her reaction and looked back to the members of the Circle present. "I think you are all covering up your ineptitude, and the fact that you stole the artifact yourselves."

Hearing this, Li Xiu spoke, "There was someone there. I saw her eyes."

Allison had been watching in the background, and her heart stuttered, *You were seen?* She made no effort to interact with Gina instead only thinking, *I'll deal with your carelessness later, my dear.*

She continued to watch as the Regent berated his underling, hearing the man yell.

"Are you defending them? You are not fit to be a hunter. You lost a precious item and are afraid for them? You would do well to remember your place, hunter Li Xiu."

Li Xiu went to speak but looked to Shrive, her fellow hunter, looking down in regret and sorrow that no one was believing either of them that there was another person there. Her attention was diverted as Ron entered the Chamber. Several of the Silver Hunters moved to intercept him, but were stopped by the Raven Hunters present.

Ron waited as the council acknowledged his entrance and was not surprised to hear the vitriolic remarks from Chung.

Ron waited until he had a chance to speak. "I apologize for my tardiness. I was in an important meeting."

Chung scoffed. "More important than this?"

Ron took no pleasure in his response. "Yes. I was where you should have been Regent. I was alerting your people to the situation."

The Regent was surprised and then angered by Ron's remarks. He ordered his people to apprehend him and Linda, their actions causing Lord Cale to stand in protest. "You are not in command of this facility, Regent, I am. You will refrain from accosting our guests."

"Guests?" The Regent looked to Cale. "They are thieves and criminals. You consider them guests?"

Cale looked stoic, taking time before answering, "They have helped with many situations involving the Raven Hunters. And from what I have been informed, your own people as well."

Allison watched as Chung moved toward the head of the Raven Hunters ready to strike but was stopped as Dr. Brentwood rose from her seat, her voice commanding and with an unnatural-sounding echo, bouncing from the walls of the council room as she raised her voice.

"That will be enough."

The whole room seemed to reverberate, even the floor, which caused Ron and Linda to look at each other in surprise. The room fell silent before Dr. Brentwood spoke again. "We are not contesting the event's outcome, Regent. Right now, we do not know how the missing item was taken. Given the incoming evidence we must look at all options."

Chung looked to Shrive. "Not only is a precious artifact missing, she attacked one of our people."

Shrive looked up to see the man's dark eyes staring through her with accusation. She had already defended herself. And having never been accused of any criminal act she was unsure how to respond. Her apprehension was sensed by the Regent who took advantage of the situation.

"She must be punished," Chung growled.

Shrive looked toward Dr. Brentwood, pleading for an answer. The catgirl, never having been in a situation such as this before, didn't know what to expect. She had always done the honorable thing. She was disheartened to see the doctor sit gracefully and take a breath,

"Unfortunately, you are correct, Regent." Dr. Brentwood looked toward her husband and around the room before returning to Shrive. The doctor was hesitant before she spoke. "Shrive Llewelyn, as of now your status as a Raven Hunter has been revoked. You will be held in confinement until this has been cleared up."

There were murmurs from around the room. Li Xiu watched as Shrive's face filled with a tormented sadness; her stomach turned as she saw the smile on the Regent's face. She had to turn away as he nodded in agreement with Brentwood's words. Tears filled Linda's eyes as she leaned against Ron, her husband looking toward Cale, seeing the man they knew as a friend look away. Ron knew that he didn't agree with the verdict.

Ron looked to Dr. Brentwood and could see the pain she fought to hide as she said, "Lord Cale, please make sure the accused is taken to a holding area."

Cale looked defeated as he fought to walk toward Shrive. Ron could see the man's steps heavy and unsure. Ron decided to say something. "Would the Council allow us to take responsibility for the accused?"

All eyes looked to Ron as he finished. Regent Chung was the first to

STEPHEN PHILLIPS

protest. "You were the one who was responsible for bringing the artifact here."

Dr. Brentwood was next. She stared at him, and Ron could see the pleading in her eyes. He could hear the cracking in her voice as she spoke, "Given the evidence, this council cannot allow the accused to roam freely."

Ron could feel the torment in her words and pursed his lips in muted anger as he nodded in acceptance. His actions were met by Regent Chung saying, "They should be imprisoned as well. They were responsible for the artifact."

Lord Cale looked to Ron with an apologetic stare before Ron produced a folded paper. "If the council will allow, I have a request from the acting Regent of Xiling Snow Mountain to allow us to continue to investigate the thefts."

"What?" Chung yelled as he quickly ripped the page from Ron's grasp. The Regent looked at the document in disbelief before looking to Ron in anger.

Ron felt a certain bit of satisfaction as Cale took the page from the Regent's hand, and spoke, "As you mentioned, Regent Chung. The item was their responsibility."

Cale looked to the Council and nodded. "The request is legitimate."

Dr. Brentwood looked to Ron. She somehow knew he did everything to try and help Shrive. And he and Linda being able to continue looking into the situation may just save the Circle from having to deal, somewhat unfairly, with one of their own. She nodded. "Then continue your investigation and share your findings with us and the Regent." The doctor stood, conflicted, and turned to look at Ron and then to her husband. "Please provide me with any information that you do have, Mr. Wilt. I will have to add it to the statement as soon as possible." She then leaned on the table as if exhausted, her words fading as she walked toward the hallway to her office, "Please forgive my departure; I have something to attend to."

Ron nodded, looking to Cale who returned a single nod. Ron said nothing, but Linda reassured her friend. "Don't worry, Shrive."

The Regent looked to his people, "We will confine our agent to her quarters."

Linda spoke up, "You have to allow her to finish being healed first."

The Regent moved toward Linda, making Ron step in front of her. His silence and stare caused the Regent to pause mid-step. The Regent's

102

hesitation made him to turn to look back at Li Xiu. "We will take care of her injuries." Ron watched as the Regent seemed happier than he should have been.

Ron stood silent as they escorted Li Xiu away, his eyes turning and becoming tormented at seeing Shrive restrained, her body language that of someone who had already given up. Linda touched his arm and could feel the tenseness in it, prompting her to ask, "Do we have a plan?"

Ron nodded, before saying, "I'll tell you while we head over to see Brentwood." He then looked to Linda, and she looked at Chung.

"Something else is going on, isn't there?" Linda said.

Ron nodded, "I'm not sure yet, but I think you just might be right."

Allison was delighted to see through her doll's eyes the shapeshifter bound in chains. She craned Gina's neck to get a better look at the poor girl's face, and let out an elated giggle, seeing the tears running down Shrive's cheeks.

"Oh, I'm not done with you yet, my dear," Allison said as she gave control back to her doll.

What is known or unknown has no substance, it is what you learn along the way that matters.

- Allister Chu, Geomage.

Chapter 14:
Hunters Disgrace

Li Xiu winced in pain as a woman pulled on her arm to set the fracture. She then began to wrap Li Xiu's arm in bandages. Usually, they would use a spell to heal the injury, but her fellow hunter seemed unsure as she finished. The healer said, "They have ordered us not to use any healing elements on you."

Li Xiu looked puzzled. She had known Biyu for some time. The woman was one of the younger hunters who now worked as a medic for the Silver Ravens. Li Xiu watched as the woman turned away. "We've also been ordered not to speak with you." There was a sad coldness in her tone.

This confused Li Xiu even more until she heard the Regent's voice from the doorway. "The loss of the *tianqiu* has been noted in your file, Li Xiu. Therefore, I recommend you return home as soon as possible. They are dispatching a delegate to retrieve the remaining artifacts in the possession of the Forge."

The Regent glanced at Biyu before motioning for her to leave. The woman followed her orders. However, instead of returning to her station, she stayed within earshot to listen to the Regent and her friend.

"Li Xiu, you have served as a hunter for several years. I'm surprised that you were so careless," Chung said.

Li Xiu said nothing, but her jaw tightened as her superior spoke.

"You have shamed your post and us with your ineptitude," Chung said. "You even fabricated some story about an invisible assailant."

Li Xiu protested, "I saw her eyes, blue—almost like the sky. She was cloaked. I'm sure of it."

The Regent moved uncomfortably close. "You didn't do your job."

Li Xiu remained silent.

Chung huffed, "It is unwise to continue trying to protect them." Then, he grabbed her chin and turned her face to look at him, "Are you a thief or a hunter?"

From deep in Li Xiu's chest, a growl came, "I have always been a hunter."

Regent Chung smiled. "Not for much longer."

Li Xiu looked puzzled at the man.

The Regent's following words sounded with a satisfaction she didn't care for. "I recommend you be stripped of your status and your memories removed when you return."

Li Xiu looked dumbfounded. She had been a Hunter for over seven years. If they took her memories, she might not be able to survive back home. She had learned so much while being a Hunter that it would remove all of the skills she needed. Seeing the confusion in the woman's eyes, Chung laughed before saying. "Don't be upset, I'm sending you back along with the rest of the things from this place."

She didn't understand what he meant, but things became clear as Chung continued, "You are going back along with everything else these people have secured in the Forge."

Li Xiu again looked puzzled, making her ask, "What else do they have?"

The Regent smiled as he walked toward the door, "I'll provide you with a list of the artifacts. After that, who knows. If you will tell the truth about your so-called attack. I may reconsider."

* * *

Linda walked alongside Ron as they headed to the Administration building. They were both surprised that the portal connecting the Sanctuary to Brentwood's office was unavailable. That was something they had never encountered. As they walked, Linda asked, "How'd the meeting go?"

She watched him shake his head. "That well. Hmm. Did Zhang have anything useful?"

Ron looked at her. "They didn't know any uses for the *tianqiu*. At least nothing obvious. He did provide a possible lead, though."

Linda's eyes perked with interest, "You keeping it a secret or are you going to let me in on this one?"

Ron tapped away on his phone and nodded. "There may be an answer, but we have to find someone to help figure that out." He then pointed to the amethyst and silver bracelets that they both wore. "Chu might know something. The problem is we have to find him."

Linda seemed happy as she asked, "Did you speak with him yet?" She saw Ron intently looking at his phone.

"Damn, no one's answering any of my texts. I was trying to see if Amanda or anyone knows anything else." Ron shook his head as they walked up the steps of the Administration building. He paused. "Chu's in hiding. Apparently, he stole a lot of precious metals from someone."

Linda looked concerned. "They didn't have any information to help find him?"

Ron replied, "No, they've been looking for him," before pressing the button on the building door, and both entered a few moments later.

The two walked toward the attendant, who greeted them by asking, "Do you have an appointment?"

Ron shook his head, "We're being nice by not barging in. Please let Dr. Brentwood know we're here. We need to discuss some business with her."

The attendant smiled back, her eyes full of determination to defend her authority of the building.

Ron smiled, adding, "It involves Shrive."

Both watch the eyes of the attendant turn frightened. Then she looked at the small monitor on her desk. Both heard moments later, "Dr. Brentwood will see you."

Within seconds the elevator behind them opened.

The ride up was quiet, and as the doors opened, they met a familiar face. Colleen stood to greet them. "Dr. Brentwood wanted to see you right away. Please follow me."

They entered Brentwood's office to see her in the corner, wiping a tear from her cheek. They kept things civil as she offered them a seat.

Dr. Brentwood forced a smile before she spoke, "That was some trick producing an order from the acting Regent." She looked at the two of them. "I guess I shouldn't be surprised. I've asked you to find some of the more difficult items that I couldn't trust to the Hunters. You both have been very proficient." The doctor's smile turned kinder, saying, "Please tell me you have some good news."

Linda sighed. "I know it was difficult to do what you did. I'm sorry you had to."

Dr. Brentwood nodded. "As am I."

Ron acknowledged her regret and added, "The *tianqiu* may be the key here. According to our sources, there have been several stolen. All of a similar type."

Dr. Brentwood looked puzzled. "How will this help Shrive?"

Ron held his hand up. "We may be looking in the wrong direction. Let's focus on what they could be used for. I think that may lead to the person who set this all up." Ron took a breath. "About the spheres, the only man that might know is Chu, but no one has seen him."

When she asked who they were speaking about, Ron and Linda both showed their travel bracelets and smiled. Linda said, "He's someone we've met before. But we need help finding him."

Dr. Brentwood nodded. "I think I may know just the person." She then tapped a button on her desk, and Colleen instantly appeared in the room.

"What do you need, doctor?" Colleen asked, giving a smile.

Ron mumbled, "She's fast."

Dr. Brentwood heard him, saying, "You have no idea." She then looked to Colleen. "Do you know where my daughter is?"

Colleen looked mildly upset. "Last I heard, she was with Amanda."

The doctor watched as Colleen looked at Linda and Ron. "What is it, Colleen?"

The woman stood tall, "Is it true that Shrive is in the dungeon?"

Dr. Brentwood nodded. "Much to our dismay." The Doctor looked toward the door. "And with the recent theft, I have asked Lord Cale to find a way to secure the more dangerous artifacts we have stored currently."

"Some nasty things in storage, huh?" Ron quipped.

Dr. Brentwood answered, "Both Cale and I are uncomfortable with everything being sent together. And I hope when you speak with the acting Regent again, you will mention that fact."

Ron nodded as Linda responded, "You're not the only one concerned about the situation. We have a theory that something else may be going on." Linda sighed, "But we don't have any proof, only strange circumstances."

Colleen shifted as she listened to their discussion. She was afraid for her friend as well. She had known Shrive since she arrived at the school. Shrive was a good friend and was always willing to help when Colleen joined the Hunters. Colleen was having a difficult time believing that Shrive tried to harm anyone. Even when taking down a suspect, Shrive went out of her way to ensure no one was injured.

The doctor could see the concerned look in her assistant's eyes. "What is it, Colleen?"

Colleen's light blonde hair tossed back slightly as she looked up to see them all staring at her. Seeing the look of worry in Linda's eyes gave her some courage to speak.

"Doctor, Shrive has never harmed anyone without provocation. And I've seen her hold back not to harm those we were after."

The doctor smiled slightly. "I know you mean well, but people can change." Dr. Brentwood nodded in thought and said, "Anthromorphs are notoriously strong by nature. Nothing seems right about any of this."

Ron sighed. "Much like what's happened to Shrive. We're sensing something is wrong, so we're working on our own theory."

Linda looked to Colleen. "We're trying to figure out how to get her out. Can you get in touch with Selese?"

"Have you tried her phone?" Colleen asked.

Ron nodded. "Yeah, no one's answering. Not even Amanda."

"That's a surprise," they all heard Dr. Brentwood say questioningly." She then looked to Colleen, "Please find Selese. She may have a way to help."

In a flash, Colleen left the room.

"She is fast," Ron said again.

Dr. Brentwood smiled. "Sylph and Elf. She would outrun a cheetah in a sprint." The doctor leaned back in her chair. "I do have an issue I need you both to understand."

The two looked at the doctor.

"That stunt involving the acting Regent was overstepping your bounds. I don't particularly appreciate being kept out of the loop regarding my people. You should have informed us of what you were planning," Brentwood said.

Linda interjected, "We're not Hunters. You have no control over us. We can come and go as we please. Besides, something else is happening here. We're pretty sure there is some third party in play. These thefts are not the Feather. It may be possible they were hired, but we're not sure they are involved."

Dr. Brentwood took a breath, a stare of power aimed toward the two across her desk as she spoke, "We can control you if needed. But we have decided not to, so far."

Ron felt slighted and looked up to spy a picture of a sylph that Amanda had done for the Sanctuary's files. The original drawing was displayed with honor on the wall of the doctor's office. Brentwood noticed his expression of realization and gave a slight smile. "I see you understand."

Linda looked to Ron as he spoke, "You're not that low or desperate to involve or threaten her."

Linda turned to Brentwood, now understanding what she was implying. "And if you did, you'd have to pay a heavy price."

Brentwood sighed heavily. "In more ways than you can imagine." She looked at them over her glasses as if relieved. "Truthfully, we would never, but the Feather would be willing to try and harm her. She has become involved with the Hunters since she arrived." The doctor looked at Linda. "Not that we haven't tried to dissuade her. Truthfully, she would make a good addition. I'm concerned that she already has a mark on her back from nearly stopping the Feather."

Linda sat tall. "You're not the only one with resources, doctor. We can protect her as well."

Brentwood smiled. "I would certainly hope so. I was only thinking about her and your safety. Honestly, having others able to work outside the circle can be quite convenient."

Chapter 15:
They Make Things Difficult

In the Shadowed Hall, a man dressed in the full uniform of a Silver Hunter appeared. The guards moved to block his path, and he stopped respectfully.

"I am here by request of Regent Zhang. I am to meet with the head of your facility about an urgent matter," the man spoke concisely.

The guards looked back before making a call. It was less than a minute before Lord Cale appeared and greeted him.

"I was not informed that you were coming. Can you provide proof of who sent you?" Cale asked.

The man nodded, holding out a scroll. One of the guards grabbed it from him and opened it.

"Lord Cale, I am Bao Zheng. I have been sent to help with the investigation of the recent theft and to aid in the return of the artifacts now in your possession."

Cale looked at the man suspiciously. "We are already working on that now. Why would they send someone else?"

Bao showed no emotion. "With the recent thefts, I have been ordered to secure some of the more volatile items housed here." He looked Cale dead in the eyes. "I trust you will assist me in doing so."

Lord Cale didn't like the unannounced intrusion, but his intuition told him to trust this man.

Bao looked to the guards surrounding him and to Cale. He made no effort to antagonize them in any way. He did however keep his stance, showing the power he held. The Silver Hunter looked to Cale, "Lord Cale, I do have another matter that may interest you, but I prefer to speak with you, in private."

Cale looked suspiciously toward the man.

Seeing his reaction Bao sighed before saying, "It involves your allies. They have, shall we say, some concerns about which my superiors seem to agree."

Cale remembered that Linda had told them of an investigation earlier and that they had concerns about Chung. And that they were working on a way to help Shrive. Lord Cale looked toward Bao and nodded. "I understand. Perhaps we should discuss this in private."

Bao smiled as he followed Cale past the guards.

Cale was surprised to see Selese reading a file as he walked in. She had taken it from the shelf behind his desk.

She could hear the man with her father say, "If she's no longer a Hunter, her element should have been removed."

Bao looked suspiciously at Selese as he turned toward her. Her father shook his head before glancing at his daughter, motioning for her to leave. She had been reading through the reports and was hoping to find something she could use to help Shrive. But, seeing the look in her father's eyes, she closed the files and put them back on the shelf.

Selese was closing a door to the cabinet when she heard Bao tell her father, "The Regents have asked that you suspend all research of the artifacts and have them ready for inspection." The man looked at Selese as she walked around the room toward the door.

"The Duànzào thinks your security is lacking, and has asked me to secure every artifact the Forge is holding on our behalf. Especially the dragon-based items. We do not need any more thieves taking things that do not belong to them." Bao said, never removing his eyes from Selese.

Her father wasn't surprised to hear Selese say, as she was leaving the room, "I know when I'm not wanted, I'll be outside."

Selese walked down the stairway leading to the dungeon, the anger welling up in her gut at the way they treated her friend. She wiped a tear from her cheek as she entered the dungeon floor.

Selese silently walked up to the cell door, carefully looking around to see if anyone was there. The golden light from the crystals lit the area. Their glow prevented any form of shadow walking. She knew her friend, and even if it was possible, Shrive was too honest to leave. Selese moved to the small window on the door—the bars made of rolled steel—and could see Shrive balled up on the bed almost like a cat, her hand grasping the necklace that hid her more feline features from most of the world.

Don't give up. You know you're innocent. We all know you're innocent.

Selese held her breath before speaking, "Hey, you awake?"

Shrive's head snapped around and she jumped toward the door. As Shrive grabbed the bars in the window, Selese could see the look in her friend's face, it was if she was already broken. "Shrive, you didn't hurt anyone. We all know this is a mistake."

Shrive looked away, "I've never been in trouble, I've always followed the rules. Why do they think I did this? I didn't do anything wrong."

Selese didn't have an answer. The same question had been bothering her as well. None of this made any sense. Whoever took the artifact could have just left with it. Instead, they went out of their way to involve her friend. She had even called Amanda, but neither of them knew any reason why a thief would even pull Shrive and push Li Xiu toward the cliff like that. But seeing her friend so despondent, she had to say something.

"I know that. Li Xiu didn't hit you either. It was that invisible thief, I'm sure of it."

A simple spark flickered in her friend's eyes, and Selese thought, *That's right, I believe you. And I'm going to damn well make sure I prove this wasn't you.*

Selese put her hands on her friend's. "You're not guilty, Shrive. You're too goody good to be guilty." She then looked at Shrive's arm to see the element she used to shadow walk. Selese bowed her head. When she returned to look at Shrive, she said, "I heard they took away your status as a Hunter. I'm sorry."

Shrive's lips seemed to tremble. Selese fought back tears seeing her reaction. She held her friend's hands hearing Shrive say, "They're removing my element later." Shrive's tears flowed from her eyes. "I've always been a Hunter. Who would do this to me?"

Selese sniffed holding back tears, "I don't know. But it seems like someone has it out for you. Do you have any idea who it might be?"

Shrive shook her head.

Selese took a moment, her mind racing through what she had read in the files on the incident. She knew Ron and Linda believed her; after all, they were there. Selese knew of nothing in the files she had gone through that would point to whoever set Shrive up. And from Selese's experiences with being a thief, the invisible person's actions didn't make sense.

If you're invisible and cloaked, it's easier to get away. Every thief knows that. You just leave.

Selese could see some hope returning to her friend's eyes, making her smile. She looked around her before speaking, "We'll prove you're innocent." Selese seemed to think, "or, maybe, I'll steal all of the evidence and then they can't prove anything."

She didn't really mean that and Shrive knew. Her friend said, "Don't get in any trouble. Everyone thinks I'm guilty, I couldn't live with myself."

Selese nodded. "Maybe you're right, bad idea."

Shrive smiled.

Then Selese thought before saying, "Well since they have all decided that you've joined the rest of us dishonest people, maybe we can work with that."

Shrive chuckled, shaking her head in disagreement.

Selese smiled seeing her reaction, and said, "Look, I know you're innocent. We just have to prove it. Besides they are all busy getting all of the artifacts together. So, I think we have some time. Tell me what you remember from the fight."

Shrive looked up. "You know everything already. You were there."

Selese nodded. "Yes I was, but let's see if you can remember anything that we may have missed."

About an hour later, Selese appeared in the small room where the vending machines were, down the hall from Amanda's apartment. She could hear the thumping of someone punching what sounded like a practice dummy as she looked out of the small entryway, only to hear the sound stop. She then shadow-walked to stand before her friend's door.

Inside, Amanda was about to go out; hearing what happened to Shrive was making her angry. She had just put on her jacket, the one with large pockets, and was startled to see a shadowy figure as she opened the door. Amanda raised her hands, ready to fight, before she realized it was Selese.

"Sorry. You startled me," Amanda said, bringing down her guard.

Selese responded, "Then maybe you should fix the light outside your door, the shadow was dark enough for me to use." She looked at Amanda, and then to where she knew the camera in the hall was, only to see the trash and recycling bins blocking the view of it. "Never know if some hunter may come calling. Or is that the reason you have the camera blocked?"

Amanda looked at her, annoyed, before smiling. She understood what Selese was implying. She only said, "Maybe, but you know."

Selese motioned, asking to come in, and closing the door, she said. "If you really want Luke to stop by more often, think about making that vending room light a bit dimmer, it'd be easier for him to drop by."

She looked to see the practice dummy Amanda used for training looking somewhat tattered. "Well, that guy didn't stand a chance."

Amanda shook her head as she laughed. "Look, I was going to go out and look around. I don't want Shrive blamed for something she didn't do."

Selese agreed. "That's why I'm here. You have some time to compare notes?"

It was sometime later, after the sun had set, when the two had caught each other up on their collective information.

"So, they are really going to take away Shrive's element?" Amanda asked to confirm.

Selese nodded. "It looks that way. Even though Li Xiu's own story proves otherwise. She told the Regent that she saw the person's eyes and was trying to see if there was more detail and was going to ask for Shrive's help."

Amanda seemed to be in thought. "Does the Regent have anything of interest in this, that we know of?"

Selese shook her head. "I was unwelcomed, so I left."

"I thought I smelled perfume as well. And I don't think either of them is lying." She huffed, "Both of those two are too honest."

Selese smiled. "Not like us, right?"

Amanda laughed. "You're not that bad Selese. Neither am I. We just see the world a little differently." She paused. "We may need some help though. And I'd like to talk to Li Xiu."

Selese could see Amanda's mind working, and said, "We can't, she's in a secure part of the sanctuary. They have her on the top floor of the maintenance building. The elevators can't take you in unless authorized, and using magic to fly or jump wouldn't work, the building's been protected."

Amanda thought for a moment, looking out the window and seeing the same design as the apartment where she lived. The small balconies close and connected to each other. She turned to Selese. "Do you know anything about the protection on the building?"

Selese did. "Yeah, the spell is a pain, But I think I can get through it, why?" Selese looked out the window, seeing the same view as Amanda. She then laughed. "You know they had to leave the fire escapes unenchanted for building regulations."

Amanda nodded as she listened to Selese. "We can't use them to climb up; you can only head down them. Even grapples won't work."

Selese looked beside her to see a familiar glint in friend's eyes, making her ask, "What?"

Amanda looked at her. "Has anyone ever fallen off them?"

Selese shrugged. "Not that I'm aware but a few years back someone painting had slipped and grabbed hold of the floor and railing to stop from falling, why?"

Amanda looked back to the window. "Think you can get past the window and door protection spells?"

Selese nodded.

Amanda smiled. "Good, then give me a few hours. I've got an idea, and it's something I've been meaning to try."

Chapter 16:
The Great Break in.

It was several hours later, and the headlights of Amanda's car lit the darkness as she returned. Amanda parked quickly and rushed to her apartment carrying several bags.

"I can't believe climbing equipment is so expensive." She produced a harness and safety line and quickly opened the packages to put them together per the store clerk's instruction.

Selese asked, "What are you doing? I told you even grapples won't work."

Amanda smiled, "But hands do. And I've been meaning to try something since Gabs did it a few days ago."

Selese looked puzzled, asking while they walked toward the building in the darkness. "Wait. What did Gabs do?"

Amanda mentioned that Gabs had climbed up and over several balconies and was standing on the railing of her apartment to jump to her own. Unfortunately, she hadn't realized that the window was locked from the inside. Amanda told Selese that Gabriella said, "She didn't want to bother me after she got back in."

Amanda and Selese stopped beneath the room where Li Xiu had been told to stay until she was sent home. Selese confirmed the order that the Silver Hunter was there to recover from her injuries.

Jumping onto the bottom rail, Amanda grabbed onto the floor above and climbed up. She repeated, standing on the top of the railing, using the base of the support above to steady herself. Finally, she hooked the harness to the bottom of the fence above and pulled herself up. They made it up a few floors, and Selese followed, complaining as they rested, "Now I know why you're in the gym so much. This is hard work without magic."

Amanda smiled. "We have a couple more to go, and then it's up to you."

"Lock, magic or not. I'll get it open. You get us up there."

A short time later, their feet landed on the balcony of Li Xiu's floor. Amanda looked around. "I thought you said this was enchanted?"

Selese nodded. "It is against magic and grappling equipment. Guess they thought no one would be crazy enough to climb it by hand."

Amanda pointed to the lock. Although they were there, she didn't want to spend more time than she had to outside in case someone was patrolling the area. Selese nodded and went right to work. It took less than a minute for her to open the door.

"That was way too easy," Selese said.

Amanda agreed, "Let's hope it was just an oversight and not a trap."

Selese opened the door slowly and carefully. Both were surprised not to hear any alarm as they entered.

The lights were off, and Amanda couldn't see anything, but she could hear Selese walking around the room, her thoughts screaming, *maybe darklings can see in the dark, but I can't.* Selese stood by the bed and could see that Li Xiu was asleep before turning on the light. It took several seconds before Li Xiu woke, startled. Then, in a panic, she shielded herself before realizing that Selese was standing beside her bed. Li Xiu went to yell, but Selese covered her mouth. The former thief quickly held her finger to her own lips. "You're not in danger. We just came to talk."

Li Xiu looked and saw Amanda approaching. "I know this is weird, but we have a few questions."

They were both surprised to find Li Xiu very accommodating.

They whispered for nearly an hour, Li Xiu telling them, "I told them that Shrive was as surprised as I was. And that she didn't break my arm. It was someone I couldn't see. And that I saw the woman's eyes. They were like blue glass."

Selese seemed annoyed, "Yeah, well, they have Shrive locked up now. So, your people want her memory erased." Selese was very angry at the situation. "And since she's been a Hunter most of her life, that would be bad."

"I'm sorry, I keep telling them it wasn't her, they just don't believe me." Li Xiu insisted. Then the hunter seemed angry, almost yelling, "Guess she and I are in the same situation."

Amanda put her hands up. "Keep your voice down. I don't want to have to rush out of here." She then looked to the door and to the window they entered through. "When I pulled you up, I could smell perfume. So, I thought maybe it was something you were wearing. But it wasn't. Shrive smelled it too."

Li Xiu told her. "I did as well. I thought maybe it was something Shrive was wearing, but if none of us was, then…."

Amanda nodded. "Someone else was there."

"There's something else. I protested the decision when I heard it," Li Xiu said.

Amanda asked what it was.

Li Xiu told her, "They want to send everything back all at once."

Amanda and Selese looked at each other. Each with the same thought, "That is not a good idea."

Amanda and Selese climbed down after speaking with Xi Liu. She told them the rest of the artifacts would be moved in the next few days. And that she was to accompany them home. That didn't sit well with Amanda, and she asked if Li Xiu could postpone their trip. The thought of all the artifacts moving as one shipment seemed odd. And the information regarding the perfume now was more proof that someone else was there fighting.

She mentioned it to Selese, who seemed to agree. "Great way to get rid of a witness when you steal everything. Maybe have her injured, or worse, killed. Even blame it on her."

Amanda was hesitant but agreed.

"I'm sure there was someone else, but why do they seem to appear so quickly?" Amanda said as she walked.

Selese turned to see Amanda deep in thought, clearly realizing that something was there but not quite able to figure it out. Amanda sensed her gaze and asked, "What?"

Selese smiled. "You have an idea of who it might be?"

Amanda stopped walking, looking back from where they came. She looked around before looking to the ground, "I don't know. All of this started only a few weeks ago. I just can't find the connection."

She looked to Selese, the night making it difficult to see. Amanda could see Selese's eyes in the darkness before she spoke. "I have to think this through. Let's head back to my place. I think it's going to be a long night."

The sound of their steps was the only thing to be heard as they headed back to Amanda's place.

* * *

The Regent stood inspecting the remaining artifacts, his fellow Silver Ravens cataloging what remained. He looked over to see Bao double-checking the records as they were handed to him.

Bao, I cannot believe they sent you. You are a good Raven, a good soldier, one of our best. It would be a dishonor to eliminate you. Chung's mind was still in thought. *But, if I must, I will. This world is not fit to be ruled by such weak individuals.*

The Regent stood silent, observing the activity all around. His mind was filled with a plan that the new Hunter was now endangering. He watched Bao as the man recorded every item before him—marking its place on each pallet. Then, Chung remembered what Bao had said.

"I am here to make sure things are returned safely."

The Feather cannot be made to wait. Fools run this world. Fools and those without magic who should serve, not lead.

The Regent looked around. He had disdain for the formalities of the group he was among. They worked with the Raven Hunters of the Sanctuary, whom he felt were undisciplined and careless. These people were no more than would-be slaves.

Chung's attention was diverted hearing Bao's voice pierce the walls of the Forge.

"Careful. If you drop that, it could incinerate everything in this room."

The Regent took notice and approached. "Bao, is there an issue?"

The Silver Raven answered his superior, "No, sir, not while I am watching. We should take that last, perhaps in a more secure casing." He then pointed to a pedestal near the far wall.

Chung's gaze followed the man's direction, and saw what Bao was concerned with. On the pedestal, what looked like a claw hung from a wire of iron. The object was still swinging from someone who hit it only moments ago.

A dragon's claw?

The Regent could see the sharpened crystals churning with the fire they held. Chung knew well the power of a dragon's claw; he reached for the coins that hung around his neck and deftly fanned through them. His thumb and forefinger were resting on a single coin. Within seconds the coin glowed red hot as flames seeped from its edges. He could feel its warmth and the fire seemed to flow through his veins.

The Regent released the coin and looked to his fellow hunter, "Good. You kept everyone safe."

Bao nodded with acceptance. The Regent seemed in thought for a moment.

"You can handle things here for the moment. I have some business to attend to. First, I want to make sure they have not forgotten any hidden rooms with our property."

His fellow Silver Hunter nodded. "I will alert you to our progress when we are finished for today."

The Regent said nothing as he walked toward the door, his eyes still focused on the dragon's claw. *I am sorry, Bao, but you have just chosen the instrument of your demise.*

* * *

Chung sat in his room, turned to pull out a small book from the desk, and flipped through it. He stopped on a page hiding a small mirror. The Regent tapped the mirror, saying a few magic words. On the glass, an image appeared. The image was of a man both Amanda and Selese would immediately recognize if they saw him.

"Mister Fierst, I am not intruding on your rest," Chung said.

Dennon's smile was sinister, "Not particularly. We have been busy preparing. To what do I owe this encounter? You were ordered not to contact us until you had information on the rest of the artifacts."

Chung's smile would have sent chills down the spine of any ordinary individual. "That is precisely why I am contacting you."

Dennon lifted his head. "Oh, you have information for us?"

Chung nodded. "We are going to have the full details shortly. But I have confirmed that most of the items can be sent in one shipment. I hope your people are willing to eliminate any witnesses this time."

"That was a misunderstanding, Chung. We try to preserve life whenever possible. But we deal with the inconvenience when it becomes a hindrance," Dennon scoffed.

Chung again grinned before saying, "We are not sure, but someone else may be attempting to take our prizes. However, they seemed focused on something unknown. It may be unrelated, but they seem to be focused on minor artifacts and the *tianqiu*. All of what they are looking for are completely useless to our cause."

Dennon nodded before reaching over to take a paper from the desk. "What about the rest of the items?"

"It will take a few days, but I should be able to have them on their way by then. Do you think your people will be ready?"

Dennon smiled. "Yes."

"Then I look forward to joining your quest. I will contact you when the time and route are decided."

Dennon nodded, tapping the mirror on his side. "You had better, Chung. We do not allow feathers to fall to the ground."

Chapter 17:
A Golden Secret

It was mid-morning when Selese left Amanda's apartment. They still had no way to prove there was another person who forced Shrive to attack Li Xiu. Selese stopped to get a coffee and was heading back to the administration building when Colleen found her.

"There you are." Selese, surprised, nearly threw her coffee in the air as Colleen suddenly appeared behind her.

Selese turned, noticing the worried expression on her friend's face. Any anger she had already melted from her as she greeted her friend. Instead, she was puzzled and asked, "Why are you looking for me?"

Colleen looked around before moving closer. "Dr. Brentwood, Ron, and Linda are looking for you. They are trying to prove Shrive's innocent."

Selese nodded. "They're not the only ones. But why do they need me?"

Colleen shrugged, only telling Selese, "From what I overheard, they need to find someone or something that may be able to help."

Selese looked past her friend, deep in thought. *They need to find something and can't. They need someone who thinks like a thief, not a hunter.*

Colleen gave a subtle smile. "Would you come back with me?"

Selese smiled, lifting her coffee. "Lead the way."

At Dr. Brentwood's office, Selese paced as Linda and Ron told her what they found. The problem was that they needed to find Chu, the same geomage who created their Amethyst gates. Her mother handed her the files she had on the man, and Selese quickly read through them.

Selese seemed lost in thought as she sat in the chair by the doctor's desk. It was a familiar feeling, since it was the same one she had spent many hours in when she first arrived. Seeing her reading in the chair brought back pleasant memories for the doctor. She didn't want to upend them but asked, "Do you know of a way to find him?"

Selese nodded. "He stole a lot of gold. A simple finding spell would work." She looked to Ron, "But, I'm sure they thought about that already."

Ron nodded, knowing the Silver Hunters had already tried, but her logic made sense to him. He also knew Chu and was sure he could find a way to mask the gold, which he also mentioned to Selese.

"Right now, we need every bit of a thief to find another thief. And I mean that in a good way," Linda said.

Selese smiled, comforted by the fact that they trusted her. She stood and silently walked to the far wall, running her hand along the shelf as she slowly paced around the room. Finally, she stopped. "The gold is too obvious. We need something so unique that only a few on the planet exist." She looked at everyone staring at her, "and hope he has it on him, or at least nearby."

Ron looked to his armband. "Too bad I don't have the last location we met with him. I've searched for it on the crystal for the last few hours."

Selese watched as Ron tapped at the amethyst gate he wore. Her mind suddenly filled with inspiration. "Wait, the amethyst gate, more of its kind, I can find."

Dr. Brentwood sat straight, smiling. "Oh dear, she rhymed again."

Ron blurted out, "So she is. I wonder why? Such a whiz, don't be shy." He turned to Look at Linda, seeing the surprised look on her and the doctor's faces as he said, "What did I just say?"

Linda said, "I really hope that's not catching."

Ron turned to see Selese shaking her head. "I keep forgetting I'm not the only one here part fairy."

Selese walked over, grabbing Ron's arm. "How many of these do you think he's made?"

Ron shrugged. "It did take him a while to make these. I don't have a clue."

Linda shook her head.

"These are incredibly rare. I've only read about them. Most geomages now couldn't make them. They all use shadow walking. It's easier and more reliable," Selese said.

Ron chimed in, "And traceable. But," he tapped the purple armband, "these aren't unless you know an exit point exactly or a duplicate." He also understood what Selese was implying.

"And we know that Chu has one. He used it right in front of us. That's why we asked for them." Ron looked to the others before looking to Selese. "If your theory is right, then there can't be many of these around."

They could all see the smile Selese showed as she said, "Then let's find out how many there are."

Dr. Brentwood smiled, seeing the grace and confidence Selese showed as she walked to one of the many books along the wall, pulling one from the shelf. The woman opened the pages, flipping through them until pausing on one. She stared at it for a few seconds before saying, "A simple low-level finding spell won't work for those. Besides, we know the amethyst gates are not traceable by normal means."

Selese said, looking up from the open book she held, "But I think we can find him with this."

Selese showed Dr. Brentwood the pages before turning them over to read the spine. *Mineral hunting, Geomage spells*. The book, worn and aging, was dated sometime before the 1900s. The magic was designed to find precious stones. Claire could see a flaw in her daughter's plan, but, as she looked up, Selese was smiling.

"This will find the gem, but also any other gem similar in composition. You'd have a lot to sort through."

Selese chuckled before answering. "That's if we were looking to find the stones. My guess is that Chu was saving time and used the same spell he used on his as he did on theirs."

"That's brilliant. You look for a stone with the very same spell attached." Dr. Brentwood looked at Linda and Ron. "If she's right, you should find him quickly."

Ron and Linda said nothing, only nodding in agreement.

Selese huffed, "There is a catch."

Linda raised her brow in a questioning gesture, which Selese was already answering. "One of you has to let me have their amethyst gate to use as a beacon. And, the spell can sometimes damage the item being used to match it, so. . ."

The couple looked at each other. Ron started to remove his armband, but Linda stopped him, "No. You do most of the traveling. She can use mine."

Ron looked concerned. If the spell didn't work as Selese had promised, they would be down one armband. That meant they would have to find other means to travel if needed. Seeing his concern, Selese said, "I just need to find its likeness. There shouldn't be any. . . complications." They all heard her mutter, "I hope he didn't put any protection on them. That might get nasty."

Linda was the first to say something, "If you think it's too dangerous, then we'll find another way."

Dr. Brentwood agreed. But Selese looked to Ron. "You're not agreeing with them?"

"I already know your answer." Ron blurted out.

Selese smiled, holding her hand out, waiting for Linda to hand over her armband.

* * *

The three arrived in a darkened hall, the stone smooth as if poured into place. As they walked, its walls glowed in green and gold as they looked around.

"I think I'll keep my gate ready in case we need to leave quickly." Linda and Selese nodded in agreement.

Linda asked, "I thought you would have put us right on top of the gate you were looking for?"

Selese whispered a reply, "When you go to steal something, you never drop down on top of it right away. You'll get caught."

Ron whispered, "Wisdom in thievery, good to know."

Both women silenced him with a glare, making Ron chuckle before they cautiously entered a larger, well-lit room.

They looked around but saw no one. Selese approached one of the tables, one displaying several gold and platinum rods melded into a twisted ring. She looked to Ron in question, only to see him shrug. Ron and Linda split and searched down separate halls that connected away from the large room, while Selese inspected the gold structure in front of her. She hadn't noticed a sudden form appear beside her.

"Who are you?" Selese heard a voice quietly ask and turned to see an older Asian man standing next to her. His long, greying beard raking over what looked like stone and metal armor across his chest. He wore a monocle of crystal.

Selese readied to fight but was confused as the man quietly and studiously held his hand out as he moved closer to her. The man's lens showed him a royal red glow from around the woman. His visible eye displayed a mix of sadness and curiosity. He inspected Selese head to toe before saying, "How? How are you doing that?"

She didn't know what he was talking about.

"Aurum pulsation, how? How long have you had it?" She could see the man looking even more sad as he continued to inspect her.

Selese's mind filled with fear; *aurum was an alchemist's term for gold*. She knew he was seeing her golden heart. Terror filled her and she yelled, "Ron! Linda! Help!"

They returned to the chamber to see Chu standing before Selese. The old geomage was startled by her scream. He stepped back, seeing her friends appear from the halls, looking angry. They moved to protect Selese. He stepped aside, almost quivering, "I'm sorry, I meant no harm. I merely want to know how it is still beating." There was a heavy sadness in his words.

Linda growled, "Back away," as Ron moved to protect Selese.

Chu stepped away in fear, a look of repentance as he sat, "I'm sorry, forgive me, I only wanted to know."

Selese felt the pain in the man's voice. She gently pushed Ron to the side. "Why did you ask how it was still beating?"

A tear rolled down the man's cheek, "because every one I've created lasted only a short while." He huffed, calming himself. "Dania. . . she was lost when I couldn't. . ." Chu's words faded.

Selese felt the tears in her eyes as the man went quiet. He looked at her. "I was creating this to try and find her again." Chu pointed to the table and the golden ring device she had been inspecting before calling for her friends.

Selese sensed felt Linda's presence and felt herself lean back against her friend. Ron moved to place his hand on Chu's shoulder.

Selese heard Linda whisper, "Dania was his wife. She was killed some time ago. He told us about her."

Chu looked to Selese. "She lost her heart to a wraith mage. But Aiden and I couldn't save her."

Selese felt panic and anger welling up in her and watched the concern in Ron's gaze as he looked back toward her. She pushed away from Linda, taking a step forward, anger in her stance, "Was it Britlan?"

Chu shook his head. "No, it was another wraith mage. He took her heart to make her. . ." Chu paused, his look angry, sad, and confused, "Is that how you lost yours?" Concern and sorrow rolled heavily into his words. "I'm so sorry, I am so, so sorry. You are so young. Whoever did this should be punished severely."

Selese nodded animatedly, causing Linda to move up to put her arms around the woman.

Chu showed sorrow and anger as he spoke, "Did you create your own heart?" He waved his hands toward the table. "If your friend needs one, then take any gold you need, take it all. Please take all you need."

Selese felt the tears in her eyes fall as she shook her head. "No, I'm trying to stop my friend from having her mind erased and her life ruined. She looked to Ron. "You said he might be able to help. Lets' do what we came to do."

Ron nodded and took a breath to speak. Chu was worse than he was when they first met him. His emotional state seemed to be waning. Ron pushed the man, turning him to look at him.

"Chu, someone has been stealing *tianqius*. . ." Ron spoke but never had a chance to finish his sentence.

Chu stood. "Is their spirit trapped in one? Where is it? I'll happily release them."

Ron grabbed the man's shoulders. "Chu, listen to me, we need to know something. We're sure her friend is innocent, and someone is setting her up. But we need to know what other uses the *tianqius* have."

Chu was silent. He seemed to be processing what Ron had said. The old geomage looked to Selese and smiled as if remembering something. Ron wanted answers and again needed their friend's full attention.

"Chu, we're sorry about what happened to Dania, but right now, we need your help. Time is running out." Ron said. He then looked into the man's eyes and could see their distance as he mentioned Chu's wife. He looked to the table. "That's why you stole all of this?" Ron looked at Linda. "You're trying to find Dania again? On another world?"

Chu wiped the tears from his face, nodding. "But I can't get it to work."

Ron shook the man in a comforting gesture. "Maybe you can help us with the problem we came with. I know it might not be a priority, but maybe we could come back later. We'll even help if we can. But, right now, we need information. Anything you have."

Chu nodded as he looked at Selese. "I'm a bad host. I'm sorry. Although, I am surprised that you found me."

Ron looked back to Selese. "She's the one who found you. She's pretty clever." Then, he looked to Chu, "and she's trying to save our friend."

Chu gave a smile, "The *tianqius* can be used several ways. One is to trap spirits and spells. But there is another they were used for long ago."

Ron huffed, "And what was that?"

Chu hung his head. "Territory. They can be used to hold a population. Or at least their will and minds. Many alchemists used them to enslave entire cities. Sometimes separating them from the world. Moving them outside this realm."

Ron took a step back. His mind reeled at the thought, and he looked up. "That would be worth it for someone looking to take over an area."

Linda spoke up, "Or the Sanctuary."

Chu laughed. "The Iron lamps would prevent that. They were created to stop all magic from encroaching. Besides, there are easier ways to control an area. For example, a simple encirclement spell and gold would work. Any geomage can do it if they know how. The only people I know who might use a *tianqiu* to encompass an area are feral witches or alchemists."

Chu slumped in his chair, "I don't think there are any left anyway."

Ron turned to Linda; it was more information than they had. But would it be enough to help Shrive? Or at least convince others to start looking for another person.

Selese moved from Linda's embrace, standing before Chu, "Maybe there are still some around. Would you know how to find them?"

Chu shook his head, "I'm sorry, I don't."

Selese looked back at Linda. "Do you think we can convince the council that Shrive was set up?"

"It's not a lot, but it's all we have," Ron said.

Selese looked to Ron, "then we go back with it and hope those morons believe us."

Ron sighed, then nodded. He started walking toward Selese, who was about to join him, when she heard Chu chuckle. Selese looked at him as the man turned up to look into her eyes. "You'd do anything to help your friend, wouldn't you?"

Selese nodded.

Chu smiled, then said, "You know, Aiden had a theory about why the hearts we made failed."

Selese felt a heaviness in her chest as she processed his words and asked, "Why did they fail?"

Chu smiled. "It was that the gold could not sustain itself. Therefore, it could not be a true heart unless the one it replaced were already one of gold."

Selese seemed confused, then looked to him for clarification.

Chu stood up. "It's simple, my dear. Your heart is still beating because you've always had a heart of gold. Regardless of what it is made of now."

Selese felt a warmth in his words and pulled against Ron as he walked by. The man who was Amanda's friend and now hers allowed her to lean on him for a moment.

Ron said, "Thank you, Chu. If you need anything, let us know."

Chu nodded. "The darker side of magic will always persist. If I find any more information, I'll send it along." He looked to Selese. "And you, my dear, no matter what people say about you, keep being who you are."

Selese smiled the entire way back through the short tunnel. She looked back to see purple light surround them and watched as the old geomage waved at them before the room vanished. She knew what they found wasn't much, but she hoped, as did Ron and Linda, that it would be enough to save their friend.

Chapter 18:
A Little Help from Fairy Friends

Gina's hands glowed as she felt the water. It wasn't physically touching her, but she felt it as it moved, the fluid action and substance as she held the wavering sphere above her.

"Excellent, you've improved a lot since last week. What have you been doing differently?" Mallie asked.

Gina smiled. Mallie had made things easier for her once they realized that her water sprite side had been suppressed for so long. Gina felt the natural flow of the water and was still wondering why she never knew about the power she had. It was also helpful that Allison had not taken control of her for the last few days. It allowed Gina to be left on her own as she practiced.

Why can I do this? I don't understand. How can I do these things?

Gina's mind began to focus on why she now had power over water and that it felt good to be near it. Her mind asked repeatedly, and finally, she forgot what she was doing. Within seconds the giant ball of water rebounded off the floor and over everyone around, including herself. She flung off the water and could see others soaked as she did. She felt embarrassed at first but then started to laugh. Her very being filled with a flippant humor that she enjoyed—her boisterous laughter filling the room all around.

Gina looked back to see the annoyed glare of a dripping wet Mallie; Gina felt herself smile. She watched as Mallie walked up, shaking water toward her, the drops hitting Gina as she continued to smile. She could hear her teacher chuckling.

"I had almost forgotten about water sprites and their humor. Always splashing trespassers as they walked by." Mallie's hands started to glow, and the water floated from those all around. Gina looked up to see the drops coalescing above her. The teacher smiled before hearing Gina say, "I didn't know you could remove water from clothes."

Mallie tilted her head. "Control of water and its element are all part of being part water spirit."

Gina watched in fascination as the water suspended above and before her. Then, she looked at Mallie and could see the woman grinning.

Mallie said, "Water spirits are playful but can also be vindictive," causing Gina to look up in concern. "What does everyone think?"

She watched as those practicing with her all put their thumbs down. Gina looked up to see the water right above her. She went to move away, but it followed her.

"No, it was an accident. I didn't mean to splash anyone," Gina pleaded.

She tried to catch her breath as the ball of water followed. Finally, she stopped, and within seconds, the ball of water crashed down over her. But instead of being angry, she laughed. Mallie walked up laughing as well. The teacher said, "All right, everyone, we're done for the day."

Gina flung water from her sleeves toward Mallie. The woman caught it mid-air and tossed it back. Then, she stood, arms crossed, before Gina, saying, "You did really well today. I'm surprised you let the water fall."

Gina was about to say something but groaned, "Ugh, waterfall?"

Mallie laughed. "Water jokes. You'll get used to them."

Gina smiled, telling Mallie that she enjoyed today's lesson much more than the others. And she didn't know why. Mallie nodded. "You've probably been away from your element for so long. But you are what you are. Nothing will change that." Mallie looked around the room. "You may just be tired. It would help if you went for a swim. It's sometimes better than sleeping."

Gina looked toward a doorway that led to what looked like a lake in the portal. Although it was nighttime, the blue sky above it was confusing. She didn't know how it was like that, but as she looked at the calm lake water, she felt its draw. She started toward the doorway before Mallie said something.

"You may want to change before you go take a swim. People might look at you strangely, even here, walking around soaked." Gina nodded and waved to Mallie as she headed to get changed.

In the locker room, Gina sat on the bench; she reached for her assigned locker but froze halfway. Then, she felt her mind fade and heard Allison's voice again.

"Hello, my little doll."

If Gina could speak, she would have said some very cross words. But instead, she remained unmoving as Allison took control of her again.

"Have you forgotten why you are there, my dear?"

Gina stood, taking the bag she had and pulled something from it. She seemed to be pulling at the air. Allison moved Gina's head to look around and moved into the shadows before pulling the cloak over her, making her doll invisible again. Gina stood still, unable to move, but Allison could sense her trying to break from her control. The old witch said, "That'll be quite enough, my dear. I'll take things from here for tonight."

It was around seven o'clock when they arrived back as Amanda waited for their return in her apartment. She was eager to tell her friends what she had learned. Selese had provided some insight into Amanda's short investigation—as did the fairies in the Grove whom Amanda asked for help. Although they couldn't directly do so, they were able to provide a much-needed account of what had happened—the forest providing new information from what she and Selese had learned speaking with Xi Liu. At least in Amanda's mind, she was sure a third party was involved. Although her newly disclosed escapade about meeting with Li Xiu in her room did cause some concern for Ron and Linda.

"Why did you take the chance? The Duànzào are not like the Raven Hunters." Linda paused, seemingly annoyed. "Here they take your memories. There they take, well, you."

Ron also couldn't stand silent on the matter, telling her that the Duànzào play far too rough, even for their liking.

After things had calmed down, Linda told her that she and Ron were sure that Shrive was innocent. The hard part was proving it with the Silver

Hunters pushing the issue. Finally, Amanda agreed to tell her that she knew Shrive was innocent, and the actions they described were not ones that Shrive would take. "After all, Shrive was a trained hunter." Amanda criticized the Raven Hunters, "Whoever it was, they were sloppy."

"Wait, how did you see?" Selese asked.

Amanda admitted that she wanted to help Shrive even more after the break-in. When Amanda went to the Grove, asking for help from the fairies, none of the fairies could believe the accusations against her friend. She told them that she watched one fairy fly quickly away, only to return with a single leaf in hand. "Then she gave it to me. They showed me what the trees nearby could see."

Ron looked at her. "What the trees see?"

"Yes, they are always watching the forest. That's how the fairies know what's happened when they're not around." Then, Amanda paused, "well, at least when they're being helpful."

Amanda told them how the fairy who brought the leaf, named Castil, had met with, as the fairy put it, "some stumpy tree, and grumpy indeed."

Linda laughed before asking, "Can you show us?"

Amanda looked at them. "Okay. But, I have to concentrate for this, so be patient." Amanda held her wooden ring and focused. Above the leaf, the image was as clear as if recorded on a nearby camera.

"You can do magic?" Linda said with a hint of delight.

Amanda shook her head. "No, enchanted leaf. Apparently, the playback only works if you're friends of fairies or trees. That's why I'm holding my ring."

They watched the images with Ron saying, "It was clear that something grabbed them both. It was a good thing you grabbed Li Xiu when she fell." Then, Ron paused. "Although you do seem to be getting into some dangerous situations recently."

Amanda became angry. They were her friends and, so far, had been on adventures without her. She felt hurt that they didn't trust her, even after all the times they had been chasing magic together.

"Amanda, we're just being protective." Linda smiled. "We're not stopping you. Just be careful. That's all we're asking."

Selese said, with a somewhat happier tone, "So, you think that'll be enough to help?"

Ron nodded, pulling out his phone. "Dr. Brentwood, I'm not disturbing you, am I?"

Everyone watched as Ron nodded during the conversation between the two. When Ron said, "We have some evidence we think you and the Regent should see," they all waited.

Ron nodded, saying, "Okay, see you in a bit," before hanging up. He could see everyone staring at him. "Half an hour." Then, he looked to Linda. "Hopefully, the information Chu provided and what Amanda has will be enough to, at the very least, get Shrive out of that cell."

They arrived to find Chung waiting impatiently. Ron explained what he discovered about the *tianqius*, which Chung dismissed. "This has no relevancy to the anthromorph's attack."

Linda spoke up, "It wasn't an attack; she and your person were grabbed. You can even see the sleeve of Li Xiu's arm crushed under something invisible."

Chung scoffed and stood. "This proves nothing. That thing will stay in its cage like an animal should."

Amanda stood, as did Selese, both yelling at the Regent, their words fueled by anger and emotion. Their tone only angered the head of the Silver Hunters. That was until they all heard the room fill with one word.

"Enough!" Ron's voice echoed almost as much as Dr. Brentwood's had earlier.

As the room fell silent, even the Regent wasn't making a sound. Finally, after a few seconds, he huffed turning to look at Lord Cale, who was standing by the door. The Regent started to walk but stopped hearing Ron's outburst.

"Regent, why do you dismiss the evidence you've just seen?"

Chung stood tall. "It shows nothing valuable."

Ron started forward as he responded. "That's interesting. Many others seem to think otherwise."

The Regent said nothing and turned to leave. Ron spoke again, causing him to pause.

"It's been my experience, Regent, that those who ignore evidence are either ignorant or have an agenda." They all watched as Ron turned toward the Regent. "Which do you think it is?"

Linda placed her hand on Ron's arm, her face full of concern. The room was silent.

The Regent smiled. "Accusations. . ."

The Regent went silent as Ron interrupted, "Accusations are not being made, Regent. I'm merely asking for your opinion."

An uneasiness filled the room as the Regent stepped toward Ron. But, he stopped, remembering that they were under the protection of the acting Regent of Xiling Mountain.

The Regent instead smiled, saying nothing as he walked toward the door. Lord Cale shifted out of the man's way as he exited. Linda spoke soon after.

"Are you crazy?"

"He's hiding something. I'm sure of it now."

Dr. Brentwood stood. "You had no right to accuse him of anything."

Ron looked at Lord Cale, who nodded, saying, "You're right. He is hiding something."

Ron turned to see confusion in the eyes of the others. "Easy, easy, if he were an honorable man, he would have argued, even demanded an apology." Ron leaned his head back. "And I would have given one, happily." Ron turned to Cale. "Instead, he chose to say nothing. He's hiding a secret. And I don't think it's about anyone like Shrive. He's made that certainly clear."

Cale looked to his wife. "I think Ron should accompany me to the Forge. If Chung is planning something, I'll need the help."

Dr. Brentwood nodded. "I'll authorize it. Keep out of trouble, please."

Ron nodded and left with Lord Cale.

Dr. Brentwood looked to everyone remaining, "While they're on their mission, tell me everything you found, no matter how small the detail."

Chapter 19:
Almost had it

As Cale approached the Forge, he could hear the commanding voice of Regent Chung giving orders. The main door to the room was wide open, but he could tell that the security spell was active with a glance, the distinctive glow of the energy surging as one of the Silver Ravens pushed against the shield. Ron could see the distinct faded veil of a glowing sheet surrounding one of the artifacts. Ron followed after him, keeping a few steps behind. He didn't want Chung to realize that he was there. At least not right away.

Ron was still thinking about the evidence they found, and if it would be enough to free Shrive. He also suspected Chung of having an ulterior motive in combining the shipment of the artifacts into one. As he walked, his mind focused on the events only to feel something brush across his left arm. He could hear something like fabric, but when he turned, he saw nothing. After pausing for a moment, he turned to see Lord Cale enter the Forge and decided to follow.

The witch could see Lord Cale looking for something in the air around him. She moved Gina away as silently and quickly as possible. *Careless, Allison, careless. Can't have your doll caught by some lumbering hunter.* Allison thought, realizing if she had let Gina speak, the rest of the words that followed, she surely should have had to find another unwilling accomplice.

Instead, Allison moved the girl to the far wall, willing her doll to climb to stay out of the way of any possible hunters walking around. The witch silently cursed, seeing Ron standing before the opening of the Forge, his stance blocking any easy way to enter. *Guess I'll have to wait for this oaf to move before I can enter.* She leaned Gina back against the wall, the cloak holding her loosely against the stones. Once she was secure, the witch waited and watched.

Ron still stood before the door of the Forge; he felt his fairy ring shift. But that wasn't his only warning as he felt the hair on his neck bristle. It was as if someone was nearby watching. He looked around, searching, but his eyes couldn't see anything.

The person who was at the cliff was invisible. I thought I had walked into someone earlier.

Ron slowly scanned around the area. He could feel something was amiss. But as he heard Chung yell out more commands, he was brought back to the task he had initially come to help with.

Chung sneered, giving a half-smile as he looked toward Lord Cale. His eyes spying Ron standing watch by the entrance. He couldn't help but notice the small vestibule that separated the main room of the Forge, now empty of its contents.

"Why is he here?" Chung asked with disdain.

Cale replied, "He's here to watch things from an outsider's view. And at the request of Dr. Brentwood."

Chung scoffed, "Ah, you allow your wife to dictate your actions."

"I trust her judgment." Cale looked forward as he continued, "Why? Do you allow someone to control yours?"

The Regent felt slighted and turned his eyes angrily as he watched the leader of the Raven Hunters give a subdued smile of confidence. He was about to remark but was interrupted when Bao approached.

"Forgive my interruption. Lord Cale, your people are quite efficient. We should have things secure to ship in the next day." Bao looked to the Regent, speaking loudly, "I would like to offer my recommendation to splitting the shipment." He watched as Ron's attention became focused on him, so he spoke to allow him to hear, "your concerns about the shipment are valid. I am glad you brought them to the attention of our people."

Bao watched as Ron nodded, but didn't move from his spot before the doorway. That caused Bao to consider something, and he made another recommendation. "Regent, I recommend we keep the security spell active while working. Those artifacts already moved are of little consequence. The remaining are the more precious and dangerous." Chung looked toward the two standing beside him but said nothing.

"Regent, Mr. Wilt has been standing guard before the door. Do you know why?" He turned to Lord Cale, asking the same question.

The leader of the Raven Hunters nodded. "Last time I was here, the protection spell was inactive. Like Mr. Wilt, I do not think that is a wise action. Although, since these are your people and property, we have considered your needs in the situation."

Bao stood with a sense of authority before sighing and saying, "Thank you for your generosity in allowing us full use of the facility. However, I agree with you. The previous removal of the alarm was a misjudgment. I am comforted that it has remained."

Chung's eyes never faltered. He merely stared on at the work being done. His years of working within the Silver Ravens and for the Broken Feather allowed him fair practice in masking his disdain for procedure. The Regent noticed Bao leaning toward him in confusion. But as the man was about to speak, Chung replied, "It will be a hindrance, but I suppose a necessity. But I can't entirely agree with splitting the shipment. We have a better way of defending it as one." And after a slight pause, he said, "And that is what we will do. Continue to do as I have commanded."

Bao's head turned slightly, his eyes looking to Lord Cale for support. The air between the Silver Hunters was not one of sympathetic nature. Bao was beginning to wonder if the Regent had a plan that was, for now, unknown. His suspicion showed in his stance as he was about to express his disdain, he but saw how his fellow hunter was reacting. Chung turned instead to say, "My apologies, my friend. I am worried about the shipment and our people. If I seem distracted, I ask for understanding."

Bao stood at attention. "I am concerned as well, but why do you oppose the idea of multiple shipments?

Chung had to think fast. He had already promised the items to the Feather and was not willing to concede. Instead, he looked toward where they had moved the dragon's claw.

Chung smiled, then appeared worried. "My friend, I have been doing this work for many years. Unfortunately, I have seen too many stolen items from multiple arrangements." Finally, Chung sighed, "It is easier to defend one shipment than two. And in my experience, less likely to lose valuable items."

Bao stared at the Regent. Although Bao was sent in to aid the transfer, he knew, as did everyone, that the Regent had the final say in all matters. So, the Silver Hunter watched as Chung motioned toward the dragon's claw.

"You are worried that something powerful such as the dragon's claw would be lost, yes?"

Bao nodded.

A sense of confidence returned to the Regent's pose. "Then we will surround it with those less dangerous or valuable. That way, the artifacts would be much more difficult to steal if attacked. It is a strategy that has worked successfully for centuries. So why would we change it now?"

Bao glanced toward Lord Cale to see the Raven hunter raise a single brow subtly. His expression made it clear that he still didn't understand why the Regent dismissed the splitting of the shipment. Then, with some distress, he complied with the command of the Regent and looked to Lord Cale.

"Lord Cale, would you help me move some of the more delicate items to be loaded when we have done so with the other items?" Bao asked, his voice filled with questions he wanted to ask.

Cale smiled. "Certainly."

As they walked to the smaller room, Bao spoke quietly, "Would your people be able to send a message to snow mountain for me?"

Cale nodded.

"Thank you. I wish to look for guidance from the council. I am still uncomfortable with all this as one shipment."

Cale whispered, "As are we."

The Regent turned to watch them walk away, his eyes keeping track as they moved the dragon's claw toward the wall. A short smile graced his lips. *Soon everything will be in place.*

A short time later, Allison, using Gina's body, crept down from the wall. She had watched the men talking but could not hear what they spoke about. Her main frustration was the man standing in the doorway. He only moved when someone walked in or out and kept a close distance between whoever it was.

"Damn hunters, there's always one that gets in the way," Allison said as she moved her doll closer and reached the door. She watched as her hand started to become visible and pulled back quickly.

"The protection spell is still active." She looked around before moving Gina closer to the wall. She kept the girl's eyes focused on Ron as he turned, seeming to hear something behind him. "This one has good ears, dammit. Why didn't she just steal the blasted thing earlier?"

Allison used Gina to look around. She moved closer to the door and waited with her hand near the entrance. As Ron moved from his post, allowing a Silver Hunter to enter, she placed her hand inside the doorway, and nothing happened.

"The field is down when they move through," she whispered with joy. She then attempted the same action as another moved from the Forge. The smile of salacious delight on her lips. "It'll be a matter of timing. But I think this doll can finally bring back what is rightfully mine."

The witch moved Gina away from the entrance and peered inside the Forge before moving closer. She could see inside the small room that connected the Forge to the Sanctuary as one of the hunters placed her prize near the wall. Gina moved closer and was startled as another hunter carrying an artifact bumped into her, the hunter dropping the item but quickly moved, catching the artifact before it struck the ground. The action grabbed Ron's attention.

"You all right?" Ron asked, moving away from his post.

The woman nodded, "Yes." She looked around. "I thought I ran into something."

Ron immediately became vigilant and started moving randomly, reaching out into the air. Earlier, he had thought someone, or something had brushed against him. Now there was another. Ron turned, yelling into the Forge, "Cale, we might have an issue."

The leader of the Raven hunters rushed toward the door, and Bao soon followed.

Allison moved Gina up onto the wall again. *Dammit, I'm not as good at this as I thought.* She seemed to think. *Perhaps I should give control back to my doll. She has proven herself sometimes capable.*

Gina felt her mind coalesce again, and she could hear her thoughts. Allison, however, was still there to persuade her accomplice. Gina heard in her mind, "The protection field will show you if you try to cross it, my dear. It is, however, open when others walk through. You will have to time things to reach the Sphere."

Gina was about to speak but whispered, "Why are there so many people in the hall now?"

Allison huffed, "I'm relying on you to retrieve my prize. Remember our agreement."

Gina looked at the hunters searching the air around them, the sight somewhat amusing to her and her mistress. However, she still had no answer as to why so many hunters were now surrounding her.

As she was about to ask what was going on, Allison spoke in her mind, "I was careless, my dear, is that what you wanted to hear?" Gina felt a twinge of acceptance as Allison continued, "You are a far better thief than I am, my dear. Now, remember our bargain. You bring me my prize, and I release you from your, uh, situation. I'll leave you to it."

Gina's mind quieted, no longer hearing her mistress in her head. She had wanted this arrangement over for some time. Gina still didn't know what the old woman had used her for many times. Only recently, however, she was left worse than when she started, which concerned Gina. For the moment, she needed to be attentive. The hunters around her might find her, and she didn't know what Allison would do if they did. She moved further up the wall silently until the hunters returned to their duties. However, the one who stood in the doorway didn't relinquish his post.

"They're going back to work; how do I get past that one?" Gina whispered.

She waited for an answer from Allison, who, for the moment, remained silent. It was several seconds before she heard her mistress in her head saying, "I was not able to get past him. Perhaps you might have a better chance."

Gina shook her head and watched, waiting for her chance to sneak in and grab the Sphere.

It was a short while later. Chung was walking around the room, inspecting the artifacts that were waiting to be moved into the truck. He was especially interested in the more dangerous ones. The Regent stopped by the dragon's claw and inspected it. He looked around and, seeing no one nearby, tugged on the small ring of coins he wore around his neck. His fingers fanned through them until he felt the precise one he needed. He spoke a few words, and when finished, the dragon's claw twitched, the elemental flames within its claws now active and waiting.

It will be a shame you have to die, my friend. But the Feather will remember you with honor. I will be sure of that. Chung thought as he walked back toward the others. Spying Bao, walking into the Forge, returning from an errand, the Regent tapped his arm as he walked by. "Bao, when we are ready, I wish you to take the dragon's claw. I do not trust our fellow hunters with such an honor."

Bao looked curiously at the Regent but nodded. Boa would be willing to handle the artifact if his superior was not confident in the others.

Gina watched as the two hunters spoke and silently griped, "I wish I knew what they were saying."

She watched as the others moved away from the Forge entrance. She was wondering what was happening. Then she heard the commanding voice of one of the hunters, "Regent Chung, Mr. Wilt, I think we're ready." Chung walked toward the dragon's claw, where another hunter waited. She stood outside the door. As Gina looked to see what they were doing, she spotted the sphere inside the inner room.

If I can get in, it'll be easy to get out. I just have to be careful.

Gina climbed down the wall and stood nearby, ready to rush into the doorway. As soon as the woman started forward, Gina mimicked her actions and entered the Forge quickly. However, her hand was behind her as the hunter crossed the threshold. And for a split second, Gina's fingers were visible.

The anomaly didn't go unnoticed by the hunter, and she suddenly turned, her arm out, striking something.

"Intruder!" The woman yelled.

Within seconds hunters rushed toward the door. Gina was in a panic. She was invisible, but if enough people were there, then she would be trapped. Ron stood in the doorway, his arms out, making it difficult for anyone to move past.

I need a diversion. Gina thought, and she moved toward the dragon's claw. She pushed it over, making the hunters pause. She scrutinized them. *They're blocking the sphere. Oh, I hate you all.*

Gina turned avoiding a hand swiping at the air around her. She knew she had to get out of there. But then she turned to see the ground around the claw glowing with fire and heard, "Dragon's claw! Run!" She watched as the hunters inside the Forge quickly moved away, retreating to the doors in the back of the room. One of the hunters rushed to where the claw lay and yelled for everyone to seal the inside doors.

"Fire," Gina whimpered, her eyes filling with terror. She looked around, her body ready to run. But as a hunter swiped toward her, she looked to the main door and made her move.

She ran through the alarm, showing her form as she passed through. Ron watched and went to chase her but stopped, hearing, "This fire will destroy everything. Mr. Wilt, we need to contain this. Now!" Ron turned to grab the large door, pulling on it to close the Forge from the rest of the Sanctuary.

Gina continued to run as she heard the door of the Forge close. The only thought in her head as she ran from the Sanctuary was, *I almost had it, I almost had it!*

Chapter 20:
A Good Hunter Gone

Ron secured the door and turned to see Bao standing over the dragon's claw. Ron slipped as he stepped on some ash left from the claw's initial assault. The artifact had now dug its talons into the stone floor through the moss that littered the entrance of the Forge. Bao used several elements to try and calm the artifact without success. Things looked grim to Ron as the Silver Hunter eventually pulled at the chain of coins around his neck, breaking it and releasing all of those it held at once. Bao threw them to the floor, and they arranged themselves into a circle. Each coin, in time, was spinning like a top. Moments later, the stone floor itself surrounding the claw within the ring ignited.

"I wasn't able to stop it, but I can try to contain it," Bao said, looking at Ron.

"How can I help?" Ron could see the man's concentration and effort as he watched the coins spinning as if tossed onto a table. They surrounded the claw and the flames for the moment.

"You closed the main door. That's good. Now we only have to worry about the fire in here." Bao looked back. "Get everyone to safety and close the inside doors. It will extinguish if the fire cannot find something to consume."

Ron looked back, seeing everyone running into the forge room itself. Lord Cale arrived by his side. "How do we stop it?"

Bao shook his head, "The claw has been angered. It will burn everything combustible it has seen and can find."

Ron and Cale looked around the room. It was almost bare, except for a few artifacts. Ron looked back to see Chung joining the others heading into the Forge. He turned to Cale, "Go, I'll follow you. Let me see what I can do here."

Bao interrupted them, "Regent Chung's element is of fire. He may be able to help."

Ron and Cale rushed to reach Chung, who was nearly inside the main room of the Forge. They yelled for him to stop, but when the Regent was asked to help, they were surprised to hear him respond, "You can stay if you want." Chung continued to rush back toward the Forge.

Ron paused as Cale went to retrieve the Regent. "Are you a coward, Chung? Bao is trying to save us all."

Chung turned angrily, his fist not entirely accurate, missing Cale by fractions. Cale then yelled, "Secure the inside door! Now!" They all heard the sound of the lock that secured the large door of the Forge itself.

Seeing the doors sealed, Chung turned to Lord Cale in disbelief. "You've killed us."

Ron turned back to see the circle of coins glowing brightly. The flames from the dragon's claw surrounded them. Ron noticed the doors that separated the storage room from the entryway, and he rushed to close one before yelling, "Bao, come on. We can shield this door and remain inside here." Ron had to look away, the light becoming white-hot to his eyes.

Bao turned, seeing Ron holding the door open, and turned before hearing the disheartening sound of the coins he once held so dearly fall, molten, splattering to the ground. Ron watched as the hunter's face filled with terror before closing the door. Ron's mind was a mix of anger and sorrow, his mouth forming words filled with the same as he said, "I'm sorry."

Ron didn't have time to grieve as the door started to smoke. He felt the fire's heat through it. Then, as the door began to glow red, he stepped back and heard the Regent say. "It knows we're here. It will come for us."

Ron asked, "What knows we're here?"

The Regent looked at Cale in anger. "The dragon's fire. It will consume all that can burn." Cale moved beside Ron, leaving the Regent behind. "I have some shielding spells, but I'm not sure they'll work against this."

Ron nodded. "Use them, use all of them." He looked at the door. "I might be able to help as well."

Cale used his elements, but the flames started breaking through as the door started to buckle. Ron held his hand up, and his fairy ring began glowing brightly. As the fire reached out, it hit the shield he produced.

"A fairy shield, how?" Chung asked. Ron only looked at him, his eyes a soft glow of white, his face lit by the fairy ring he wore from beneath his shirt.

Chung stepped back. "You're not a FOF? You're one of them?"

Cale turned as Chung looked at Ron with disdain. Cale could see the disgust in the Regent's eyes and raised his fist, striking Chung securely, knocking the man unconscious.

Cale turned back to Ron. "I'm sure he had something to do with this."

Ron nodded, doing his best to hold the flames at bay, "Me too. The problem is proving it." Then, he looked to the Regent, now prone on the stone floor. "Maybe if we survive this, we take him out into the desert and leave him there."

Cale half agreed, then joked, "Could you imagine the paperwork on that?" making Ron chuckle. He then looked to his elements. "Let me see what else I've got and see if we can survive this. Then we'll deal with him."

Dr. Brentwood arrived along with Linda and the others. But unfortunately, the door was still sealed from the inside.

"We need to get them out," Amanda said with some urgency. But then, she turned to Linda to see actual fear in her friend's eyes. "Can't we get inside? Maybe we can get them out," she asked Selese.

"No!" A very adamant command escaped Dr. Brentwood. "You will do nothing until we know the fire is out."

Amanda looked at the doctor then glanced toward Selese, who started toward the door. Seeing this, Dr. Brentwood again yelled, "Selese, no! It's a dragon's claw. It won't stop till everything it can find is burned. If you go in there and it's still awake, it will consume you."

Selese watched as her mother fought to contain her emotions. She realized that what they were facing inside the Forge was far more dangerous than she understood. She looked at Amanda and shook her head. Amanda watched Linda and could see her far-off stare as she stood, rolling the fairy ring she wore between her fingers. Her expression of concern became joyful as they heard the door to the Forge unlock.

They could hear coughing as Ron pushed the door open; Cale had pulled Chung from the floor and carried him through the door. The remaining hunters soon followed.

Linda rushed to Ron, inspecting him. She noticed the burn on his hand and asked, "Are you okay?"

Ron nodded once, then looked toward Dr. Brentwood as Linda used her ring to heal his injury.

The doctor then asked, "Did we lose anyone?"

Ron nodded several times, anger in each short nod, before saying, "Bao tried saving us."

The doctor looked to Lord Cale, who approached. "It was quick." She turned away, her eyes closing in disgust and sadness, understanding his implication.

Amanda rushed over, hugging Ron. "I'm glad you're all right."

Ron looked her in the eyes. He was going to say something but instead remained silent while he put his arm around her.

Selese did the same to Cale.

Dr. Brentwood joined Cale and Selese. She held him longer than she usually would. She only released him, asking, "Do you know who did this?"

Cale nodded, and Dr. Brentwood looked to Ron, but when she asked, all Ron said was, "Not here. we need to go somewhere more private."

Dr. Brentwood looked to Cale, who nodded in agreement.

It was several minutes later as they entered Dr. Brentwood's office. After activating an element and a quick wave around the room, to prevent their words from being heard, she watched the others as they sat.

"That should dissuade any prying ears or other senses from hearing us," Dr. Brentwood said as she walked to sit in her chair. "Now, you said you know who did this?"

Lord Cale looked to Ron before he spoke, "We don't have a way of proving it, but we're sure it was Chung. The dragon's claw was secure. Someone had to activate it." Cale leaned back, the soft chair wheezing as he spoke to the ceiling, "There were only two fire element users in the Forge. Bao and. . ."

Ron spoke, his voice confident, "Chung."

Everyone looked around as the new information came to light. The doctor nodded. "The acting regent must be told."

Cale then spoke, "Bao asked to send a message to snow mountain before this all happened. He was concerned about Chung's recent decisions as well. He was waiting to hear back for guidance." He then looked to Claire, "I'll make the call. I'll take responsibility for Bao."

Ron chimed in, "Make sure they know Bao tried saving everyone. Maybe mention that Chung was running away instead of helping." Then, he looked to Linda. "I'll call Zhang. He should know as well."

Dr. Brentwood sat tall. "Before either of you do anything, first, we need to figure out how this started."

"Someone passed through the spell surrounding the door. One of Bao's people saw them. They set off the alarm." Ron looked to Linda. "I saw a figure pass through the same spell as I rushed to close the door. So there is definitely another player in this. And I don't know if they are even associated with the Broken Feather."

Ron leaned back in his chair. "Either way, this is way out of control. And we still don't know what the connection is."

Amanda stared forward. Selese took notice and asked, "Okay, what is it?"

Amanda looked up to see everyone staring at her and suddenly felt the room's weight on her. First, she looked to Selese, then to Ron.

"Whatever it is, and I'm sure Claire and Cale would agree, you're already out of this. Both of you. You are not going anywhere near the Silver Ravens now," Ron said.

Amanda sat tall, as did Selese. They were both about to speak when Linda said, "It doesn't matter if you have information. Tell us now, and we'll take it from here."

Amanda looked hurt and glared toward Ron, who said, "You're not going to change my mind or any of ours. So, you might as well tell us what you figured out. Whoever is playing this game is playing way too rough. Being burned alive wasn't exactly on my bucket list."

Amanda chuckled at his poor attempt at humor. "That's not funny."

Ron replied, "You're right. It's not." He sat forward, "I'm serious, Amanda. Neither you nor Selese are getting involved with the Silver Hunters from this point on. So, you might as well tell us what you figured out."

Amanda felt hurt, but she knew Ron and the others were trying to protect them. She understood and shifted, "You're right."

Ron looked puzzled, but Amanda cut him off as he was about to speak.

"You're right about us not getting involved with the Silver Hunters from here on. Because I'm sure the Broken Feather is behind the Regent. Whether the Silver Hunters know it or not. This has their way-of-doing-business stink all over it."

Amanda looked to Ron, "You're also right about there being another player."

Ron nodded. "Okay, how are you sure?

Amanda looked around the room. "You said that one of the Silver Hunters set off the alarm, right?"

Ron nodded.

Amanda looked to Lord Cale, "Ron also said that he saw someone and even started to chase them before he had to head back and close the door."

Cale and Ron agreed.

She then looked to Selese. "The dragon's claw would have been one hell of a prize. Imagine the damage you could cause. But instead, whoever it was, ran soon after being discovered, right?"

Selese nodded. "That makes sense."

Amanda continued, "So if they weren't after a dangerous item like that, why were they in the Forge? How many of the *tianqiu* were stolen? We already know they can be used for something else. Maybe whatever they were after was related." There was a pause as Amanda thought, "Maybe they are just using the Silver Hunters, the Feather, or whoever is moving stuff as a cover. If you think it's too dangerous for us. Maybe we could focus on that instead?"

Ron raised his brow, "What's the catch?"

Amanda felt hurt but could see Linda giving her the same look. She looked at her friend and could see the concern in her eyes. "Alright, we'll stay out of their way. And we'll let you know if we come across anything big."

Linda smiled. "That's all we wanted to hear."

Amanda looked to Dr. Brentwood to see her watching them.

"We know we can't stop you from getting involved, Amanda. Heaven knows we tried to dissuade you enough. But, we are working together on this. Even if it seems like we aren't," Brentwood said. The doctor leaned forward in her chair, pointing to Ron and Linda, "Amanda, Selese, Ron, and Linda have been keeping us informed of everything they've found." Dr. Brentwood seemed to think for a moment and made Linda and Ron laugh when she said, "Well, mostly informed about what they've found."

The doctor sighed with relief. "You have been involved with us since you arrived. And, at times, taken a step away from all of this. You have helped a lot since too. But," Dr. Brentwood leaned back, "things are getting out of hand. We could use all the help we can get. Especially since this is beginning to look like more than one case is happening simultaneously."

Ron looked to Amanda, "So, what's your next move?"

Amanda thought, "I think we should look at the Forge. I think. . ." Amanda paused. "I'm sure that this has to do with Shrive. It seems like the other thefts are focused around her."

Cale looked to his wife. "They have to clean the area first."

"No!" Amanda insisted. "I want to see where it was. And if they left anything behind. Even if it's ash."

Linda looked toward her young friend in concern.

Amanda huffed, "I'm not looking forward to it, but I need as much information as possible. Even if it's not pleasant." She looked to Selese. "Our friend is being framed, and I'm damn set on finding out why."

Magic in itself, is not evil, like water it is a force of nature. Any creature without either cannot survive.

- Donna Hessian

Chapter 21:
Almost Had it

Gina sat on the edge of her bed. Hours had passed since she returned, but her mind was still stirring from what happened.

"Stupid, stupid, you were almost caught," the woman berated herself. "But you almost had it. You were steps away. If it wasn't for that damn alarm spell, that hunter. . . and that. . .fire."

Gina lay back, her eyes staring at the flat ceiling. "I was almost free." She turned to the clock. *It's nearly three in the morning. How long did that witch have me hanging there?*

She lay there, feeling the exhaustion in her muscles. Finally, she had enough strength to look around at the sparseness of her apartment. Except for a bed, a small table, a chair, and that damn mirror Allison had sent, nothing was around. She could see the dark all around. Early morning had come, and a simple flash of light from outside grabbed her attention. She heard thunder as another flash seeped from around the blinds causing her to walk over to open them. Dust fell from the slats since they had been closed for the most part since she arrived. The glass in the pane was smudged and dusty as another flash of lightning filled her sight.

"It's been so long since I've seen a storm," Gina muttered, looking down, her eyes searching as if trying to remember something that wasn't there. "Why does it seem so long since I've seen a storm?"

Her voice filled the darkness, Gina's mind realizing she had not turned on the lights since she arrived. The only light she could remember was the one from the mirror Allison used to communicate with her.

It seemed like time stopped as Gina noticed the rain hitting the glass outside. Her hand touched the window, and she watched as a tiny shimmer of the storm's moisture on the outside followed her hand.

It feels alive.

Gina's mind found solace in the collected water that mimicked her hand's movements. She looked out into the lights of the causeway and could see each drop as it splashed against the pooling water. She felt the fear that drove her from the Forge fading. It wasn't a fear of being caught. It was of that fire, that living fire that wanted to do nothing but destroy.

Gina looked at her reflection on the glass, wondering why she thought the fire spoke. Its crackle and growl of destruction were terrifying to her. She felt her heart racing as she thought back to the Forge. The girl shook her head, trying to break the fear that filtered into her thoughts. She looked back into the rain and watched as a giant ball of water now hovered before the glass. But as she stared, her mind began to drift as Allison once again called on her.

Gina turned to see the mirror again aglow and hesitantly walked toward it. Her heart felt defeated again, seeing her mistress overlayed on her form.

"Ah, you returned, my dear. Were you successful?" Allison asked, her voice confident and patient.

Gina shook her head. "No, but I was close. I was close enough to grab, but. . ."

Allison glared through the girl's eyes. "Why didn't you take it?"

Gina huffed, "There were too many people. You can't steal something when there's security all around it. That's just being stupid. There were a dozen hunters or more, and there was the. . . fire . . . that fire was th. . . there."

Allison could feel the fear in her doll, even though the spell she used to control her did not allow such. She was about to discipline her, but hearing the distress in the woman's words, she felt a twinge of compassion. Allison then processed what Gina had said, *fire?* Allison sighed. *All water elementals fear fire. And air to some degree, but never earth. I had forgotten that. Even the spell I'm using cannot override primal instinct.*

Allison shifted in her chair, and Gina watched her image again clear in the looking glass. She then heard her mistress say, "You are quite right, my dear. You made an excellent decision. Please continue."

Gina told her what she had seen and heard and told her mistress of the artifacts being moved.

"I overheard someone say they were leaving in two days. I'm sure I can get it by then." Gina smiled. "I'll try again later today. If they are cleaning up, I don't think they'll have much security around." Gina conveniently forgot to mention that she was the initial cause of the alarm in the first place. And seeing her mistress's reaction, she felt vindicated in omitting that fact.

Allison sighed before smiling, "The other items are of no concern to me, my dear. I only want the sphere. The Feather can have their war. They will mess things up and destroy themselves, and I'll still be alive and here long after they're gone."

Gina sighed in relief as Allison stood. "Try to have it as soon as possible, my pretty little doll. Your window of opportunity is growing short, and I am becoming impatient. But I promise I will release you if you do this for me."

Allison waved across the mirror as Mack walked in with a tray holding a teapot and cup. He placed it beside his mistress and poured.

As he handed the cup to Allison, he asked, "Will you release her?"

Allison took a sip before answering, "She is gaining strength again. I can feel it when I draw on her energy." Allison looked to her servant. "I will release her from her body when she returns." She looked toward the sealed door behind the bookcase. "But I'll need the Sphere of Lieben to do so."

* * *

The Forge had only a few people inside. They examined the piles of ash and dust left behind from the dragon's claw. Thankfully, the Forge had protected the additional artifacts from the claw's rage. There were others in the room behind continuing to pack and catalog things. All of this, of course, at the insistence of Regent Chung. Ron stood outside the Forge, again taking a post to ensure no one entered. The alarm spell was again in place as a precaution. Chung looked through the doors to see Ron standing guard, the Regent feeling disgust welling from his gut. *Damn hybrid, I thought you were only a FOF. You, like the others, are a disgrace.*

Chung looked back, his mind repeating what he learned while becoming a Silver Hunter.

There are four elements, Fire, Water, Air, and Earth. The Regent scoffed, "This place is a mockery. The five pillars, Bah!"

To him, there were only four elements to be respected. But Spirit, that had no opposite. To Chung, fairies and those associated were to be associated with air or Earth. They were nothing more than a perversion of one of the primal elements. And he watched this man protect him from the living fire of the dragon's claw.

"I would have relished defeating that dragon's claw." The Regent mumbled, causing one of the other nearby hunters to turn and ask what he had said. Chung dismissed the woman and turned to see Ron again staring at him. *When this is done, I'm sure the Feather will take care of you.*

Ron watched as Chung turned away and heard Amanda telling Selese something as they walked up.

"Did they move anything?" Amanda asked.

Ron shook his head, "Only in the main part. Everywhere they think our invisible person was, was left as is."

Amanda looked inside the door to see tape laid out, appropriate for any crime scene. She nodded to Ron, and she and Selese stepped through the door. Selese looked toward the sphere she had procured earlier still on its stand. *I really hoped that would have burned.* She followed Amanda, and once inside, they stood before the tape, and Amanda seemed saddened, "It's hard to believe someone died here." Amanda looked to the pile of ash that was once Bao. She could see the splattered metal of the coins he used nearby all around.

Amanda turned to see a tear on Selese's cheek before she wiped it away. She briefly looked at Amanda, "Sorry, it's not right what happened."

Amanda agreed, fighting back tears as well. But then, she heard Ron say, "It's okay, you don't have to do this."

Ron stood beside them, clearing his throat. Then in a somber tone, his voice almost cracking, he said, "Bao was honorable. He was a good man. He didn't deserve this."

Selese turned away, her head down, and Amanda nodded quickly. Her lips rolled over her teeth before she said, "I understand." Amanda then looked up, taking a breath and releasing it, her eyes alert as she scanned the scene.

"You know what you're looking for yet?" Selese asked, causing Amanda to shake her head quickly.

"Not yet, but there has to be something."

Amanda looked to the floor. She knelt. Amanda touched some of the ash that covered the floor toward the wall. "This was from the paperwork, right?"

Ron nodded, "Yes." He didn't know for sure, but wanted to spare Amanda the knowledge that she may have just picked up some of Bao's ashes.

Amanda looked at the ash. "It's very fine, like powder. She looked down to see an almost exact copy of her fingerprint in the small pile. Her mind acted quickly, she looked to Ron asking, "Where was the intruder standing?"

Ron pointed toward the front of the wall, and Amanda quickly ran around to look at the area. She leaned over the tape looking at the ground. Both Selese and Ron noticed the expression on Amanda's face. They watched as Amanda held her foot over some ash and looked down again closely. "I wear a size nine. The other woman, the hunter, what size shoe does she wear?"

Ron looked around. He rushed back toward the Forge room and found the woman while Amanda continued to examine the footprint.

"There's no tread. Almost all shoes, sneakers, all have some kind of tread." Amanda said, "that's about a size eight, and this one looks like fabric."

Amanda looked toward the woman as Ron brought her over, "What size shoe do you wear?" Amanda asked bluntly.

The woman answered, "Ten, why?"

Amanda smiled, "Our intruder, I'm pretty sure wears size eight shoes, without a patterned sole."

The woman looked to Ron for an explanation, he just shrugged his shoulders. Amanda huffed, "Look we have something. We just have to find someone who wears shoes with fabric on the bottom."

Selese shook her head. "That's unlikely." Then she turned to look at the sphere she had stolen, and remembered. She looked to Amanda, "A good thief would cover their shoes or use something different, but not fabric it's too slippery. Unless. . ." She turned to the sphere again.

Amanda joined her friend again, "Would you cover your shoes?"

Selese nodded, "Yeah, but I'd use a texture. Like I said, fabric is too slippery." They watched as Selese growled, "I can't believe I didn't see that."

Both Ron and Amanda asked what she was talking about.

Selese pointed to Amanda, "I'm glad you're on our side." Selese huffed, "there are only four types of people who can use a full invisibility cloak, and I mean the full outfit."

Amanda smiled, "okay, who?"

Selese gave a nervous chuckle, "well, me for one. The second would be a trickster, a spirit that causes trouble for others. The third would be a full-blown assassin." Selese seemed to be in thought, growling in frustration, saying, "I wish I could remember the fourth."

Ron chuckled before sending the woman he brought over away, "so, Amanda, do you have any ideas?"

Chapter 22:
I Have a Theory

It was about noon when Selese found Amanda in the practice area watching Gina. Luke was nearby, leaning against the wall. Even from a distance, Selese could tell Amanda had that *particular* look in her eyes, and it wasn't the one she usually saw when Luke was around. She deduced Amanda was there for another reason.

Selese became curious. After the Forge, even Selese knew Amanda suspected something. The facts needed to help Shrive were beginning to add up since their meeting with Li Xiu and the information she provided. Even Ron, Linda, and Dr. Brentwood were convinced another player was in the mix. However, they still didn't have undeniable proof or any that others wanted to hear.

Selese walked up, seeing Luke turn to give her a smile. Then she looked to see Amanda staring at Gina practicing.

"Uh oh, she's got that look again," Selese said, making Luke smile and nod before he spoke. "She's been studying what's been going on for almost an hour."

Amanda turned. "What are you two talking about?"

Selese chuckled. "You know. That look, the one you make when you know something's off, but can't quite figure it out, yet."

Amanda turned to see Luke nodding in agreement. "Selese's right. You do have a certain stare when trying to figure something out." Her eyes glinted with annoyance and anger before Selese interrupted.

"Easy there, Mandy. I'm used to figuring out people. If lover over here is seeing it, then it's pretty obvious." Selese chided her friend.

Amanda bowed her head, chuckling. "It's that obvious?"

Selese smiled, saying, "Yep, now spill. What do you see that we don't?"

Amanda looked toward the practice area. "I think she's holding back. I've been here for other practices, and people really seem to try. Even new scroll witches. But something is different with her." Amanda paused. "I've seen others like her not realize and overcompensate. But with her...." Amanda shook her head slowly, "even when dealing with others, part-sylph, fairy, and sprites, or whatever, they all either seek out or stay near their element when injured or tired."

Selese agreed, adding, "We all do. She would benefit from being near water if she's a water elemental. So, what's the catch?"

Amanda looked at the two of them, "Have either of you seen her near a lake or stream? Or even a pool? I haven't seen her near anything like that, even a faucet or sink. She always heads back to her room."

There was silence between them as Gina ended her training. Then, finally, Amanda started toward the area; she had some questions floating in her mind that needed answering.

Noticing Amanda walking toward her, Gina smiled, waving to invite them over. She felt out of place coming to the school, and Amanda was the only one who even attempted to make her feel invited. Also, she felt uncomfortable seeing Luke close behind her. Allison had warned her that he was a Raven Hunter. Even confirmed with Selese who he was and found out that he was Amanda's beau. Gina felt a little jealous of Amanda for that, but she noticed that Amanda seemed to care about her well-being.

As Amanda walked up, she said, "Looks like you're getting better."

Gina returned a smile; she felt the caring in Amanda's words about her progress, and seeing the others with her made her feel a bit more at home.

"Yeah, I'm starting to get the hang of some things. I don't know why I never did any of this before. I mean, it feels like I've been missing things. Like, like I've been lost forever. At least from what I can remember. But, weirdly, I don't know why I stopped."

Gina felt a wave of sudden anger, which faded quickly, her change in expression noticed by Amanda. The quirk now gave Amanda more questions, but she held back. The training facility was not the place to ask them, especially since she wasn't one of the hunters.

"You'll figure it out. Most elementals usually do fairly quickly," Amanda said, then noticed something in the air. She discreetly sniffed. *That scent, I think it's the same as the one I smelled when I grabbed Li Xiu at the cliff.* Amanda smiled, "You'll get it soon, I'm sure. You just need practice." She then looked around and, with an animated sniff, asked, "Is that a new perfume you have on Selese?"

Selese looked at Amanda, confused.

Amanda looked at Luke, "Nah, it's too girly for you, or did you want to tell me something?"

Gina laughed, seeing the expression Luke gave her before she spoke up, telling them. "It's probably me. I had some allowance left and bought something for myself."

Amanda moved closer. "It's lovely. What's it called?"

Gina paused, thinking for a moment, "oh, uh, Brise de Renoncule. It felt familiar, like it reminded me of something. I just can't remember what it was."

Amanda smiled, "well, it smells wonderful. And I'm sure you'll remember." She then looked at her phone as if it rang. She seemed to scroll through, saying, "Oh, sorry, forgot an appointment." She leaned in, telling Gina, "I was supposed to have some sketches for a client. I still have to finish and send them."

Again, Amanda smiled, giving Gina some encouragement before turning and starting toward the door. Luke and Selese said their goodbyes and followed close behind. As they exited, Amanda quickly ducked around a corner, pulled out her phone, and started searching for something.

Selese looked at her questioningly. Amanda must have sensed her stare and briefly looked at her.

Selese said, "I thought you were taking time off from the business you started. You were only doing projects for Ron and Linda."

Amanda nodded.

Luke watched her response and asked, "Then what are you doing?"

Amanda stared at the screen of her phone and gave a smile. "She did say Brise de Renoncule, right?"

Selese confirmed, and Amanda grabbed Luke's arm, pulling him along, "Come on, I want to check something out."

Luke protested. "Where are we going?"

Amanda turned. "Shopping. Now come on, let's go."

Selese followed quickly. "I knew you found something."

A few hours later, on the drive home, Amanda sat in the back seat with a look of resolve now in her eyes. She held onto a small bag with something she had purchased. Selese had asked to be in the front, which was acceptable to Amanda, who needed to put something into her phone. She also needed time to think.

When she finished, a message from Linda appeared to steer clear of Regent Chung and that they would explain later. Selese looked back, "I'm surprised you bought that. That was an expensive gift."

Amanda agreed. The small vial of perfume cost her almost $220. She was thankful not to have expensive spending habits. But she was still wracking her brain over the price. Now that she had the perfume, she needed to confirm her theory.

"Luke, can you get me in to see Shrive?" Amanda asked.

Luke looked back. "It may be tough. She's still locked up. She's not supposed to have visitors."

Amanda looked concerned. "She's never done anything wrong. So why are they treating her like this?"

Luke huffed, "The Regent insisted. He mentioned something about her being a danger." But then, Luke paused, "Personally, he only changed his mind when he found out she was an anthromorphic."

Amanda watched Selese roll her eyes before saying, "You mean she's locked up because she's a catgirl? So the man doesn't like people who are part fairy or catgirls? There's something wrong with him."

Luke gave an acknowledging playful nod.

They both heard Amanda mutter, "The guy doesn't like catgirls. So that's another strike."

Selese turned, intrigued by her remark, "You find something else?"

Amanda looked to see Selese staring back and said, "I think Linda and Ron found something. I'll have to check in with them. But I need to see Shrive first." She then briefly held up the small bag with the perfume.

Luke warned her that vials were not allowed in the dungeon, so Amanda sprayed a little of the perfume on herself. She then read aloud the message from Linda, "Chung is insisting that you and Selese be held for questioning. He thinks you or she had a hand in setting this up. We're working on a solution. Best stay clear of the hunters for a bit. We'll let you know."

We were the ones who tried saving Li Xiu. So what does that bastard want? Amanda thought. Her train of thought was interrupted as Luke asked, "Okay, you used that, now what?"

Amanda looked up to see his eyes in the rearview mirror, and she said, "I hope I'm wrong, but if Shrive answers the way I think she will, then we may have a problem."

Selese turned around. "You know who did it?"

Amanda didn't want to accuse Gina, but the perfume was a dead giveaway. So first, she needed to confirm the scent was what Shrive also detected. From there, she hadn't decided on what to do yet.

Amanda said, "Maybe. But If I'm right, we'll need some help."

In her apartment, Gina tied the cloak together, covering most of her body. She looked into the mirror to see only her head floating in the reflection. Feeling slightly silly, she smiled, walking back and forth, making light of the situation with only her head as amusement.

The situation felt normal, even relieving, as she made expressions in her reflection. But then her mind seemed to fight against her, as no memories of why she thought it was amusing appeared.

Gina paused, and the smile faded from her face. An air of regret filling her eyes as she tried to remember. Her action brought nothing more than a question, *why can't I remember anything from before Allison took me in?*

The thought of her benefactor reminded her of the task she was given. "I have to get that sphere, and maybe she'll leave me be," Gina muttered.

Gina looked into the mirror again, half expecting to see Allison's face suddenly appear. Instead, she was relieved when only her floating head smiled back. Gina reached back, grabbing the hood, and a glint of the thief she was, appearing just before the hood made her vanish completely. The only thing to be seen was the door to her apartment open and close. It was around dinner time, and she figured it might be possible to sneak in and steal the sphere. She hoped that no one, or at least a few people, would be in the Forge.

"It was by the left wall, about twenty feet in. I hope they didn't move it," Gina said. Only the darkness heard her words as she headed out into the night.

Chapter 23:
An Innocent Friend

Amanda and Selese waited nearby as Luke headed up to get permission for them to see Shrive. Selese was pacing, her impatience growing as Amanda leaned against the wall in quiet thought.

"Why is he taking so long?" Selese asked in frustration.

Amanda agreed that it was taking longer than usual, but she suspected Ron and the others were dealing with the fallout from Bao's death.

"Selese, we have to do this their way for the moment. I don't like waiting any more than you," Amanda said with a stern annoyance.

She was about to voice another objection to the situation when Luke appeared around the corner. Amanda could see his expression a bit somber as he neared.

"They're dealing with the fallout from the fire?" Amanda asked.

Luke nodded, "yeah, apparently Bao sent a message just before it happened. The entire *Yín yā lièrén* is in an uproar over Bao Zheng's death."

Amanda sighed. "I can't blame them. They probably want to blame us for it too."

Luke nodded in agreement but seemed distracted. Amanda moved closer, touching his chest, "What is it?"

The Hunter sighed, "They wanted us to bring you in for questioning. They think you're involved."

Selese yelled, "What?"

Amanda nodded. "Yeah, I heard. Ron and Linda were trying to change their minds." She turned to Selese. "My guess is they think we set this all up."

Amanda scoffed, remarking, "Probably think a FOF and someone who's part fairy are criminal masterminds trying to make them look bad."

She turned to see Luke concerned and asked him what it was.

"They're still trying to prove you didn't. I'm supposed to bring you back, but. . .you know," Luke responded.

Amanda smiled, stroking his cheek. "You can do that after we see Shrive." Then, she looked at him questioningly, "Anything else?"

Selese also watched as Luke rubbed the back of his neck, his voice almost cracking as he said, "They took her Hunter and shadow-walking elements while we were gone."

Amanda's face showed sadness and frustration as Selese yelled, "Why?"

She turned to Luke, tears in her eyes, "She's innocent. Why did they do that?"

Luke reached out, pulling her close. "I know she's innocent, but Chung insisted."

Amanda's voice muffled as she leaned into Luke, "She's innocent. I'm trying to prove that. I'm doing my best. Why won't they leave her alone?"

Selese put her arms around her friends. "Bastards. I don't like any of these other hunters."

Luke looked up. "I don't like this any more than you two, but we have to play by the rules here."

Amanda held up the small vial, her voice filled with barely-masked anger and determination, "If Shrive answers how I think she will, then maybe I'll be able to tell you who the thief and the person who attacked Li Xiu really is."

Luke scoffed, "You can tell Dr. Brentwood who it is. She's going to meet us there. And they're not going to allow you in with that."

Amanda pushed away, yelling, "I know!" She then opened the vial and tossed a few drops on herself. "I'll leave it here with my phone and anything else they want me to leave." Amanda turned to hand the vial to Luke. "Are we going in or not?"

Luke nodded, and they started down the hallway that led to the dungeons.

* * *

Dr. Brentwood stood outside the cell, where Shrive sat quietly sobbing. The leader of the Circle wiped a tear from her face. Her voice was a whisper as she said, "I'm so sorry. I did not want to do any of this. I'm sure you're innocent. But the Regent insisted."

Shrive said nothing as she sat quietly balled up in the corner. Shrive didn't hear the doctor's words. She was still dealing with the removal of the elements that made her one of the Raven Hunters. She had been with them for most of her life and Shrive knew she was innocent. She was even thankful that Lord Cale hesitated before he removed them. She knew that they didn't like this. But, with the bit of evidence there was and the insistence of Regent Chung and Yín yā lièrén, it had to be done.

Shrive could hear Selese yelling. Her voice filled with anger as Shrive said, "Tell them to go away. I've never even stolen anything. I'm not a criminal. I don't want to see them."

Brentwood turned to see Selese walking into the small hall that led to the cells. She could see the determination in both her and Amanda's strides as they neared.

"She's not taking this well. I'm not sure she'll see you," Dr. Brentwood remarked.

Selese's pace quickened, and she landed her hands against the solid iron door. She said nothing as her eyes searched for her friend in the cell's darkness. Instead, she only heard Shrive say, "They took my element from me."

Amanda overheard Shrive's words, and her mouth quivered in sadness as she approached the doctor. Finally, Amanda asked, "Did Linda or Ron talk to you about the Regent yet?"

Brentwood raised her brow, not answering Amanda's question right away. She instead nodded, only saying, "The Regent insisted we do this to prove that we are not harboring any factions against the Yín yā lièrén. And if I recall, we asked you and the others to remain out of this, Amanda."

Amanda smiled. "So they did, good. They warned us to stay away from Chung. They suspect he caused all of this." Amanda looked all around, "I can't believe there are dungeons in the Sanctuary."

Dr. Brentwood glanced at her, "They were built before the Sanctuary. Part of the old estate. Technically, they are surrounded by the Sanctuary. These were built before the Circle was founded. The administration building is above us."

Amanda nodded, hearing the doctor's words, but her thoughts were focused on how she could help her friend, "I think we have a way to prove someone else was there."

Brentwood suddenly became interested. Her words were marked with hope. "Good. Because we had to convince the others that neither you nor Selese were even involved until that night. Thankfully, Ron and Linda have friends in high places."

They heard Amanda say a quiet thank you and headed over to see Shrive. As they walked, Dr. Brentwood asked, "Is that a new perfume?"

Amanda nodded. "Yes, the same one that the attacker wore, if I'm right."

Dr. Brentwood said, "Hmm, that'd be difficult to prove."

Amanda nodded, "Shrive and I could smell it." She looked to Brentwood. "Maybe a few of the other Hunters did as well. And Li Xiu certainly did. She confirmed it when we spoke with her."

Brentwood stopped, putting her hand on Amanda's shoulder. "She's been in isolation. When did you speak with her?"

Amanda looked the doctor in the eyes. "Yesterday; we met in her room."

Brentwood suddenly became very concerned. "That's impossible. The Regent told us that she's seen no visitors and wanted to keep it that way. Plus, the building is secure."

Amanda smiled. "Not as secure as you would think. I found a way in, and Selese helped. Don't worry, no one saw us. Although I have a feeling if they did, we wouldn't be talking on the outside of these cells."

"Amanda, please stay out of things this time. I'm aware Ron and Linda have already warned you."

Amanda scoffed, "They did, but one of my friends is being set up. If you think I'm going to stand idle, think again."

Amanda walked forward, meeting Selese at the cell door, holding her friend's hands.

"Amanda, my dear, you are more focused than you should be on this.

I hope you'll be able to survive the consequences if you're wrong," Dr. Brentwood whispered.

Amanda tried sounding cheerful as she said, "Hi," to try and cheer up Shrive. Her friend meekly looked up for a moment before returning her eyes to the stone floor. Selese moved to the side as Amanda looked in through the iron bars. Shrive made no motion to look at her.

She's really not taking this well, Amanda thought before turning to Dr. Brentwood. "They're wrong. She's innocent."

Dr. Brentwood nodded, "I know, but our hands are tied on this. With the attack on one Hunter and the death of a representative, we're in a precarious situation." They all heard what sounded like a scuffle from Shrive's cell and were startled as the cat girl threw her weight against the iron door.

They watched as Shrive smelled the air animatedly and heard her yell, "She's here! that's the same scent I smelled when my arm was grabbed."

Knowing what Amanda had planned, Dr. Brentwood asked, "Selese did you tell her anything?"

Selese shook her head. "No! I was just trying to cheer her up a bit. I told her we're working on trying to get her out of here."

Shrive was looking around, and she turned part cat to make her senses more heightened. "She's here. Please don't hurt them."

They watched as Shrive gripped the bars, her claws extended around them. Amanda put her hands over hers. "It's okay, Shrive. That's me. I'm wearing the perfume."

"Wait, you were wearing that when we were attacked?" Shrive asked.

Amanda shook her head, "No, But I have a suspicion now who our mystery attacker is. But I have to prove it to one other person first." She turned to the doctor. "Can you get us in to speak with Li Xiu?"

Dr. Brentwood considered telling them no, but seeing Shrive's reaction, she was willing to play along. The doctor stepped back, "I can pull rank and get you in. They did rush us on removing Shrive's element. Maybe we can return that discomfort."

She looked to Amanda. "What else would you need to prove this?"

Amanda looked to Selese. "Everyone who was there has to be in the same room. I mean everyone who was at the cliff. And who was there investigating."

Selese said, "Good, and we can tell them about the perfume."

"No!" Amanda yelled, "For this to work. They have to notice it themselves. If we coax this in any way, the Silver Hunters won't believe us."

Amanda looked to Shrive. "We're doing our best to prove your innocence. I know you are, but they're making it difficult." Amanda watched as Shrive reached up, gently holding the necklace she wore to hide her feline features. Then, she looked at Dr. Brentwood. "They let her keep her necklace?"

The doctor looked pained as she nodded. "It was a courtesy. The Regent wanted us to take all of her elements, but…" the doctor paused, "he found her true form repulsive. So he allowed her to keep it."

Amanda looked back to Shrive as the woman looked away. *Shrive, we need to get you out of here.* Amanda thought, then her eyes filled with resolve as she looked back at the doctor. "Can you arrange for everyone who was at the cliff to be there?"

Dr. Brentwood looked to Shrive. "It'll be difficult but give me a little time. We'll message you when we can. Would that work?"

Amanda nodded.

They all heard the guards enter, "Time's up. You need to leave."

Amanda nodded and followed everyone. "Don't give up, Shrive." She turned forward, "Because we sure as hell won't."

Chapter 24:
The Hunters don't need to know

The death of Bao Zhang by the dragon's claw still had everyone on edge. The artifact was made inert by Chung, who claimed that he was able to calm the claw to sleep for years. Ron didn't believe Chung; however, his people took his word over theirs. He still believed Chung had caused this whole situation in the first place. The stress of the case made any interaction between the hunters very difficult.

That fact, and that Chung seemed to be driving the conditions for the shipment of artifacts to move faster, was not sitting well with any of them. This circumstance forced Ron to call in a favor to get a meeting with the leadership of the *Yín yā lièrén*. The information Zhang provided helped, but the remaining task was no small feat. The only concern now was convincing them that Chung was not someone to be trusted.

"This is not going to go well if we're wrong," Ron said, looking at Linda.

Linda nodded, "I know, but if Zhang's information is correct, I think they may have someone from the Feather on their staff and not realize."

Ron clicked on the button for the video conference and called Zhang. When the man answered, Ron, said, "Zhang, sorry for the early call. I presume you've heard the upsetting news."

Zhang nodded. "I think we may need to talk."

Their friend took a few minutes to get everyone on the call.

Ron apologized again for the early hour but that this couldn't wait. "Acting Regent Zu, as you know, we were asked by the Circle to be independent observers for the transfer of the artifacts. And honestly, ladies and gentlemen, we have concerns."

"It is not your place to dictate our actions," one man said.

The acting regent replied, "Counsel Xi, please allow him to continue. I see no reason why this would affect our plans."

The other counsel quieted as the acting regent said, "Please continue, Mr. Wilt."

"As I mentioned, we have concerns. Regent Chung has requested all of the artifacts be transported in one shipment. I am not a strategist, but that seems like an odd request."

Counsel Xi interrupted again, "Then you know your place. We should convene."

Zhang now spoke. "I disagree. Mr. Wilt has helped us in the past in recovering several dangerous artifacts and individuals. So let us listen to his concerns."

Xi again attacked. "This man is a foreigner. He is not—"

"That is enough, Counsel. Let the man speak," Zu spoke with authority.

Ron waited until things quieted. "Thank you, acting Regent. As I mentioned, putting everything in one shipment was a concern. And truthfully a good way to allow the Broken Feather or any other organization to steal them easily. So I would recommend at least splitting the shipments. But as I mentioned earlier, I am only a consultant."

Ron waited for a response.

Counsel Xi interjected, "You are only a consultant. And you have said you are not a strategist. So then why are you requesting this meeting?"

Ron sighed. "Please forgive me for my next statement. I do not wish to accuse anyone, but we have seen something like this before."

Counsel Xi went to speak but was cut off by the Acting Regent, "Quiet! Or I will terminate your connection, Xi." Zu paused. "Please continue, Mr. Wilt."

Ron Looked at Linda off-screen, the concern on his face reflecting what he was thinking.

"Gentlemen, I do not have hard evidence, but what I have found, I hope, may be enough for you to split the shipments at the very least," Ron told them.

"What is the concerning information?" Zu asked.

Ron took a breath, "Regent Chung is in charge of the transfer, and there has been a recent attack on one of your people. And the death of another, I do not feel that the two are connected. However. . ."

"This is preposterous, Regent I—"

Ron watched as Zu terminated the link for Xi's connection. Zu said, "Please continue."

Ron watched Zhang remain emotionless on the screen. Ron continued. "Regent, you are aware of the theft from the Forge a few years ago, correct?" Ron watched the Regent nod. "With respect, and I hope I am incorrect in this matter, from information received from counsel Zhang, there is possible evidence that Chung may not be entirely truthful in his dealings."

Ron watched the Regent sit taller, hearing him say, "Regent Chung is loyal. Are you insinuating that he may not be?"

Ron's shoulders dropped, "Regent, the only evidence I have is that Regent Chung has not used any of his government-allowed stipend for travel in the previous years. Again, I apologize and hope that the decision on the shipment is a judgment mistake, and I truly hope I am wrong. I do not know what his living conditions are, but that this seems to be an unusual circumstance." Ron sighed before continuing. "Regent, the theft from the Forge was accomplished by one of its highest-ranking members. Unfortunately, it was too late that they figured out he was part of the Broken Feather. There were subtle clues, but no one took them to mind. For Regent Chung, I would like to know how he is paying for the transport and lodging he is currently enjoying."

Ron held his breath. His dealings with the *Yín yā lièrén* had been more difficult than others they worked with. Ron watched as Zu sat tall again. "You will apologize if you are incorrect, Mr. Wilt."

Ron nodded, "Publicly, if I need to. But, truthfully, I hope I am wrong."

Zu nodded. "As do I, Mr. Wilt. Counsel Zhang!"

Ron watched Zhang sit tall. "Sir."

Zu ordered Zhang to investigate the financial dealings of Regent Chung further and that he would speak with the remaining counsel on the separation of the shipments. "Mr. Wilt, you would be correct in separating the shipments. From a military outlook, that would be less efficient but more secure. We will contact Chung shortly to separate the shipments."

The video for both Zhang and the Regent closed, but Ron didn't look happy. Linda asked, "What now?"

Ron shook his head, "I don't know. We're betting our reputations, maybe putting our lives on the line here. I just hope they don't wait on the shipment. It's supposed to go out tomorrow."

* * *

In Amanda's apartment, she and Selese waited for the others to contact them. Both were sitting quietly and reserved, and the time that passed felt longer than it really was. They had just come from seeing Shrive and were concerned at how their friend was taking having the element that made her a Raven Hunter erased. Seeing her curled in the corner when they arrived wasn't putting either of them in a talkative mood. Selese sat on the small sofa that Amanda had bought when she arrived at the school, and with her almost ready to graduate, Selese was sure Amanda had other priorities on her mind.

Selese knew Amanda suspected someone. With Shrive acting the way she did smelling the perfume, Selese was sure who she suspected. Most of the trouble started after Gina had arrived. But seeing the woman struggling to use her powers made Selese and Amanda both unsure of accusing her.

"What if we're wrong?" Selese asked.

Standing at the window, Amanda looked down, shaking her head. "That's been bothering me as well." She looked toward Selese. "When I talk to her, she seems innocent. Like she was lost. But, in the Forge, and when Shrive and Li Xiu were attacked, she seemed to be a different person."

Selese sighed before saying, "Some people can hide like that."

Amanda now sat opposite her friend. "I know. But there's something." Amanda paused, her expression one of deep thought.

Selese noticed, asking, "Uh oh. What is it?"

Amanda shook her head. "This doesn't quite add up. I've watched her move. And I've watched the fight at the cliff over and over. If it's her, she moved differently."

There was silence as Selese contemplated Amanda's words. Finally, she only said, "Maybe she fights in different styles."

Amanda leaned back, "I thought about that. It's possible, but even if she did, her body moved differently altogether."

Selese leaned forward. "What do you mean?"

"Let's say I knew like five different fighting styles. And I was deciding on which to use? How would I choose?"

Selese thought for a moment. "The most appropriate, right?"

"Yes and no. I'd use the one most appropriate for the situation and one with which I was comfortable. Everyone is like that. You choose the movements that your body does the easiest and most efficiently. That's inherent to all humans. Well, at least all with human in them." Selese raised her brow toward Amanda. "I know, I know, not an accurate description. I just want to include everyone." Her statement made Selese chuckle.

There was a minute or so of silence as Amanda thought. Then, finally, she looked over to see Selese patiently watching and asked, "You think I'm wrong?"

Selese shook her head. "I understand what you said. I just think Gina is lost. That's why she acts the way she does. Trauma will do that to you."

Amanda leaned forward, her chin resting in her palm as her elbow leaned on the chair arm. She took a moment before agreeing with Selese. "I'm having trouble with that as well. But the evidence looks like it's her. She doesn't remember her past, and she is just learning that she can control water." Amanda looked toward the window. "It's like a part of her is missing."

Amanda and Selese both remembered Tyler from when Amanda first arrived, after the *Effigy of Tarnus* was stolen and Dennon Fierst escaped. Tyler had returned but seemed to be missing memories. So when they brought him in for questioning, they discovered that a part of him had been ripped away. That part was the one that held his magic.

But Gina was different. Her magic was there. She just didn't know it existed.

"How do you forget a part of yourself?" Amanda asked, not expecting an answer.

"You don't. You might temporarily forget, but eventually, you find it again. It's always a part of you. Maybe Gina had some trauma that made her forget for a little while." Selese said.

Amanda chuckled. "You really do have a heart of gold. You're defending her even though we're trying to prove she's the one who attacked Li Xiu."

Selese nodded before saying, "On a side note. . . How did my mother take being told that we already spoke with Li Xiu?"

Amanda side-eyed her. "I don't think she liked it. But I don't think she was as surprised as she should have been." She paused. "I meant to ask you earlier, did you remember who else uses the invisibility cloaks that would have a footprint like what we found?"

Selese shook her head. "I wasn't really thinking about it; I'm more worried about Shrive."

Amanda said nothing, only nodding in agreement. They continued to discuss their next move but returned to their friend again. Selese said, "Did you see her? Shrive looked awful."

Amanda nodded. "Yeah, her element being taken really did a number on her." Amanda looked away, "It would have been easier if maybe she really was a criminal."

"That's a horrible thing to say."

Amanda put her hands up. "I know, I know. I was just thinking how this would be easier if she were at least partially guilty. But unfortunately, someone is purposely trying to frame her. And I think the person behind it is either the thief that set the Forge on fire or someone she's working for." Amanda stood in frustration. "And I can't prove either right now."

Amanda threw her head back, "All the evidence points to Gina as the cause. But there is also evidence that it's not Gina. The only thing we have is the damn perfume."

Selese could see the frustration Amanda was going through. She didn't believe that Gina was totally guilty either. Amanda herself said that it didn't seem like her at the cliff. The woman also showed no evidence of being a thief.

Amanda walked to the window. She leaned against the outer frame. "It's not making any sense. Why does it seem like it's a different person if it is her?" Amanda thought out loud.

Selese remained silent.

Amanda stood straight. "Is that possible?" She looked back at Selese. "Maybe we are dealing with two people." Amanda sat, her hands animated as she spoke. "What if it is two people, one body. Maybe she's being controlled."

Selese didn't want to believe what she heard. "That'd be horrible."

Amanda continued. "Do you know of magic or any way to control someone. Maybe erase their memories?"

Selese shook her head. "Other than what The Raven Hunters use, no."

Amanda asked, "Do you think the Sanctuary library would have something?"

"If they did, it'd be restricted."

Amanda huffed, looking at the floor, "Let's see how our meeting with Li Xiu and the others goes first. I don't want to go down that rabbit hole just yet." Amanda paused, then looked to Selese with a smile. "Although, it's not like we haven't been in a restricted area before."

Wind, like change, comes when you both hope and least expect it. The world of humans is increasing every day, a mix with all that we can discern. We must act to protect both magic and non-magic before one overwhelms the other.

- Alex Pertu

Chapter 25:
That One Way to Prove It

The hallway reverberated as Regent Chung objected. "This is highly irregular. Li Xiu is to be punished for not performing her duties."

Lord Cale had just spoken with Dr. Brentwood and disagreed with the Regent. "I do not think so, Regent. We have investigations to perform here as well. You may be from a more disciplined facility, but we all have the same function."

Cale paused as they arrived at the door to Li Xiu's room. "We are all protecting those with magic and without. This incident may be an attempt to attack the artifacts. Or possibly something else. We have to be certain."

Chung scoffed. "I highly doubt that. And if it is, it will be your responsibility to protect us all." The Regent referred to the shipment of artifacts he was pushing to leave the Forge returning to the Snow Mountain facility.

"I was to understand that you have allotted a small force to protect the shipment along the way. Was I misinformed?" Cale looked at the Regent questioningly.

The Regent seemed uncomfortable at his remark, and Cale noticed that. The concerns the others had were now becoming more concrete. *Ron, Linda, It's good that you're on our side.*

Chung finally agreed. "You may speak with her. But I will be present."

Cale nodded. "Fair enough. We'll bring her to the interrogation area so we can all be comfortable." A hint of sarcasm was noted in his statement. "We'll use one of the larger rooms."

The Regent looked curiously toward the leader of the Raven Hunters as he knocked on the door to Li Xiu's room.

The Regent stood nearby, his mind more concerned about the shipment than where he was. He had walked past the interrogation area but stopped when one of the silver hunters ran toward him.

The man handed him a note. "It's from Snow Mountain. New orders."

The Regent opened the note as the man stepped back, and his eyes filled with anger. *Is the council ordering me to split the shipment? No, I don't have time to alert the Feather of the change. Bao was a good man; it is a shame he had to die. But the Feather needs to take their place among the rulers of this world. He may be honored when we are triumphant.*

"Those damn fools. I have everything planned. I can't stop now," Chung muttered; his teeth gnashed together. *Fools, we should be the ones running the world, not those politicians.*

He motioned for the hunter to approach. "The orders are to move quickly, and we want to move quickly. First, make sure the alarms are off for the Forge entrance. That will allow us to move without having to stop for every artifact. You have my authorization."

The hunter nodded and left to relay the Regent's orders.

Chung looked at the note before looking around and placing it in his pocket. However, his concentration was interrupted as Lord Cale walked up beside him, asking, "Everything alright?"

The Regent nodded. "An update from our command. Nothing important. I've ordered the threshold alarm you have across the door of the Forge removed. That way, we can move the items quickly."

Cale didn't like the idea of removing the alarm, but the Regent had a right to request it. As for the note, Cale could tell he was lying, but with the imminent interrogation of one of Chung's people, he felt it prudent that he did not press the matter.

Li Xiu sat in the middle of the long table in the interrogation room. There were other Silver Hunters behind her, and she could see Amanda and Selese along the side away from the table. She did not see Shrive anywhere, and that concerned her.

As she sat, she asked, "Where is Shrive?"

Chung had entered the room with a smug remark, "Where a traitor belongs, in a cell." She could see the look Lord Cale gave as the Regent spoke.

Li Xiu looked to her superior. "But I told you I don't believe it was her. She seemed as surprised as I was when I was pushed over the cliff." She pointed to Amanda. "She was fast enough to keep me from falling."

Chung huffed, "You allowed a weak, untrained civilian to aid you? Even more reason to reprimand you."

Amanda shifted and was about to speak, but Selese put her arm across her to stop her. Her friend side-eyed her and shook her head in silence. Amanda understood and remained silent.

"Hunter Li Xiu, you were at the attempted theft and the cliffside, correct?" Chung asked.

"Yes," Li Xiu replied.

"And who else was at the same location?" Chung asked.

"Shrive and few other hunters," she answered.

Amanda watched Chung nod. *Bastard is going to try and blame Shrive again.*

"So, in both instances, you and the female anthromorph known as Shrive, were present," Chung remarked.

Cale took exception, giving a warning. "Careful Regent, we have rules here. If Shrive is guilty, she will be punished for her offense, nothing more."

Chung smiled, looking briefly at Lord Cale with a stare of condescension. Then, he returned his focus to Li Xiu. "We have witnesses stating that the feline—"

Cale interrupted, "Shrive, or Hunter, Regent. That is your last warning."

Chung smiled, saying, "Such subtleties are wasted. But the Hunter known as Shrive attacked you."

Li Xiu hesitantly responded, "Yes. But she was surprised when her arm moved. It was like she was fighting something, but not me. And when her arm was near, I noticed her pulling as if being held. And her hand was never around my other arm. So, whoever broke it, I'm sure it wasn't Shrive."

Amanda stretched, causing the Regent to briefly look at her before returning to Cale, muttering, "Your people need discipline."

Amanda stood, then walked toward the other two from the Silver Hunters and nodded silently, greeting them. She stopped momentarily and watched as the woman on her left seemed to sniff the air. Amanda had used the perfume again just before entering the room and wanted to see if anyone else recognized it. The Hunter quietly asked, "Where did you get that perfume? I meant to ask you back at the cliff."

Chung, overhearing the exchange, said, "You wish to add something to this interrogation, Hunter?"

The woman stood at attention. "No, Sir, forgive the interruption."

Chung rose, walking toward Amanda. He raised his hand, about to strike. But as his hand came down, Amanda blocked it, pushing it aside. The action caused the Regent to fall off balance. He turned to see the fairy ring around her neck glowing.

"The FOF and thief, why are they here?" Chung asked angrily as he walked back to the table behind Li Xiu.

Amanda watched Cale stand and say, "Gaining evidence for their own investigation."

"For what? To prove that that thing is innocent?

Amanda nodded and pointed to the hunter before saying, "And she just proved that."

Chung huffed. "You are wrong, FOF."

Seeing Amanda's fearlessness, Li Xiu was about to yell at her superior, but as she took a breath; she could smell the perfume. "Regent, the attacker is here. It's the same perfume. I can smell it." She then started looking around.

Chung laughed as he sat in his chair across from Li Xiu, watching her searching for nothing. Her arms swung around, trying to find something that wasn't there.

"I am beginning to question your allegiance, hunter Li Xiu. What are you looking for?"

Li Xiu stood. "The attacker is here. It's the same fragrance. I'm sure of it."

Chung scoffed, pointing to the Hunters at the wall. "She just proved who was wearing that perfume." Chung looked disappointed with Li Xiu. "I will recommend that you be dismissed from the Hunters when we return."

Li Xiu was about to defend herself but remained silent. Amanda, however, didn't.

"Regent, with respect, your conclusion is wrong," Amanda said with impunity.

The Regent smiled. "Oh, please tell me how I am incorrect. You are not even a hunter; you are a pet they keep around."

Amanda felt the sting of his remark but kept her calm. She walked to the table, standing beside Li Xiu. "Your other hunter and Li Xiu just proved there was another person there."

The Regent looked confused but asked, "How so?"

Amanda smiled, "Because I wasn't wearing this perfume then. I just bought it."

Cale looked to Amanda. "You know who it was?"

Amanda nodded. "I believe so."

Chung suddenly remembered his duties and asked. "Who was it?"

Amanda lowered her head, "I'll tell you." She looked to Cale. "But I really hope I'm wrong."

Gina had made her way to the Forge unseen, the cloak hiding her from all who passed by. She climbed the wall as she had done before and waited. The cloak and gloves held her in place so she wouldn't exhaust herself.

I could have used this when breaking in to steal food. Wait? Where did that memory come from?

As Gina waited, she overheard one of the hunters order them to remove the alarm spell across the door. She had been watching them securing items on several pallets, and they all waited to be moved. Gina scrutinized the hunters as they pulled a pallet through the doorway. No alarm sounded. *Now's my chance,* Gina thought as she climbed down the wall. Gina moved closer, quickly testing the entrance as she placed her hand inside before removing it. This time she could not see her hand.

She glanced around the frame, the sphere still on its pedestal, and waited for her chance to take it. Gina carefully moved inside, keeping to the wall on the side where the Spere resided. She paused, looking at the packaged artifacts, and began to wonder why the items were being moved. But as the Sphere came into view, her thoughts returned to her mission again. She moved as soon as she had an open opportunity. She waited and looked around to ensure no one was watching before slipping the cloak over the sphere. The Sphere of Lieben vanished from view.

I hope this doesn't have an alarm. Gina thought as she gently lifted it from the pedestal. To her relief, no alarms sounded, and she made her way back through the threshold into the hallway of the Forge.

Chapter 26:
Finally Have It

Gina's heart pounded as she ran toward her apartment. Nestled securely in her cloak was the item she was sent to retrieve. *Maybe that witch will let me go.* Her mind filling with a sliver of hopefulness, and the thought of freedom she only recently was begging to have. With stealth Gina quickly made her way into her room. As if by instinct, Gina sat across from the mirror and waited. But nothing happened.

She stood and moved toward the light switch, but stopped, fearing that someone might see her with the sphere. In a moment of inspiration, she wrapped the sphere in the cloak. To her amazement it remained invisible. She placed it on the floor near the mirror, tucked as close as she could so the small bundle would not be kicked as someone walked by. Gina moved to face the front of the mirror again.

Gina waited, then reached out tapping the mirror's surface, but nothing happened. She pleaded with her reflection, "C'mon, c'mon I have the damn thing, answer me."

Still nothing happened.

Gina looked around, her teeth biting onto her thumb nail. She had the item she was sent for and didn't know what to do. She had stolen the Sphere of Lieben, with nowhere to go. She remembered that Allison's assistant, Mack, had dropped her off. She didn't have a car or any means to head back. In fact, Gina couldn't remember where the mansion was, or if she knew how to drive. She looked to where the cloak hid the Sphere. "What do I do with this?"

Gina looked at the sphere, her mind confident, but confused. She had the prize that Allison wanted, but then gave a sigh of relief. "At least if someone comes looking for it, they won't see it right away."

She tapped the mirror again, but nothing happened. In frustration Gina sat on the bed, the covers fluffed by the intensity of her actions. Gina held her head down mumbling, "I hate that woman. The one time I need her to actually show up, she's nowhere to be found."

* * *

Back in Massachusetts, Allison walked into her office. She had returned from processing the paperwork that officially transferred the mansion and possessions to her new identity. She also had some additional paperwork drawn up to allow Gina to inherit her fortune.

"Those greedy little people. All thinking they can take advantage of a poor little niece who just lost her lost great-aunt," Allison said before giving a salacious grin. "They're all fools." She laughed, then looked at the packet of new papers, "Gina my dear, when this is through, I think we'll have to end our current bargain."

The witch turned, looking into the mirror, she pulled at the wrinkles on her face. "The question is, do I take your youth, or your body?" And without a care she said, "No matter, I'll figure it out once I have the Sphere."

Allison tapped the mirror and said, "Let's see what my little doll is up to."

The image in the mirror was dark. Allison realized that Gina was probably asleep, she touched her earring, and willed the girl's eyes to open. Allison then sat her up and shook Gina's body, causing Gina to wake, "Wha, what's happening?"

Allison guided her to the mirror. "You sleep too much, my little doll. Give me an update on your progress. I am growing tired of waiting."

Gina went to move but was unable. "Mistress, I have it."

Allison, amused, said, "Oh, you have a present for me?"

Gina tried nodding but Allison remained in control. "Please, mistress, I have the Sphere."

Allison stood, "What? You, have it?"

"Mistress, I need my body back, please," Gina pleaded.

Allison released her earring and Gina fell to the floor. With her returning strength, Gina crawled forward, sweeping her hand for the invisible cloak. When she found it, she held her hands up and wrestled to unwrap it. Allison watched as the sphere appeared in Gina's hands.

Oh, my precious little doll, you did retrieve it, Allison thought.

Gina held it to the mirror and pressed it against the glass's surface, only to hear a distinct clack against hard glass. She tried again, with the same outcome, "Why isn't this working?"

Allison yelled, "Stop! You stupid doll. You'll damage the sphere."

Gina looked up in surprise, then asked, "Then how do I get it to you?"

Allison shook her head. "The Sphere is an alchemic, my dear. It cannot be ported like any simple magical item. You will have to physically bring it here." Allison's expression turned to a mix of emotion and concern. "Were you able to remove it without setting off any alarms?"

Gina nodded. "They were moving a bunch of stuff and I think they turned everything off."

"You think? No one followed you back, did they?"

Gina shook her head. "I came back a few hours ago. Why? I don't want to be caught with this."

Allison tried calming Gina. "My dear, I don't think they know it's gone. But we have to hurry. Why don't you drive home?"

Gina looked in the mirror with fear in her eyes. "I don't have a car, And I can't remember If I can drive."

Allison thought for a moment. When she took the girl's memories to prevent her from trying to escape, she didn't think how invasive it would be.

You've been alive for centuries and you still make stupid mistakes, Allison thought as she berated herself.

She said, "Hold on." She rushed to open her office door. "Mack! My office. Now!" Her voice echoing with authority through the entire mansion.

The sound of someone falling downstairs and the familiar grumbling and cursing of her assistant now filled her ears with entertainment.

"Mistress, what is it?" Mack said as he followed her in the door.

Allison pointed to the mirror. "She has the sphere."

Mack looked on with elation, "Put it through the mirror."

He heard Gina yell, "I can't."

Allison put her hands on Mack's arms. "It's an alchemic, Mack. It won't work. You need to go up there and get it, now!"

Mack looked at the clock. "But it's just past 2 a.m."

Allison glared at him, and the silent growl in her eyes told him nothing more than what he needed. His only response to her was, "Yes, mistress, give me a few minutes to get dressed."

Allison then ordered Gina to leave and wait near a small café almost a mile away. She was instructed to wear the cloak and to make sure no one saw her leaving. Gina agreed and did as ordered. The only sense that someone was outside was the movement of a small bush as Gina headed to the location.

* * *

The door to the cell opened and Shrive meekly walked forward. The evidence Selese and Amanda had gathered was enough to allow Shrive to be freed, at least for the moment. At the insistence of the Silver Hunters, Shrive's element making her a Raven Hunter had been removed earlier. The element to allow her to shadow walk was as well.

Amanda was nearby watching Li Xiu as she viewed the reunion of these two friends. She heard Li Xiu say to Selese, "You did so much to prove she was innocent. And to prove I wasn't lying."

The hunter smiled. "You're not a thief, just someone with a heart of gold that others mistake for a thief."

Selese looked over at Li Xiu, only to see the Silver Hunter wink. Selese then realized that she knew about her gold heart. But that fear of knowledge didn't stop her from staying near Shrive, "I did, with Amanda's help." Selese pointed to herself, asking, "How long have you known?"

Li Xiu pointed to Selese's heart, "It's in your file back home. I never thought that it was both literal and figurative."

Selese's eyes widened, "It's in my file at your sanctuary?"

Li Xiu nodded.

Selese shook her head, her voice filled with disappointment, "Great, so at least a few thousand people know. Oh, that's not unsettling."

188

Amanda stepped forward. "Not easy keeping a secret like that is it?"

Selese nodded, then pointed to the chain that Amanda wore. "Seems like you've got a similar problem."

Amanda disagreed. "Nothing like you. Mine you can see. Yours is, well, inside."

Selese smiled then returned her attention to Shrive who had been silent the entire time. Amanda moved forward, hugging her, "Sorry we took so long. Those idiots kept getting in our way."

Selese then hugged her friend. "Sorry, I should have broken you out of there as soon as they walked away."

Shrive shook her head. "No. they would have hunted us both down."

Amanda agreed, looking around. It felt good to get Shrive out of the dungeon, but they weren't able to do it before they removed some of her elements. Trying to be positive, she said, "We can get them back."

Shrive looked angrily toward Amanda, making her step back. Shrive growled, "I can't get it back."

Amanda looked to Selese for an answer and watched as Shrive's eyes filled with tears. Li Xiu stepped forward. "It's the same for us. Her shadow walking element can be replaced. But, for the other we take an oath to receive that element. If it's removed, it's an indication that we have broken that oath. The magic it was made from is no longer able to be used."

Amanda looked to Shrive, "You mean once you're a Raven Hunter, you can't leave and go back?" She then watched all three shake their heads.

Amanda felt sorry, then her chest filled with anger and frustration as she looked to Shrive, "I wish I could have figured things out faster."

Shrive reached out to put her arms around Amanda as tears fell down her face. She knew Amanda and Selese had worked as fast as they could to get her out. She knew the real criminals were the ones who framed her and those who took away what had become a part of her life. She spoke softly as she held onto Amanda, "It's not your fault. It's those bastards who did this to me."

Amanda held onto her for a short time as things quieted, she looked around at everyone and sensing the defeat she decided to stand tall. "It doesn't matter. Selese is not a Hunter. I'm not. And we figured this out all on our own. So, screw them."

There was silence as Shrive looked to her friend. She could see Amanda standing there, the anger she held now a source of power. A will that was a part of her, it was something she hadn't noticed until this moment. *She's as good, if not better, than any hunter. And she can't shadow walk or use magic.* Shrive thought before saying, "You're right, we don't need them."

Selese said, "They couldn't stop us, even face to face."

"That's right. Amanda even inspired me stand up to Regent Chung," Li Xiu said.

Amanda looked at them all. "Really?"

Li Xiu nodded. "I was ready to fight him if he attacked you."

Amanda stood dumbfounded. She could see them all looking at her. Her friends, old and new—they all had the same look. That was cemented when Selese asked, "So, we got her out. What's next?"

Amanda chuckled nervously. "Well since it's been really stressful. And it seems that everyone is busy with moving everything, maybe we should just go out and celebrate."

Shrive smiled. It was the first time Amanda had seen her do so in days. She felt hopeful until Li Xiu said, "I can't. I've been ordered to accompany the artifacts back home." She looked to Amanda. "I'd rather go with you."

Amanda smiled; she understood that Li Xiu had a duty to the Silver Hunters. She shook the woman's shoulder. "Okay, we'll celebrate. And, after you're done, come back and we'll all celebrate again."

Li Xiu smiled, a subtle laugh of excitement and anticipation as she walked away. She knew it would probably be her last days as a Silver Hunter, and she didn't know if she would still have the capability to return. She was good at hiding her disappointment, but she felt a twinge of hope as Amanda said, "Maybe we should keep an eye out for them, just in case."

Shrive looked to Amanda. "As she said, you don't have to, but I've worked with Ron and Linda enough to know when there is a job and when there's a big job." She looked to Selese. "And my instincts are telling me that maybe they'll need our help."

Chapter 27:
Bad Things Happen

The Regent stood at the entrance to the Forge, his stance impatient.

Hurry, they're waiting. Bao put my plans behind. The Regent looked around. *This needs to go out now. I don't want those two to be a part of this. They'll ruin my plan.*

Chung walked quickly alongside the last pallet, pushing it to force the hunters to move more rapidly. He had arranged a time and location for the attack to occur. The Broken Feather was not an organization you made wait; Chung knew that. His erratic behavior didn't go unnoticed by one of the Raven Hunters overseeing the loading of the truck. He quickly moved away to contact Lord Cale to tell him of his observation.

The Regent sighed with relief as he watched the truck's door pull closed. The Magic seal applied to the lock, and the entire vehicle now gave him an opportunity. He quickly reached out to touch the security lock, grabbed one of the coins he used to access his magic, and spoke. The spell he weaved was known to many of the Silver Hunters.

"Why are you attaching a tracking spell to the lock?" the other hunter asked.

Chung was ready for any inquiry, as he answered, "Just in case the truck is delayed or stolen, we can track it. Also, if someone tried to change the lock, the spell would attach to them, and we'd know who it was."

The Hunter nodded. It seemed like a good idea. The woman understood and decided not to follow protocol. Instead, she returned to her duties, leaving the Regent to his task. However, she didn't know Chung's true intention. The spell itself was only trackable by the Regent. However, he attached the spell to a crystal as the Regent returned to his room to gather his things. Taking the book from earlier, he opened the same page with the mirror. Within seconds the imposing image of Dennon Fierst appeared.

"Chung? Are you calling to tell me that the shipment is not being sent?"

The Regent shook his head. "My friend, the shipment is on schedule. I only wish to provide you with a means of tracking it, in case they divert to another path."

Dennon watched as the Regent held the crystal in one hand and his other to the mirror. He heard Chung's words, and an exact duplicate of the crystal appeared in the air before him. This was unlike any crystal he had seen. The form was like an apparition. He looked at the form and returned to see Chung staring back through the mirror.

Seeing Dennon's confusion, Chung said, "I presume you know how an eidolon works?"

Dennon grasped the item, its ghostly form like air to his touch. He looked to Chung, "And what is its use?"

"It will expire when I desire it. It will allow you to track the vehicle for a time and when everything's complete, it will fade. No evidence. Forgive me, my friend, but I cannot trust you to have the original. If it were to be found, there would be. . . questions."

A cynical smile appeared across Dennon's face. He knew how to hide his own tracks while working with the Feather. His admiration for Chung now became prominent. "Regent, I am surprised you have not joined us earlier. Why the change?"

Chung nodded. His words filled with regret, but not for what he was about to do. "I am nearing the end of my tenure as Regent; Zheng has already taken many of my duties. I am to retire shortly, but not by my choice." The Regent looked up to see Dennon staring back. "I also feel that this world has become too polluted by the weak." A sinister smile graced Dennon's face as the Regent continued, "The world has been too free with its power. It needs guidance."

The Regent heard the subtle evil laugh that escaped his new compatriot. Dennon held the ghostly copy of the crystal and said, "If you have planned well, then this should be simple. It should ease the loss of any life. We do hate to waste good scroll witches, and hunters. I'll alert one of our people there to keep some of the more troublesome hunters busy. Chung, make sure you check in with a hunter named Faulkner before leaving."

Chung sat back. "We'll be leaving shortly. Have everyone ready." He looked over his shoulder. "Things should go as planned, as long as those two don't get involved. They have been a nuisance since before my arrival."

Dennon's demeanor became serious, asking, "What two?"

Chung sighed in frustration before saying, "Ron and Linda Wilt. Are you familiar with them?"

The Regent watched as Dennon's knuckles turned white as his grasp on the ghostly crystal tightened.

"I am, Chung. I am very familiar with them and that FOF they keep around." Dennon growled.

The Regent could feel the man's anger through the glass. He agreed with Dennon. Both they and Amanda had been of much annoyance the past few days. "I see you have had interactions with them before." Chung finished placing his belongings into the small bag he had brought. "I have them, for the moment, secured. But that FOF you mentioned was able to free one of their friends."

"Friends?" Dennon asked.

"An anthromorph; her name is unimportant. The creature was in a cell until they convinced the Raven Hunters to release her."

Dennon returned a stare of angry concern. "Do not underestimate them, Chung. They have prevented several of our attempts to obtain items and people. Unfortunately, that FOF is the one that nearly captured me."

Chung shook his head. "They are mere individuals. They do not have the resources or power to defeat us."

"You may think that, but they have a lot of power behind them. They are all FOFs. The two are also part fairy. That alone gives them allies that we cannot secure."

"You mean the fairies would help them?"

Dennon nodded. "Do not underestimate them. Although fairies

cannot leave their forest, they may still come to their aid. Make sure they are busy before you leave."

Chung smiled as he slung his bag over his shoulder. "Do not worry, my friend, they are out celebrating the release of their friend." He picked up the small book, "And I moved up the shipment time. So we will be on the way well before they find out."

Chung closed the book, placed it into his pack, and walked toward the door. *Now, I hope none of the Feather mistake me for a Hunter.*

* * *

Shrive was laughing as Selese choked on her drink. She was trying to beat Ron in a drinking contest to see who could finish faster. The display was not one of competition but more to ease the trauma that Shrive had to endure as a prisoner. And for the moment, it was working.

Amanda sat nearby, watching their friend laugh for the first time in the hours since she was released. She was concerned that the aftermath of her wrongful imprisonment was something she didn't know how to cope with. She had only known Shrive for a few years, but they quickly became friends. Selese looked over, smiling. She could see Shrive was reserved and said, "So, you going to join us or what?"

Shrive's smile widened. "I don't think I can beat either of them."

Selese watched her friend pull back. She was sorry about what had happened, and Selese knew what it was like to be locked up. Selese, unlike Shrive, always escaped. She always found a way to get out. However, she hadn't stolen anything for the last few years, at least not without permission. And even though she was innocent, Shrive was still concerned about what others would think of her no longer being a Raven Hunter. Selese could see that and offered her some words of comfort.

"Shrive, no one's going to think less of you. And if they do, screw 'em," Selese said, making Shrive look seriously toward her. Selese's smile flattened. "You are innocent. We all know that. That's why we went to all this trouble."

Amanda watched as Shrive looked around before saying, "Hey, I asked her to help me break into one of the most secure buildings on campus." Amanda leaned in. "And she was happy to help."

Shrive looked around the table to see them all looking at her. Linda smiled, saying, "We knew you were innocent, even Dr. Brentwood and Lord Cale. But the Regent insisted you be detained." Then, Linda leaned toward Ron, "I don't think he likes people who are not entirely human."

Linda's statement brought stares of confusion from the three friends. Amanda spoke first, "I know he doesn't like me. He seems to think a FOF is a bad thing."

Linda nodded. "So we heard." She looked to Shrive, "But I don't know if Lord Cale told you what the Regent said when they were all trapped by the dragon's claw."

Shrive shook her head. She knew Lord Cale considered Ron's suggestion to take the Regent to the open desert, even if he was joking. She didn't know for sure and was curious. She asked what the Regent had said and waited for an answer. Ron was quick to reply.

"I sealed the door and decided to use something that Roween taught me. I created a fairy shield." Although Ron shook his head, "that fire from the dragon's claw was tough, but I held it back till it burned out."

He told them how Chung looked on in disgust at Ron as he turned, seeing his eyes glowing dimly with fairy light. Shrive said, "You mean he thinks there's something wrong with that?"

Ron chuckled. "Apparently. But truthfully, I wouldn't take his opinion for much. We both think he's part of the Broken Feather."

Shrive looked to see Amanda nodding. Shrive said, "We should tell someone. They might come after Amanda or Selese."

Selese threw her arms around her friend, mockingly saying, "Oh, Shrive, we didn't know you cared. Thank you so much." Selese pulled back, her smile one of jest and actual appreciation. She then said, "The Feather will eventually make a move. I have a feeling we are the least of their worries right now."

Ron spoke up, "Let's hope."

There was a bit of laughter before Selese said, "The Raven Hunters have been keeping them on their toes." She looked around then pointed to Amanda. "Speaking of Raven Hunters, where is he?"

Amanda paused briefly, then her eyes filled with a glint of comprehension before she started looking around, saying, "You're right, I invited him. Where is he?"

She then looked at Ron and Linda, "I don't see any hunters here at all."

Ron looked around, his expression concerned, before looking at his phone. "Do you have any messages from Cale or Claire?"

Linda shook her head. She turned to Amanda. "You have anything?"

Amanda shook her head.

Ron and Linda both became very concerned. "There are no hunters here at all." But then, he paused. "I wonder if they moved up the time."

Shrive felt the obligation of her former vocation and asked if there was a problem. Ron looked at her, "I hope not. Hopefully, the Silver Hunters can handle this on their own." He looked around. "Then again, why are there no Hunters around at all?"

"Maybe they were called in. But, I mean, none of us are Raven Hunters, right?" Shrive said.

Ron looked to Linda, who was already dialing Dr. Brentwood. Amanda followed, dialing Luke. They had the same expression hearing the same thing from both, and almost in unison, "They just left?"

Ron asked, "You mean they left? Did they split the shipment?"

Linda shook her head. "No, Chung insisted on using one truck."

Ron leaned back with a sigh of frustration. He looked to Selese. "Can you shadow walk?"

Selese nodded.

Ron looked at Linda. "Good. I think we should all pay a visit to the Sanctuary. Now."

They were all in agreement and walked toward the end of the restaurant, the area covered by stairs, and within the shadows, they vanished.

Their disappearance did not go unnoticed by a man sitting at the bar, who said, "Did you see that?"

The bartender looked to where the man pointed before grabbing a bottle from the shelf behind him, "Here, let me freshen that up for you, on the house."

The man smiled, taking a drink. The bartender smiled, hearing the man say, "Wait, what was I talking about again?"

Chapter 28:
Enemies Attack

Selese stepped from between the columns of the Shadowed Hall. Amanda and the others trailed behind. They had used the magical entryway many times, but, to their surprise, no one greeted them. Instead, the hall itself was without guards and very quiet.

"Oh, come on, no one's here to stop us from coming in," Selese said. "Really? They always hassle me when I show up."

Ron looked around, "Selese is right. Something's not right."

Everyone remained alert as they walked toward the main hall of the Sanctuary. To their surprise, no one greeted them there, either.

"This is really starting to worry me," Selese said, making everyone nod in agreement. But then, they were startled when a hunter appeared from the darkness that led to the Forge.

Selese watched him smile as she walked closer. Yardley was one of the new Raven Hunters. He wasn't cleared to be sent out into the field yet. Selese took a chance and asked him where the guards for the Shadowed Hall were.

Yardley looked back. "All available Hunters are in the gathering hall. The guards, too. they were supposed to send replacements. You mean no one's watching the Shadowed Hall?"

Ron looked behind them. "It's never unguarded. Who's handy? We can watch things till someone gets there." He turned to look at Amanda and Selese. "Who's fastest? We need to tell the others and get someone here, now."

Linda turned to him. "With that shipment going out. This isn't good."

Ron nodded. "Yeah, perfect set up for an attack."

Selese turned to look at Shrive, and both sprinted toward the meeting hall. Amanda headed toward the offices while Ron and Linda headed back to the Shadowed Hall. They could hear Ron yelling, "This seems like a setup; be careful."

Ron and Linda arrived at the Shadowed Hall. He kept watch as she and Yardley looked around the room, the giant pillars causing shadows everywhere. As Ron listened, he only heard the footsteps of the two people with him. Yardley stopped beside him as he finished his round, "There no one here." He raised his brow. "Someone's going to be in trouble."

Linda now stood before him, and she continued to look around. "Guards can't leave the Shadowed Hall unless ordered, right?"

Yardley nodded.

Ron looked around, then to Linda, "What are you thinking?"

Linda gritted her teeth. "Maybe the guards are still here."

Ron turned, his eyes vigilant and alert. "There's only columns and darkness. So, you didn't find anything, right?"

Linda shook her head. "Nothing obvious."

She walked by him to inspect one of the columns, her hand running along a straight crack feeling its history. She then looked around, and her eyes filled with a terrible stare. She then ran to another column. Then to another, suddenly, she stopped her hand leaning against the stone column as she looked up. Ron watched as she closed her eyes then turned to look at him with tears, "They're still here."

Ron quickly joined her, and she pointed up. What Ron saw was horrific. It was one of the guards turned partially to stone and half melded with the rock of the hall itself. The guard was still there in the Hall, and anyone could come and go as they pleased. Yardley looked up and felt his stomach drop, "That looks like Navarro. He was one of the new hunters assigned to guard the hall while the others were meeting."

Ron, stating the obvious, said, "This is bad." He was about to speak again when he heard a cry of pain as someone came through the shadows.

As Selese arrived at the meeting hall, Lord Cale was nowhere to be found. Instead, another hunter was giving a briefing of the recent activities throughout the Sanctuary. Selese and Shrive paused in the doorway as a few of their fellow hunters or former fellow hunters greeted them.

Selese walked toward the front, and when the man paused to turn a page on the report, she spoke, "Kerr, who's supposed to be guarding the Shadowed Hall?"

The man looked toward her. A puzzled look in his eyes as she asked the question again. The man stuttered, "Navarro and Faulkner, why?"

Shrive took her cue seeing Selese taking charge, "because no one stopped us from entering? There's no one guarding the Shadowed Hall."

Kerr looked at her, confused. "They were ordered to cover while we were giving this briefing."

Selese said, "Ron's hunch? Something's not right." She turned, looking at the hunters to see them staring at her. She turned to see Kerr look down at the page about to continue.

"Are you all stupid? We just told you no one is guarding the Shadowed Hall. Send someone there, now!"

It took Kerr a moment to realize what she had said. He then ordered several hunters to immediately head to the Shadowed Hall. Selese yelled after them, "Ron and Linda are there doing your jobs. Try not to kill them."

Shrive walked up to some of the hunters in the front row, spoke with them, and they followed her. But Kerr objected, "You can't take any Hunters with you. You're no longer a Hunter."

Shrive turned the anger in her cat-like eyes, causing the man to flinch as Selese said, "And we're still doing your job. Get up off your asses, everyone."

The entire room stood, and followed Selese's commands. She noticed that all of the available Hunters were in one place. To her, that was a problem. Someone wanted everyone in one location and away from the Shadowed Hall.

They all heard, "something's not right. Has anyone made sure the Forge was secure before coming here?

When no one answered Shrive ran off toward the Forge. Selese motioned for them to follow. She brought the other Hunters as she followed Shrive when they arrived at the Forge. To their surprise, the door was closed.

Selese turned to her friend, "I thought about it being a target, but it looks like they secured it. So it's not our mystery thief."

Shrive turned her cat-like ear. "There's yelling. It sounds like it's coming from the Shadowed Hall." Suddenly the alarm of the Sanctuary blared around them, the two ordering everyone to follow as they headed back toward the Shadowed Hall.

It took them less than a minute to arrive and they could see Linda trying to heal an injured hunter. The man's arm looked as if it was turning to stone. Selese and Shrive quickly rushed in to help.

"This one's bad. Someone take her to the infirmary. We've got more coming in." They heard Ron giving orders.

Finally, Amanda arrived, asking, "What happened?"

She immediately started helping some of the injured as Ron replied, "the truck was hit. There are still people out there and a lot of injured." Ron paused. "Half of them turning to stone."

Selese realized what it was, "petrification!" She reached out, grabbing onto the woman's shoulder, and after a few magic words, the stone started to recede. It took some concentration, but she was able to reverse the effect. She looked to Ron, "Get any geomage we have. I'll show them how to reverse it."

Ron yelled the order and asked Amanda, "Did you find anyone?"

Amanda did. In fact, she had spoken with Dr. Brentwood and was returning to tell them to watch the Shadowed Hall until the guards returned. She was surprised as the doctor appeared behind her.

"What happened?" Dr. Brentwood asked one of the Hunters. She wasn't surprised to hear of the attack, but she did fear for Lord Cale. She watched as Selese started to reverse the stone on several hunters. The doctor knew reversing a petrification spell was difficult. Nevertheless, she watched Selese do so with ease. *You learned a lot more in my office than I fear I have.*

Dr. Brentwood watched Shrive turn to her feral form to hoist up two hunters as they walked from the shadows. Their injuries were more physical, the blood filling her senses as she handed them to others waiting nearby. Ron and Linda worked together as a team, the hunters following their lead. *It seems like you all work well together,* the doctor thought.

Dr. Brentwood moved to stand nearby Ron. "Do we know how bad it is yet?"

Ron turned to shake his head. Selese had shown the other geomages how to reverse the petrification, and she was looking at Ron for direction. She could see her mother speaking with him, and one thought entered her mind, *Oh no, Cale.*

Selese rushed toward them. "Is Cale back yet?"

The doctor looked to Ron, who said, "I haven't seen him."

This prompted Amanda to ask, "What about Luke?"

Dr. Brentwood answered her question. "He was sent to secure the Forge. Unfortunately, the Silver Hunters left it open and unguarded."

Shrive said, "We were just there. It was closed."

The doctor looked to Shrive. "We need to make sure everyone's all right." She then grabbed Amanda, and they started toward the Forge.

Selese was about to follow when they heard Ron yell, "You two over here."

Shrive and Selese quickly joined Ron, who looked into the darkness, "we don't know what it's like on the other side. But we need to find out." Then, he turned to Linda, "Think you can cover here?"

Linda looked back. "If it's too dangerous, head right back, I don't want to have to chase after you again."

Ron nodded.

Selese was about to shadow walk, but Ron stopped her and tapped his armband. "I don't want to use shadow walking right now. Not until I know it's not a trap." Within moments, a purple glow engulfed them, and they disappeared.

Linda sighed, whispering, "Be careful, all of you."

Amanda arrived at the Forge. She pounded on the door, her effort bringing no sound in return. Dr. Brentwood arrived soon afterward; her breath heavy. "I'm not as young as I used to be," she muttered as she held her hand to the door, glowing. The sound of metal and stone moving rang all around them like machinery as the door to the Forge unlocked.

They heard the other hunters yelling as they rushed to squeeze through the door as it opened. "Dr. Brentwood, what's going on. Why is the alarm sounding?"

Amanda didn't give the doctor a chance to answer as she threw her arms around Luke, knocking him back. The doctor became annoyed. "We don't have time, Amanda. We need their help."

Amanda looked back quickly, letting Luke go, bringing several questionable glances from his fellow hunters. The doctor resisted laughing as she spoke, "The truck was attacked. We have injured coming in."

Luke asked, "How bad?"

Amanda answered, "A lot of them are being turned to stone."

Luke looked to the others. "We were investigating one of the alarms going off when the door was closed on us.

"Did you see who it was?" Dr. Brentwood asked.

Luke shook his head. "The person keeping guard was shoved into the Forge before the door was closed."

Dr. Brentwood looked around, "We can investigate later. But, right now, we have injured, and we don't know how many or how badly."

"We should go help. There's nothing to do here that can't wait," Amanda said.

The doctor nodded. "All right, everyone, let's see if we can help."

Chapter 29:
The Witch wants Some Fun

Mack stopped to get gas. He had forgotten to do so the last time he arrived at the school. Allison ordered him to wait for Gina at the nearby diner. But first, he needed to ensure they had enough fuel for the return.

"Damn witch thinks this is easy. I do all the driving. Shopping. Cleaning of that mansion. And what do I get for this?" Mack muttered as he looked down at the glimmer of his heavy gold watch. And that gold chain that made him almost immortal. "Oh, that's right, she pays me too," Mack whispered as he chuckled. "Can't wait till this charade is over. That doll of hers is becoming a lot of trouble."

Nearby Gina could see Allison's car but didn't see Mack. *He's here. Now I can get rid of this thing.* Gina thought as she ran toward the car. The only indication of her was the puffs of dust from each step she took.

Gina grabbed the door handle and pulled, causing the door to swing open. She wrestled with unwrapping the sphere and was startled as Mack appeared from around the car. Her surprise caused her to nearly drop the prize as Mack ran right into her. She held onto the sphere; it was still invisible as Mack looked around. She watched as his eyes locked onto the ground just before her, and she froze.

Mack knew some tricks the Raven Hunters could use and a simple cloaking spell. He held up his gold watch and used the reflection to scan the area.

Nothing? That usually works countering invisibility spells. Then Mack remembered that Allison had given Gina a woven cloak. He looked around before whispering, "Gina?"

Gina removed her hood in a huff, saying, "You need to watch where you're going. I almost dropped this thing."

Mack snarled back, "It's not like I could see you." Then, his mind returned to the item he came to retrieve. "Is it in one piece?"

Gina wrestled with the cloak, revealing the prize their mistress had sought. She handed the sphere to him and stepped back. Mack quickly opened the other door and retrieved a box. And when opened, it was lined with soft velvet padding. Mack gently placed the orb and it sank into its fabric slowly. Gina sighed in relief, but both were startled hearing someone around the other side of the car. He smiled then sniffed the air, "Are you wearing perfume?"

Gina became annoyed. "Ugh, I left it in my room. Allison probably won't let me leave to get it again. I liked that perfume."

Mack scoffed, "What? Did you drop the bottle on yourself? Or is it that strong?"

Gina tilted her head, giving the man a very cross stare. They were both startled as the attendant came around the car.

"Hey, you may want to avoid the school right now. I heard there was an. . . ." The man's voice faded as he saw Gina's head floating without a body. Gina turned to the man, her eyes filled with anger as Mack groaned indigently. The man whispered in a stutter, "G-ghost, ghost!" before Mack held his hand out, giving a snap of his fingers, freezing the man in place. He approached, holding his hand before the attendant's face, and tapped his watch.

Suddenly an image floated before his hand and the man's head. Mack slowly moved his hand to the left, watching the images change. Gina could see the last few seconds of the man's memory. She watched as Mack stopped on a particular image and closed his hand, the image then shrank, and Mack tossed it aside. Mack opened his hand again, and new images appeared. This time they were of a scene of Mack paying the man. He motioned for Gina to get into the car, and she complied. She was going to remove the cloak, but her hands hesitated, and Gina felt her mind start to fade.

"Well, well, my little doll. You didn't disappoint me after all," Allison muttered as she used Gina to open the box holding the Sphere. She looked to see her assistant adjusting the memories of the attendant, "Mack, what are you doing?"

Mack smiled. "He saw something he shouldn't have."

"Then kill him. It's not like you haven't before," Allison replied.

Mack sighed. "Mistress, you seem to miss the point. I have won cases like this easily. It's more challenging. Not to mention entertaining and more practical than killing." He looked to her then back to the attendant, "Also, he was about to tell us something. I thought it might be important. It was about the school."

That news intrigued Allison, and she placed the box back into the car. "Then please continue."

Mack looked at Gina. "Uh, you do know that only Gina's head is visible, right?"

Allison swung the hood of the cloak over Gina's head and, with unseen hands, motioned for Mack to continue. Annoyed, Allison said, "Go on, Mack."

Mack stepped back, and with a snap, the attendant started to move.

"What was I saying again?" the attendant asked.

Mack helped his memory, "You were saying something about the school?"

The man remembered. "Uh, yeah, there was a big truck accident. And there's police or like secret service all over the place. You'd have a hard time getting through there right now."

Mack smiled. "Thank you for that. I'll steer clear of the school. Did you bring my change from the hundred I gave you?"

The attendant looked baffled but reached into his pocket, looking at the gas pump. "You got about forty-five, gave me a hundred. We don't usually take those, but it seemed good, so I owe you sixty-two and change."

Mack smiled. "I'll take the sixty, and we'll call it even."

The attendant gave Mack the money before walking away. Mack turned as Allison removed the hood, exposing Gina's face. She looked toward the direction of the school, and Mack heard her say, "You know, although I do not believe the Feather should be in power, I am curious about how their little attack went." Mack watched as Gina's face again disappeared and heard the shuffling of feet while watching footsteps appear in the sand before breaking into a stride.

As Allison used Gina to run toward where the attack happened, Mack growled as he closed the passenger door, "You sent me up here to get this damn thing, and now you want to explore. Make up your mind, witch."

* * *

Ron, Selese, and Shrive faded into the landscape, surrounded by a purple light. They could see the truck on the side of the road. Its side was torn open, and what remained of some of the hunters lay on the ground. Selese rushed to the nearest, who was almost entirely turned to stone and went to work. She looked up, hearing Ron say, "See if you can help anyone else."

Selese nodded as Shrive followed Ron heading toward the truck.

As they approached, they heard Lord Cale yelling orders. They watched as the hunters around all complied. As he ran up to Cale, Ron asked, "how many injured?"

Cale turned to see him and Shrive slowing to stop. "We had over forty, and I don't know how many of the Silver Hunters, that fool Chung wouldn't tell us anything. And I can't find him anywhere." The frustration in his voice was inherent as he said, "He's probably gone with them, or he was a coward and headed back to the Sanctuary." Cale then looked to Shrive. "We could have used you here." The regret in his voice almost debilitating.

Shrive looked to her former leader and knew what he had to do was not of his choosing. She looked around. "I can grab anyone injured. But I can't shadow walk."

Ron turned to her, "Shrive, go help Selese; she can shadow walk. Get any injured back to the Sanctuary."

Shrive looked to Lord Cale and watched him nod. She then rushed back to help Selese. Ron watched her as well before turning back to Cale. "How many?"

Lord Cale knew the man wasn't asking how many were injured but how many were lost. The leader of the Raven Hunters shook his head. "I don't know yet."

Selese was on her fifth hunter as she reversed the petrification. She was happy when Shrive picked up two of them from the ground. She watched as Shrive looked around, helpless.

Oh, right, you can't shadow walk, Selese remembered. She then grabbed her friend, and they disappeared into the shadows of the trees.

Allison had finally arrived; she could not hear or feel the heart quickly beating in Gina's chest. The constant running had pushed the woman to near exhaustion. Allison felt Gina fighting for control but remained in control of her body. Her curiosity about the attack took precedence as she watched Ron work with Lord Cale using his amethyst gate to transport several people at a time. She watched as several hunters and Selese and Shrive appeared in the shadows across the way.

"They let you out. Humph, they must be desperate." Allison craned Gina's head to look at the damage to the truck and the hunters still lying around. She muttered, "Looks like the Feather did a number on you, my friends. I'll have to do something about that when my plan is in effect."

Allison returned to Shrive, "Well, I am probably done with you. My doll retrieved the property you stole from me." She then leaned back. "This is entertaining. Maybe I'll sit and watch for a while."

Ron did his best to bandage one of the Silver Hunters' injuries. He could hear Lord Cale giving orders but could see several Silver Hunters working to save their teammates from being turned to stone. So he wasn't surprised when Selese pushed him aside to start the reversal process. He could hear her complaining, "Don't they teach geomages anything useful anymore?" He chuckled, realizing that she and Shrive were helping more than anyone who called themselves hunters.

Selese started reversing the spell on another Silver Hunter, only to be pushed aside by another of their team. The woman, also a geomage, was working to save her friend. Selese looked on in anger as she righted herself. However, the woman only glanced over. "You're not a Hunter. You shouldn't be here."

Selese watched as the geomage struggled to stop the petrification. The woman again pushed her, yelling, "Get away!"

Selese shot back, "Why won't you let me help? I can do it faster."

The Silver Hunter looked at her, "We take orders from our commander, not some thief."

Selese stood, anger in her voice as she changed her appearance into Chung's, her voice the same as his as she yelled back, "There, I look like him, and I'm telling you to move so I can help."

The altercation didn't go unnoticed by Allison. *Another shapeshifter? And she changed so effortlessly.* Allison leaned forward; *I don't think she even touched an element, did she?* Allison continued watching as Selese changed into her usual self and treated the man on the ground.

Allison huffed, as she sat Gina down on the ground. *Foolish old witch, you attacked the wrong shapeshifter. Oh, that was stupid. That other wasn't a shapeshifter. She was an anthromorph.* The witch shook her head and made Gina smile, *Over six hundred years, you still make mistakes. Oh well, maybe I can still have some fun.*

Allison moved Gina closer and waited. She watched for an opportunity to strike. She was still invisible and knew she had the element of surprise. She checked the pockets of her doll and found nothing—*stupid doll, not even a small knife. I should have made you carry one, so I could use it when needed.* She then watched as Selese turned into a mockery of Chung, his features exaggerated, almost comical, as she went to help another hunter.

"She does it so fluidly. I wonder how?" Allison muttered as she leaned forward.

The witch's mind was a flurry of thoughts. *That would be a helpful attribute. However, I have the sphere back. Perhaps my little doll has outlived her usefulness.* She then had a moment of inspiration. *I can bring her in, find out how she does it, and take it from her.* She then paused, *or take her body, whichever is easier.*

Allison removed the cloak's hood hiding her doll and moved into the open field. She turned her head, looked at the hunters, and yelled. Her voice grabbed the attention of Shrive. Shrive looked at her and said, "Who's that?" Shrive then sniffed the air, "Wait, that perfume."

Selese looked over. "It's Gina, and why is it only her head showing?" She then stood, saying, "She's the thief. And I think she's the one who framed you."

Allison could hear them both and made faces and hand gestures that she realized they couldn't see. Allison laughed at herself for a moment. Then she watched as the two started toward her. "Okay, that's what I want you to do."

She then turned, running into the forest. None of them heard the pleas of the woman on the ground, who said, "No, Shrive, it's a trap."

Allison ran as fast as Gina's legs would allow, leading them away from the others, her mind thinking, *I hope Mack still has the car nearby.* She was elated as she spotted the vehicle through the trees. She slowed as she approached the edge, pulling the cloak over her head. She then stopped and waited for the two chasing to catch up. As Selese stopped at the edge of the trees, she looked around, breathing heavy, as was Shrive. Neither of the two noticed anything before both were struck from behind with enough force to make them unconscious. Mack turned to see the two women fall. "What the hell?" Mack muttered before he started walking to investigate.

He was surprised to see an arm of each lift into the air as they started being pulled across the ground. Then, Mack heard the voice of Gina yell, "Mack, get something to bind these two. I'm bringing home a couple of extra gifts for myself."

Mack did as instructed, tossing the two into the car's trunk. He watched as Gina's face appeared, seeing the woman's eyes with tears rolling down her face. This prompted Mack to say something about her face. But, when Allison looked into the side view mirror, she said, "This doll must be allergic to something in the forest." She turned to Mack, removing the cloak that kept her invisible.

"Let's head back. I want my prizes as soon as possible," Allison said. Then she pointed to Selese. "I'm particularly interested in this one. She seems to have some unique abilities. Bring them all back, Mack. With the Sphere, I may be able to use them all." Allison said before she gave control back to Gina.

The girl looked to Mack, "Why'd she make me hurt them?"

Mack smiled, then shrugged. "It doesn't matter. You heard the mistress; we're heading back. Now!"

Night and shadows are ours, but we long to grasp the light. We are the silent who plague your thoughts, and give substance to dreams.

- Darkling saying.

Chapter 30:
Someone's Missing

In the Shadowed Hall, Dr. Brentwood and Amanda helped as more of the injured came in through the shadows. Amanda recognized Li Xiu and quickly helped her into one of the beds before someone took her to the infirmary. Amanda had turned to see Linda relieved as Ron and Lord Cale appeared from an amethyst gate. She approached, asking, "Is that everyone?"

Cale nodded. "Everyone who was injured. The rest are investigating and cleaning up the whole mess." He looked around, "Where's Selese and Shrive?"

Amanda hadn't seen them return, but she was busy helping the injured hunters. She was happy to see Luke appear from the shadows. He approached Lord Cale, saying, "It's going to take a while to clean up, but it looks like we don't have to worry about doing much inventory. They pretty much took everything powerful." He looked to Ron. "Even the dragon's claw."

Lord Cale looked to Luke. "Did you find the regent?" Luke shook his head.

The whole room heard Ron growl, "Sometimes, I hate being right."

Linda put her arm around him. "They beat us for the moment. Are we sure it was the Feather?" She then looked around, "where are Selese and Shrive? Are they still out helping?"

Luke shrugged, "I came back to report in, then head out again. This whole thing is a mess and a half. I can't tell if it was the Feather or not. It certainly has their mark on it."

Lord Cale agreed before looking at Ron and Linda. "We should go back and investigate. Let things quiet down here."

Linda gestured to Ron. "I can help the injured here. I'll stay. You go. Find out what you can. Besides, if it was the Feather, maybe they left clues on where they took everything."

Ron nodded, tapping Luke's arm, and she watched them disappear again. Lord Cale stepped into the shadows and soon followed. Amanda looked toward her friend and could see Linda staring before hearing her say, "Let's help those here first. You can investigate later. After everything's calmed."

Amanda didn't like the idea of staying behind, but she reconsidered joining the Raven Hunters, seeing the injuries. She pushed aside her confusion, allowing her to focus on the task as she helped the injured. Amanda looked to her side and could see Li Xiu unconscious.

Linda was nearby, watching Amanda as she looked toward Li Xiu. Then, she motioned toward the Silver Hunter, seeing the concern and conflict in Amanda, "Go see if she needs anything, I've got this one." Linda tried sounding reassuring, but knew the questions Amanda was asking in her thoughts: *Do I want to risk a life like this?*

Amanda looked down at Li Xiu, and the other Silver Hunter, annoyed that she was standing by her teammate, said, "What do you want, FOF?"

Amanda didn't let her anger answer. Instead, she replied, "It doesn't matter if I'm a FOF or not. She's a friend. I came over to see how she was."

The woman's expression suddenly filled with remorse, "Sorry, she has a concussion. And we lost more than we should have."

"Losing one is too much. We shouldn't have lost any," Amanda said. "Was she awake recently?"

The Silver Hunter nodded, "Yes, but she fell asleep and hasn't woken up. That's the concern. I'm trying to heal her."

Amanda held her fairy ring, but nothing happened. Instead, she touched Li Xiu's hand. The contact caused Li Xiu to wake and sit up quickly, startling Amanda, "Regent? Where's the Regent? They attacked him. Is he alright?"

Amanda gently pushed Li Xiu down, saying, "Easy, worry about yourself first. You were hit pretty hard, from what I heard."

Li Xiu swayed in the bed, her eyes replaying the incident before her, "They used some device on their wrists. It was like a watch."

Amanda thought, *A watch, wait, oh no,* before she yelled, "Linda!"

Linda appeared from around the corner. "What is it? What's wrong?"

Amanda told her, "They were using scroll watches. It was the Broken Feather."

Linda nodded. "I should tell Dr. Brentwood."

Li Xiu grabbed Linda's arm. "Wait, Shrive and Selese, are they back?"

Amanda looked at Linda. "No. We thought they stayed back to help investigate the attack. Why?"

Li Xiu shook her head. "I watched them run after something in the forest."

Amanda felt very uneasy at this new information, and when she heard Li Xiu say, "It was a floating head. I'm sure it was the one who attacked us."

She turned to Linda to see a worried expression on her friend's face. Amanda only nodded and followed when Linda said, "We have the tell the others. Now! Come on."

* * *

Shrive felt a sharp pain in her shoulder as it was forced into the lock of the car trunk, her catlike eyes adjusting quickly to the darkness. She could see Selese, her arms bound before her. Shrive also found herself in a similar situation. But, unlike Selese, she transformed into her more feral form, her claws making quick work of the bindings.

She quickly worked to free herself and pushed against the roof of the trunk. It wouldn't budge. She worked to release Selese and, while removing her bonds, noticed a faint glow from behind her. She twisted to see the internal trunk release glowing softly in the darkness and went back to working on releasing Selese.

Shive shook Selese, whispering, "Wake up, come on, wake up."

Selese stirred. Her eyes fluttered as she moaned from the pain of being hit. Shrive covered her mouth. "We don't want them knowing we're awake. Yet." Selese nodded in understanding.

"Where are we?" Selese asked. Shrive didn't know, nor did she know how long they were unconscious. They didn't know where they were or who had taken them. Selese looked around. Her eyes adjusted quickly, just as Shrive's had. Being part darkling had its advantages. One was the ability to shadow walk without the use of an element.

"Let's get out of here," Selese said, grabbing her friend.

But, as she tried to shadow walk, she felt a stabbing pain as if her head had hit a wall. Then, they both watched a glowing symbol appear on the trunk above. Selese looked at it, saying, as she held her head, "Wonderful."

Shrive looked to her friend. "What? You can't shadow walk?"

Selese shook her head. "We're locked in a steel box with a travel seal. I can't shadow walk out of here."

Shrive looked around. "I found the latch. We can climb out."

"It seems like we're going pretty fast. It probably wouldn't be a good idea to jump out at high speed. We're going to have to wait till they stop or slow down. Till then, I think we're along for the ride." Selese seemed to think. "Besides, I'm curious who kidnapped us. It seems like everyone's been trying to make us pay for something."

Shrive nodded. "So, we're waiting?"

"For a bit, but I think we should get out when we can. Till then, let's get comfortable."

Inside the car, Gina sat quietly. Mack spoke on the phone to his mistress as she reminded him of what Allison had told her about obeying commands. Gina had fulfilled her task but was still under contract. Although the witch was pleased with the return of the Sphere of Lieben, she warned both Mack and Gina about not returning quickly. Reminding her doll that she had no say in the actions the witch used her for, although, this was the first time Gina objected to Allison's commands. The witch also began to feel the effort it took to control her doll.

"Mack, when you return, have Gina come directly to my study. I feel I may need to make some adjustments." Mack heard over the phone as he relayed the order to Gina as she sat quietly in the back. The Sphere she procured belted securely in the front next to Mack.

Mack looked in the mirror and could see the sad expression on Gina's face, and her silence. He thought it was because of the actions Allison had her perform to abduct the two hunters now sealed in the trunk. He didn't know what his mistress planned for those two, but if she wanted them alive, he was sure it would probably be unpleasant.

A few hours passed; the only stop was to refuel. Shrive and Selese did consider escaping, but both wanted to know who had taken them. Since Shrive couldn't shadow walk, they would have to rely on Selese to port them out together. Neither knew where they were headed and if there would be any shadows available to use. So, for now, they decided to stay put. Both were hoping to find a better opportunity in the future. Thankfully they didn't have long to wait.

They felt the car slow, swaying as if riding a semi-paved road.

"Seems like we've left the main road," Selese said.

Shrive agreed and moved to open the latch for the trunk. She looked to Selese, who nodded in agreement. Shrive pulled the release pushing up, forcing the trunk open. Inside the car, Mack was vigilant, noticing the rear hood open. His reaction was to slam on the brakes, causing Selese and Shrive to impact the trunk lid hard. The impact knocked Selese out. But, as Mack accelerated to close the trunk, Shrive was only stunned and rolled out onto the dirt roadway. Selese fell back into the trunk as the back shut securely.

When the car stopped suddenly, Gina lurched forward, making her complain. Her remarks were stunted as Mack revved the engine, pushing Gina into her seat. The loud thump of the trunk lid closing made her turn to see one of the people she helped capture rolling on the ground.

"Mack, we have to stop," she yelled.

The driver knew otherwise. "That's not the one Allison wants."

Gina turned to see him staring back at her in the rearview mirror. She suddenly felt remorse for the actions Allison had made her do, "They're Hunters. They'll come after me."

Mack smiled, seeing the familiar stone pillars that marked the shield boundary, "Not to worry, my dear. That one was dropped off outside the barrier, this one we'll bring in. She won't be able to follow. Remember, no Hunters can cross the barrier."

* * *

Along the road, Shrive groaned as she tried to stand. Her landing was ungraceful after falling from the trunk dazed. She looked around to catch her bearings before searching for her phone. She sighed, "I never got it back before all this started, dammit." Shrive turned, heading into the sparse nearby trees along the road. "Where the hell am I?"

Shrive ran deeper into the trees. She touched her arm by habit when she approached the shadow of the tree only to have nothing happen. She felt stupid remembering that they had taken her element to shadow walk. Shrive growled, her anger and feral form causing it to sound more menacing, making several small animals flee around her. She watched the dust starting to settle from the car as it drove down the long roadway. Shrive changed to her feral form, then to that of a large cat. Her dark fur blended in with the shadows as she followed the trail, hopefully, to find Selese. Spying something along the roadway, Shrive decided to take a look. She cautiously walked over to the stone pillar by the edge of the wooded area. She could sense magic from it, but as she circled it, nothing happened.

Shrive turned to look down the roadway, "Guess it's my turn to get you out of trouble." Shrive then thought, *I hope those pillars are not some kind of alarm.*

Chapter 31:
Shapeshifter's Secret

Mack sent Gina to see Allison before grabbing the box with the sphere. He opened the trunk to see Selese unconscious, unceremoniously throwing her over his shoulder as he pulled her from the car. The two items seemed weightless as he carried them up the stairs toward Allison's office. Mack gave a humorous chuckle before kicking on her door.

"Delivery for the witch of the house," Mack said, waiting for his mistress to open the door.

Allison opened the door giving an amused glance mottled with annoyance. "Must you do things like that?"

Mack chuckled again as he carried Selese into her office and through the door to her spell room. "You sent me up there for this, and I brought back some souvenirs." Then, Mack turned, "One of these days, someone is going to catch you."

Allison smiled, tapping his nose. "They would have caught you and the girl. I was nowhere near there."

Mack's smile faded. "You're not worried I'd turn you in?"

"Perish the thought. Besides. . ." Allison brought her hand up, fingers outstretched. Mack fought to control his hand, which held the bracelet she gave him, from lifting. Her words were soft but confident. "I can stop you from doing anything. Whenever I want."

The witch closed her hand to examine her fingernails, releasing him.

"I control you. And you'd turn to dust the moment that chain broke. You're a wise old man, older than you should be, remember?"

Mack's eyes showed no defiance. "What do you want with the girl?"

Allison turned her head to look at Selese slumped in the chair where Mack had placed her. She sighed with happiness. "My little doll is starting to fight back; I think it's time for a new toy." Allison moved to lift Selese's face to look at her. "I'm not a fan of the dark hair, but she has such a special gift. That would make up for her shortcomings."

Mack growled, "Speaking of, where is your other doll?"

Allison motioned toward her office. "Sitting where she should be."

The witch said a few words, and Selese started to float above the chair. Within her spell room, the furniture moved to accommodate her actions. From another room, a bed rolled in, and Allison placed Selese onto it. She motioned toward the wall, the old books sliding out of the way as a metal collar flew from behind them—the item glancing off Mack's head before she caught it. The man leaned over in pain, and Allison mocked him, "Mack, you make being injured such a drama. You're nearly indestructible with that spell."

Mack groaned. "It still hurts, you know."

"I can take any sense of feeling away if you want." Allison's eyes turned cold, "Any sense. Understand?"

Mack stood straight, his eyes down to the floor, "Yes."

Allison said nothing as she pulled the item apart, splitting it into four identical collars. She used her magic to place them over Selese's wrists and ankles. Once set, they shrank, grasping onto her limbs tightly. The witch then held a small looking glass, its crystal lens glowing softly as she viewed through it. She ran the item across Selese's body.

"Hmm, I don't detect any elements or spells." Allison stood tall. "Some minor magic but nothing obvious."

"What are you looking for?" Mack asked.

Allison turned, a sinister smile across her lips. "Her secret to changing form at will." She turned to look at Selese again. "I watched her use it, so elegant, so fast, so easy. If I know how she does it, I can take it."

She looked to the door where the bed came from. She pointed, and the bed rolled away toward it with Selese, Allison following behind, but she stopped at the door.

"Take her to the MRI. I'll be in shortly." She ordered the bed before looking at Mack. "I suspect her ability is more a physical anomaly. I'll have to run some tests." Allison looked to the box containing the sphere. "I have what I need now. Once I find out how her abilities work, I'll not need my other doll. I'll need you to prepare additional transfer papers."

"But I've just filed the ones for Gina," Mack protested.

Allison paused, seeming to think. "Perhaps you're right. If my new toy doesn't survive, I'll still need my old one. Good thinking, Mack."

Mack nodded; he knew that meant Gina had outlived her usefulness. He had seen Allison do this before during his years of service, even having to dispose of the husks once she finished. But now he knew he'd have to deal with whichever body lasted the longest.

He huffed, looking to the door where Selese was sent. "You need me to set anything up?"

Allison shook her head. "My lab can work on its own. And certainly, more efficiently than you can."

Mack agreed, then looked toward the door, his eyes involuntarily drawn to movement at the window. Allison, catching his distraction, asked, "Are you alright?" He looked back at her before replying, "There were two of them. One fell out of the trunk before the shield."

Allison sighed quietly. "No Hunters can cross the boundary, you know that, Mack."

Her servant agreed as he walked toward the window. He heard her say, "I suspect the other was an anthromorph. Besides, she'll never get in if she's outside the shield."

Mack looked out into the yard, missing the silhouette of dark fur lithely pressing against the building beneath after jumping to the ground from the sill. He turned to look at Allison, his eyes filled with concern.

"Oh, for heaven's sake," Allison said, pushing him out of the way to open the window wide. "There is no one out there, Mack. Now, come on, I have a new doll to break."

"Don't you mean break in?" Mack said.

Allison said nothing, only returning a smile as she walked through the doorway, Mack following as commanded.

On the windowsill, a large, catlike shadow appeared. *Okay, Selese, let's see how we can get out of here together,* Shrive thought as she moved toward the open door where they had taken her friend.

She heard the witch say, "I have no other means, Mack. We'll have to rely on science to figure out how she can shift so quickly. We'll use the MRI I procured for my other experiments."

Shrive cautiously moved through the door to investigate. On the other side, she found a vast room. Its size was exponentially more significant than the Sanctuary. Along its border were smaller buildings. Some looked like shops and houses. Everything looked old but in good condition. Her mind wondered, *Is this an entire city?*

She moved quickly toward where she heard the two and, within a few strides, had caught up to them. She paused behind a potted plant crouching down to use it as cover. She could see them walking into what looked like a hospital, Shrive overhearing the man say, "I thought it was just that room you had back here."

She heard the woman laughing before responding, "Mack, do you remember that small city I took over about two hundred years ago?"

Shrive could see the man confused, and she took a chance to move closer. Shrive followed them through several rooms when she heard the woman say, "Good. No one was supposed to remember it. I've been stealing buildings, things, and even people when I needed them. This place is where I keep them all—my secret quiet place. No worries, no people unless I bring them, and no hunters can find it. I took it the last time I used the ring of *tianqius.*"

Shrive froze, her ears perking in attention, *she's been stealing the tianqiu. She's the one who framed me.* Shrive jumped onto a wall, and even larger than most house cats, she could walk it easily. She lay down to blend into the shadows as she continued to listen. She watched them place Selese into a large medical device. Shrive noticed Selese's body twitch as they moved her closer to the machine.

They paused, moving away as they loaded Selese onto the trolley that led inside the machine's opening. Shrive's cat eyes focused on Selese's breathing, and she didn't like what she saw. Concerned, Shrive jumped from her perch to move closer. The bright lights and sparseness of the room made it difficult for her to stay undercover. She moved as close as she could but remained hidden. Shrive watched as the woman pressed several controls, and then she heard a sound that caused her blood to freeze. Her eyes were wide, hearing the scream from Selese as she was lifted off the bed, her chest being pulled toward the top of the machine. Shrive could see the vacant look of terror and pain in her friend's eyes.

Shrive yelled, "Stop!" The man turned back, searching before the blaring sound of alarms drowned out her voice. The ground beneath the device suddenly sprouted rocks through the smooth, shining floor, the machine lurching to one side, and Selese fell back onto the bed. Shrive could only watch as the woman slammed the controls nearby.

"Mack! Why didn't you check her for metal before we put her in the machine?" The witch yelled.

"Me? I'm a lawyer, not a doctor. This is your toy. Why didn't you check?" The man shot back.

The witch raised her hand, about to discipline her servant but looked at Selese. There was almost a glimmer of pity as she moved to pull Selese from the machine. She held her hand to Selese's face and gently looked her over. "She's still alive. She's very resilient." The woman looked to the floor and the stones protruding through it. She looked at Selese again. "She caused this. I'm sure of it."

Shrive heard a weak moan from her friend and moved closer, readying to attack. The bright lights showed the fur now matted around her eyes. *I'm getting you out of here.*

Shrive rushed toward the witch, her claws extended and her feline form becoming larger and more human, but she was unprepared to feel the full force of Mack's arm across her throat. Shrive fell to the ground, gasping for breath as Mack locked his arms around her.

"I thought I heard a cat earlier." Then, he looked at Allison. "She must have come in through the window."

Shrive fought back, tearing at the man, her claws slicing deep, only to have the same injuries fade. Allison took one of the collars from Selese's leg and split it again. She replaced it before throwing it to her assistant.

"Collar her, Mack," Allison yelled.

Mack did as ordered and snapped the collar around Shrive's neck. Allison then grabbed one of the light stands and, with several words, transformed it into a long pole with a heavy base. She looked to her assistant, "Bring her here! This pining pole will hold her while we finish."

Shrive fought the entire time as Mack dragged her to the post. He pushed her with all of his strength against the metal. When she impacted, bands of metal unraveled from the stand, binding Shrive's hands and feet. It then pulled her back and lowered Shrive to her knees.

Allison took a breath. "Well, that was exciting." She turned to Mack, pointing to Selese. "Bring this one to the other room. I'll deal with our feline savior."

Mack rolled Selese into the next room as Allison looked down at Shrive. "Like your friend, you have been resilient, my dear. But, then again, most anthromorphs are."

The witch leaned down, Shrive yelling and growling. Allison could see the anger and fear in her captured pet. "You won't be able to transform with that collar. Why are you trying to save your friend?"

Shrive's eyes were defiant, her growl guttural as she looked into the witch's eyes. Her action brought amusement to her captor. "You were clever enough to get here. I could always use a good house cat."

Shrive continued to fight the bonds holding her as Allison stood. "Take her to my office, place her out across from my other doll. Maybe the sight will persuade Gina not to cross me as she has been trying to."

The steel base sprouted legs, making a metallic clanking as it walked toward Allison's office.

Shrive yelled, "Let her go."

The witch smiled before saying a few words—another piece of steel from the pole wrapped around Shrive's face, covering her mouth.

Allison walked toward the door of the next room. The witch's voice chilled as she said, "You think you have power in my house? Think again, little cat. It is good for you that I am more interested in your friend. Otherwise, I'd make myself a new coat."

Chapter 32:
Things are not Good

Linda and Amanda arrived where the truck was attacked. They could see the remaining Hunters looking around as they continued their investigation. Amanda watched as Luke climbed from inside what was left of the trailer. She grabbed Linda's arm, pulling her along as she rushed toward him.

"Luke! Have you seen Selese or Shrive recently?" Amanda asked.

He shook his head, climbing down from the wreckage. He stopped, hearing Ron complain, "It's a mess in there. It'll take days to figure out what they took."

Ron looked to Cale. "Tell your people to be careful. I wouldn't be surprised if there was a trap set for us in there." He looked toward Linda. "Probably waiting for someone to move the right item."

Linda agreed. "We have another problem."

They told Ron and Cale that Selese and Shrive had run after something in the forest but that they hadn't returned. Lord Cale was rightfully upset, but he still had a duty to make sure what remained of the shipment was made safe.

"I'll send some of the hunters to help find her," Lord Cale said.

Luke was willing, and Cale didn't dissuade him. But as they started to walk from the back of the wreckage, one of the Hunters fell, pulling at the door, causing it to shift. There was a chilling howl as the wind started spinning around the man. The air turned to a pillar and became darker before finally engulfing the Hunter. As it moved away, what remained of the man was only tattered clothing and a skeleton.

Cale needed a moment before yelling, "What is that? Everyone, pull back."

Behind her, Amanda heard a new voice, "It's a black wind. A spirit difficult to kill or contain."

Amanda turned to see Li Xiu walking toward them as she asked, "Black Wind?"

Cale watched the pillar of air moving slowly in a circle. His eyes remained focused on it, waiting for its next move. Then, finally, Li Xiu said, "Black wind spirits are elementals that can take the very breath from you and use anything it picks up to strip the flesh from your bones."

Lord Cale looked to Ron, "They're difficult to kill and contain?" Cale paused. "Can it engulf this entire area if it wants?"

Li Xiu nodded. "Right now, it's choosing where to strike."

Linda heard Cale growl lowly and knew he was thinking about his missing daughter. She looked to Li Xiu. "How do we stop it?"

The Silver Hunter looked at her blankly, "You need an air element, I think. I've never faced one."

The feeling of defeat was overbearing now for everyone. As the creature dashed toward them, Ron held his arms across himself. His fairy ring glowing brightly, and the creature bounced off the shield he created, stunning it.

"That hurt it, but I doubt you'll be able to contain it," Lord Cale said, looking toward the pillar of air retreating slightly.

Amanda asked Li Xiu, "Do you know anything about this thing?"

Li Xiu shook her head. "I've only seen pictures. I don't know if we can even kill it."

"Selese and Shrive are missing, and now this," Amanda growled, causing Lord Cale to look toward her.

The Hunters stood their ground, each shielding themselves as the creature attacked. All knew the elemental would continue until it was destroyed or captured.

"We have to find a way to stop that thing. We still have to find my daughter and Shrive," Cale said.

Cale's concern wasn't lost. They all knew the two were in danger. Cale, in frustration, yelled over the sound of the wind howling around them, "If we could only get rid of the damn thing?"

Hearing this, Amanda saw Ron deflect the creature back into the field, noticing his coat sleeve becoming tattered by the creature's fury. She could see the Amethyst gate, and she had an idea. She turned to Linda. "Can you make that gate go someplace really remote?"

Linda paused, processing what Amanda asked. "I think so. Why?

Amanda told her about her idea. "What if we use a gate and send it to the Antarctic or something?" She turned to Ron, "You mentioned that Linda could track you and pull you from a location if needed, right?

Linda looked at her puzzled before realizing that she had never told Amanda about the Amethyst gate and that she deduced that it was possible from her actions earlier. Linda turned to Ron, before looking back at Amanda. "You two go, search for Selese and yell if you find trouble." Amanda looked to the Hunters all around her. "I can help here."

Linda's eyes became more caring. "Go find Selese. I have a feeling she's in danger." Then, she looked at Li Xiu, "You're injured, but you can help Amanda." Amanda was about to speak when Linda moved closer, "Please, Amanda, you have to go. If something goes wrong here, you'll still be able to try and help Selese and Shrive."

Amanda felt her friend's words and agreed as she pulled Li Xiu to the side. "Where did you see them go?"

Li Xiu pointed, and she and Amanda disappeared into the forest.

Ron stood beside Linda. "One of us is going to have to go through the gate for it to follow."

Lord Cale approached. "Have you done this before?"

He watched them both shake their heads slowly. Then, finally, he heard Ron say, "We've never had to do it on purpose before."

* * *

Allison looked at the screens from the Xray, the dark blob in the center of Selese's chest. She seemed surprised, asking, "Is that a metal heart?"

Mack inspected the screen, "Diffraction analysis shows it to be elemental number seventy-nine. What is that?"

The witch smiled, looking back at Selese. "The dream of all alchemists, Mack. The dream of all alchemists."

Mack looked at her, his brow furrowed. "And that is?"

Allison smiled, reading Selese's vitals. "This woman has a precious heart, Mack. Our thief literally has a heart of gold."

Mack seemed confused. "So? She's a thief that does good things?"

Allison crossed her arms. "Something happened to her original heart, Mack. I think that was made for her." The witch moved closer. "And it's still beating. Oh, my word, Mack. This is a wonderful find."

The witch placed her hand over Selese and spoke magic words, the vitals on the screen improving. "I've healed her. At least some. I don't want her to die. At least not until I figure out why her heart is still beating." She looked back toward the room from earlier. "I'm sure she's a geomage."

"That explains the new stone floor," Mack said, bringing Allison to turn her head and glare at him before looking back at Selese, saying, "Hmmm, gold is malleable. I wonder if it's somehow combining with her essence?"

Allison looked to the sky with a delighted expression, "She is literally a thief with a golden heart. I must study her more." She turned to Mack. "Bring her to my office. I'm going to have a conversation with her feline friend. I must know where she got that beautiful heart."

* * *

Mack and Allison entered her office to see Shrive against the far wall. Allison turned to look at Gina sitting in a chair, her back straight and smiling.

"My dear, as you can see, this is what happens to those who challenge me," Allison said, seeing no reaction from Gina.

Mack waved his hand before her face. "What did you do?"

Allison happily explained how her doll just needed some convincing and an additional spell or two. Allison then touched her earring. "She won't resist me again. I've made sure of that."

Mack looked down at Shrive. "What are we doing with her?"

The witch looked toward her cat-like prisoner, annoyed. "Maybe she knows how the other got her heart." She looked to the spell room. "Bring that one in."

Mack immediately obeyed and rushed to retrieve Selese. As he wheeled the bed holding her, Allison pointed to a spot next to Gina. "Put her there. When she wakes, she'll see the same as my other doll. And perhaps they will all understand that they are now mine to do with as I please."

Selese's bed was placed next to Gina, the support attached to equipment behind. Mack was surprised to see his mistress caring about the shapeshifter in any sense. To him, she was dead weight and should have been removed. He had even thought about taking her heart for the gold it was made. However, he had no say in the witch's plans.

Allison walked over, shaking Selese gently to wake her, before holding her hand over Selese's head and speaking some magic words. Mack didn't understand them. His mistress's voice faded as if it was not spoken by someone but by something ethereal. He watched as Selese's vitals jumped.

"What did you do?" Mack asked.

The witch sighed, "I healed her. Well, mostly healed. I want her softened up a bit. If that cat doesn't tell me what I want, then perhaps her friend will."

"You can't torture her. She's still in pretty bad shape from the MRI. Probably some internal injuries," Mack noted.

Allison knelt before Shrive and grabbed her chin, forcibly removing the metal band covering her mouth before roughly pulling her face to meet her stare. "Where did she get her gold heart?"

Shrive remained silent, her cat eyes staring at the witch defiantly. Allison smiled before plucking one of Shrive's whiskers. Shrive twitched, howled in pain, her cat's eyes filling with tears, and she started to thrash around to move away from Allison. The witch reached back, and a small knife flew to her from her desk into her hand. Allison gently dragged it across Shrive's face, then to her side, where she pushed its point in her partially fur-covered arm. The tip drew a small amount of blood, making Shive whimper silently.

"Tell me how she got it! Or the next will be much deeper." Allison threatened. Her lips formed a smile of delight. She looked at the blade, "Your blood has a familiar scent. I wonder if your condition is one of my former accomplishments? Oh well, it doesn't matter. Tell me what you know."

Allison's stare turned cold as she again pushed the blade into Shrive's arm, causing her to yelp out in pain.

Selese stirred, hearing Shrive's cries, and drowsily opened her eyes to find her friend being tortured. Selese could feel the pain Shrive was enduring as she watched the woman grab hold of an area of fur on the side of Shrive's face near her ear. The witch pulled it, making Shrive cry out again, "Tell me where she got it!"

It took all of Selese's strength for her to speak, "Leave her alone. . . ." But unfortunately, Selese's voice faded quickly as the pain in her chest caused her to lose consciousness again.

Mack turned, hearing Selese speak, "She's awake." He looked more closely at Selese. "I think."

Allison rose, walking over slowly to see Selese again unconscious. Allison looked between her two new toys. "It seems this one actually cares about what happens to the furry one." She moved closer to Selese. "Are you awake, my dear? I have a few questions for you."

There was no response from Selese, making Allison look at the monitor behind her. "She is unconscious." She turned to look at Shrive. "It seems the howling of this one woke her. Perhaps we need to make things a little louder."

Mack stepped back; he had killed many in his very long life but watching his mistress torture these two now made him afraid.

Allison grabbed the fur on the side of Shrive's face and pulled with all her strength. Shrive cried out as clumps of fur were now in the witch's hand.

The pain caused Shrive to whimper, "Please stop. I'll tell you."

Selese's eyes opened as she again heard Shrive's cry. Mack heard Selese weakly say, "Stop hurting her."

Allison stood. "What did she say?"

"She said stop hurting her, I think," Mack answered.

Selese turned her head to the side and saw Gina sitting beside her. As she tried begging for help, her pleas were nothing more than whispers. Selese's eyes pleaded with Gina, and her heart sank, seeing that smile on Gina's face. And hope was starting to fade as a tear rolled from Gina's eye. Selese knew she, Shrive, and Gina were now in trouble.

Selese tried changing shape, but the bonds still held, their magic causing her to struggle, bringing Allison to her side, "Oh, you're awake."

Allison looked back at Shrive. "Our playtime is on hold, my cute fuzzy toy."

Allison leaned over Selese. "How did you get this beautiful heart?"

Selese tried to speak but was still weak from the injuries from the MRI. So her words were nothing more than a whisper. She then heard the witch say, "What was that, my dear? I can't hear you."

Shrive, fearing for Selese, yelled, "Aiden Hoff gave it to her after a wraith mage took hers."

The witch stood looking at Shrive. "That old geomage is dead, my dear. He couldn't have given her this heart."

Selese spoke as loudly as she could, her words no more than a hush, "He died after giving it to me."

Allison looked to her assistant, Mack, who looked puzzled at his mistress's reaction. His curiosity making him ask, "Do you know how he did it?"

The witch shook her head, "And he's dead. Unfortunately, I can't extract that information." She looked to Shrive, and a smile grew across her face. "It'll take time to reverse how her heart and abilities work. So, this one, she'll be spending some time with us. Who knows, maybe she'll be my next vessel? I have my sphere back." Allison looked to her wall where the Sphere of Lieben again resided. She turned, looking at Shrive, an expression of curiosity on the witch's face.

"This one may still have some use. Maybe she can tell me who the thief was that took it in the first place. They are Raven Hunters, after all. So, it couldn't have been her. But, on the other hand, maybe this one knows which shapeshifter did take my property."

She again crouched in front of Shrive. "Tell me, my dear do you know all of the Raven Hunters and who they have dealings with?"

Shrive said nothing, only looking away.

Allison smiled. "Oh, good, you do." She then produced the blade she held. "Then, my dear, you are going to tell me everything. I want the shapeshifter who stole from me."

Anyone can have a heart. Caring, warm, or apathetic. It is the latter that is most dangerous. An apathetic heart is one open to welcome the darkness in us all.

- Aiden Hoff

Chapter 33:
Friends in Need

Amanda's heart raced, not from running through the forest but from the worry about her friends. Li Xiu used her coins to find the direction they had gone and followed the trail quickly. When they arrived at the forest's edge, Li Xiu could no longer track them.

"The trail ends here. Whatever or whoever took them covered their tracks." Li Xiu noted.

Amanda looked around, her concern and frustration growing. They searched for evidence of any kind to the whereabouts of their friends but found nothing but tire tracks. Now, Amanda was sure that Selese and Shrive were in danger.

"Maybe we can find the same tires that made these tracks," Li Xiu said.

"There are dozens here. And we don't know which one took them. Or even if they were taken in a car," Amanda said.

They paused as they figured out their next move. Then Li Xiu thought about her interaction with her new friends and the once-thief with a heart of gold. That gave her an idea.

"I think I might be able to find her."

Amanda asked her how.

Li Xiu pointed to her heart, "Her golden heart, there can't be many of those around."

She held up one of her coins. Its inscription was of a finding element. Li Xiu held it to her eye, looking through the hole in the center, and images appeared. "I see one in the northern UK."

Amanda dismissed that since it would have taken too long to arrive, and she surmised that Li Xiu's magic would have detected a trail if they had shadow-walked.

"Where else?" Amanda asked.

Li Xiu continued, "I see one north of here. I can see a large house in the distance. Also, I see a gold glow, but...." Suddenly Li Xiu stopped and grabbed her head as if in pain. "I can't look through it. It hurts. It's protected by something."

Amanda consoled her. "You do have a concussion. But my guess is that someone is hiding something."

Li Xiu shook her head. "It hurts to look closer; something is protecting the house. I can't see any further than what's there. But I can see a location for us to shadow walk."

Amanda agreed, and within seconds they arrived near the mansion. "Look, there's an open window," Amanda said as she started toward the house. They were a short distance away. Li Xiu was several steps behind when Amanda stopped, noticing a bright glow from her fairy ring. Amanda turned, and the light was so bright that it escaped from around her collar. As Li Xiu moved toward her, the Hunter suddenly stopped as she ran face-first into a barrier.

Li Xiu placed her hands on the barrier pushing with all of her strength. However, she was still not able to move any further. Amanda joined her friend, waving her hand through where Li Xiu's hands were held in the air.

"There's nothing here." Amanda was perplexed and then remembered the same thing had happened to Ron and Linda. "I think we're going to need help," Amanda said. But she turned, only to hear a bloodcurdling cry from the mansion.

She pulled out her phone and dialed Linda's number. To her relief, her friend answered quickly.

"Linda, we need help. We found Shrive. I don't know about Selese yet. But Li Xiu can't get through some kind of barrier."

Linda could hear Shrive's scream through Amanda's phone.

Amanda turned her head to the sound, the hood of her fleece slapping against her face, "Hurry, it sounds like they are torturing her."

On the other end, Linda yelled into her phone, "Amanda, do not go in. Wait till we get there. I beg you do not go in. Wait for us."

Amanda yelled, "Bring everyone, Luke, Cale, whoever you can, and get here fast." There was another scream of pain from the mansion. Amanda hung up, looking at Li Xiu. "I'd rather you watch my back, but go back and bring anyone here, fast!" Amanda then turned to pause briefly before running toward the house.

Hearing Amanda hang up, Linda was shaking, "Ron! Amanda's in trouble!"

Ron ran over.

"Amanda is in trouble. She said someone was torturing Shrive."

"Dammit, can't she stay out of things for, oh, c'mon, we have to find her." He turned to look at all the Hunters around them, "Cale, Amanda found Shrive. They're in trouble. We need as many people as you can spare."

They quickly grabbed as many Hunters as they could, Raven and Silver, that were willing. The force grew. But for the moment, they didn't know where to go.

"Didn't she tell you where she was?" Cale argued.

Ron sighed. "Sometimes that girl doesn't think ahead." He turned to Linda. "She's reckless. That's why we stopped taking her on adventures. But…" Ron's voice became more caring, "She's still a good person. She just doesn't always think about the consequences."

Ron dialed Amanda's phone and waited. "She's not answering."

Linda spoke up, "you don't think—"

Ron shook his head. "She's probably heading into trouble and isn't picking up. Did she say she was with anybody?"

Linda thought for a moment. "She said Li Xiu couldn't get through some kind of barrier."

"You mean like a trap?" one of the Silver Hunters asked.

Linda shrugged. "No idea. She just kept telling me that someone was torturing Shrive." Linda's heart sank. Looking at Ron, she asked, "How do we find her?"

Ron growled. "I knew I shouldn't have argued about not putting a tracking spell on her. Roween even warned me about it."

Just then, Li Xiu appeared from the shadows. She ran over. "We need help. Now!"

Ron grabbed her. "Where are they?"

Li Xiu, out of breath, motioned for them to follow, and she grabbed Ron before shadow walking to the location. Ron looked around to get his bearings as he stepped from the shadows. He then tapped the stones on his bracelet, and Linda soon followed with several hunters.

Linda walked up. "Anything?"

Ron shook his head, "It's quiet. I don't see any sign of Amanda either." He motioned to follow as he started toward the house.

Several Hunters ran toward the house and suddenly stopped. Several were knocked to the ground, encountering the same barrier as Li Xiu. But as Ron and Linda walked right through, their rings fluttering and glowing. The two looked back. "You guys figure out how to get past that shield." Ron turned toward the house and then to Linda. "Looks like we're going in blind again."

Amanda had made it into the house. She searched carefully for Shrive, her ring allowing her to avoid several traps. *Someone doesn't like visitors.* Amanda paused, listening for any cries for help or from Shrive or Selese, but there was only silence. She placed her hand against a post only to hear it creak as she leaned against it. She lifted her hand quickly away; *I hope no one heard that.*

Allison looked to the door of her office, her eyes scanning the opening.

"Mack?"

Her assistant stood, saying, "She's passed out again. You should really go easier when torturing people. It'd be faster getting answers out of them."

Allison's eyes were ablaze. Her stare would have burned a hole through him if he wasn't indestructible. She looked at the door. "Did you check the house?"

Mack looked to the door. "No. I've been here with you the entire time."

Allison looked to Shrive, "Go look. The house just gave me a warning. We've another guest lurking about." She looked to her desk. "Take a blade from the drawer, just in case."

Mack touched the top drawer of Allison's desk, and it came alive, lurching at him. What looked like a large mouth full of metal teeth snapped down onto his arm, severing it. The man pulled back a grunt of pain as his arm quickly grew back. He looked to his mistress to see her smiling. All he heard was, "Oh good. The trap is still awake. Wrong drawer, you moron. Now, go and find out who else is here."

Within moments Mack was through the office door and into the hallway's darkness.

The witch looked at Shrive, "Let's see if we can draw out our intruder." Allison then took the small knife she held and plunged it deeply into Shrive's side, making her cry in pain. The blood from her endeavor covering her hands and arms. "That's right, my little kitten, scream for me. I want your friend to come running." She looked to her spell room. "I think I'll wait till Mack gets back to continue." She looked at the blood on her hands and arm. She reached up, motioning to her shelf the exact words she used to bring forth the collar. But nothing happened. "Don't tell me Mack never placed them back. Now I have to go get one." Allison then disappeared into her spell room.

Amanda searched and opened what looked like a small door, realizing it was an old laundry chute. "I don't want to go in there. Have no idea where that goes." She paused, hearing Shrive's cry, and looked down a dark hallway. "What is it with bad guys and dark corridors?" she muttered, only to have a man appear from the darkness, rushing toward her.

"There you are," Mack said, rushing toward Amanda.

She moved quickly out of his path and could feel his collision with the wall as the room shook. She expected him to be bloodied from the force, but as he turned, she saw he had no injuries. The man rushed her again, and she couldn't move fast enough this time. The man grabbed her wrist, his grip tight. She clawed at his hand, and she watched the scratches heal instantly.

"I'm immune to injury, girl."

Amanda heard that and realized something. She pulled back her arm, "Good. Then I don't have to hold back." Her fist landed a direct blow to his throat, causing the man to release her. The witch's assistant was unable to breathe for the moment, allowing Amanda to get away.

Stupid, stupid. Amanda realized she was in trouble and briefly glanced back to see the man had already recovered and was chasing her. Amanda went to turn into another room but slid, her body hitting the wall, the plaster giving way above the small door from earlier. *It's hollow. If it's a dumb waiter, then the whole thing is hollow.* Amanda remembered when Linda showed her some drawings of old houses with similar designs while they weren't chasing magical beings. Amanda's mind quickly made a plan. *If he's immune to injury, then I don't have to worry about killing him.*

Amanda continued to run and made her way around the rooms, checking to make sure the man was following. She heard him yell, "I'll bring you to my mistress. She'll use you like the others."

Not likely. Amanda thought and suddenly headed for the exact spot where that small door was. She slowed and taunted the man. "They'll arrest you for kidnapping and expose you when I get out of here."

Mack was becoming annoyed, his anger taking over, and he rushed toward her, yelling, "I'm immune to injury. I'll crush you."

Mack planned to throw his full weight against her, hopefully injuring her. But Amanda was waiting for exactly that. As he came a few steps away, Amanda dropped down, kicking one foot out, tripping him. The man hit the wall with his total weight and crashed through the plaster. He didn't fall, but he was off balance. Amanda took a chance, pulling his feet up, and as she felt his full weight, she released him. She heard him cursing, and it suddenly stopped as he hit the basement. She heard nothing over her own heart beating but turned to the dark hallway.

Amanda took a breath, muttering, "You better be there; I'm running out of ideas."

Chapter 34:
You Hurt My Friends

Amanda could see Shrive slumped over on her knees inside the office. There was a hospital bed to her right with what looked like legs. She cautiously moved closer to peer into the room and quickly scanned around the corner. She saw no one and quietly moved toward Shrive, her feet quick, then slid low across the floor. She started working on releasing Shrive, then looked down, her knees sitting in a pool of blood.

"My God, Shrive you're bleeding," Amanda muttered, then quickly pulled off her fleece top to place over her friend's wounds. The pressure made Shrive wince in pain. Shrive's eyes looked toward her and filled with tears, her voice quietly pleading, "Get us out of here."

The quiet whimper was tearing at Amanda. Then she heard Selese moan and stood quickly, only to see Selese trying to speak, but Amanda couldn't hear her. Instead, Amanda could see the glowing rings similar to the one around Shrive's neck holding Selese in place. Amanda also noticed Gina sitting with an unnatural smile on her face. She motioned for her to help, but Gina remained motionless in the chair.

Who is this witch? Amanda thought.

Amanda worked to free Shrive and was able to remove one of her bindings. The metal made a clanking sound as she moved to free Shrive's hands. As she worked, Amanda could see Shrive's cat ears face forward. She heard Shrive say, "Hide, she's coming back."

Amanda looked around; there was no place to hide in the office. Then she looked over and saw a small spot behind Selese's bed. It wasn't ideal, but she had no choice. Amanda moved as quickly as she could and tucked in behind the back of the bed. She crouched down, her blood-soaked pants cinching tight against her knees.

If I attack her, she may hurt Shrive or Selese. She then looked to see Gina's back and craned her neck to see her still smiling but now with streaks of tears running down her face. *I bet she's innocent,* Amanda thought as she heard the woman loudly talking as she walked into the room.

"Mack! Did you find the intruder yet?" The witch yelled. Amanda couched lower to see if she could tell where the woman was walking and could hear her footsteps moving toward the door.

"Mack?" Allison yelled again. She heard no response from her assistant.

The witch walked toward the bed. She could see the tears on Selese's face. Allison smiled. "You don't like me hurting your friend? Aw, you must really care about her." The witch moved closer. "Don't worry, you're both going to be here a very long time."

Allison stood, looking at Gina, then back to Selese. "I was going to use you, my dear. But I may have to change plans if I can figure out how this one's powers work."

The witch returned to Shrive and knelt. She again picked up the knife. But as Allison looked at her hands, the blood from her earlier torture of Shrive had started to dry. She smiled. "Well, it looks like I've got blood on my hands. Do you know the best way to get rid of it?"

Shrive said nothing.

Allison smiled, saying, "you get them wet again." This time the knife dragged deeply, cutting across Shrive's side. Shrive howled in pain, making tears stream from Selese's face. But as the tears rolled down, they drifted away from her cheek and toward her ankle. Selese watched as several drops from her and several from Gina floated down. Selese turned to see the smile on Gina's face but a stare of sadness and grief in her eyes. Selese returned her eyes to see the water enter the collar seam, and there was a loud sound of metal snapping. If Shrive weren't crying out, the witch would have heard it. Selese moved her leg, and the restraint slipped away from her ankle. Selese watched as the water moved to the other side, releasing her right leg.

They all heard Shrive cry out as the witch again asked, "Who stole the sphere from me?"

Shrive remained silent, knowing it was Selese, and she didn't want any harm to come to her friend. Selese was already in bad shape. Allison was becoming frustrated. "You are stubborn." She pressed on the wound she had just inflicted, and her hand hit something soft. Allison grabbed the item and held it up, unraveling a hooded cotton shirt.

Allison stood. "I know you're here. Show yourself."

Amanda stayed put, and Selese looked at the witch. The witch approached. "If you're not going to save this one, maybe you'll save the other. As the witch neared, Selese pulled her legs back to kick, the full force of her feet landing against the witch's face. Allison fell back, stunned. That moment of disorientation allowed Gina to break Allison's hold on her.

Gina rushed forward, a mixture of sadness, grief, and anger now focusing on her keeper. Gina pushed her back. Allison tumbled over her desk. But as she went to steady herself, her hands grabbed the trapped drawer causing it to open and bite down on her arms. But as with her magic, the witch was not harmed. Instead, the drawer bit down with enough force to trap her holding fast to the blood on her arms.

She tried to pull free. Her words were defiant, "You stupid thing. Oh, what was that release command?"

Amanda could hear her foe trapped and sprang from her hiding spot, rushing toward the witch. Allison turned, surprised to see her attack. "It's the FOF, oh, sh—" Allison's words ended as Amanda's fist contacted her face hard, causing the witch to slump down, her arms still trapped in the drawer. Gina stood, her eyes yelling obscenities toward her captor as Amanda went to help Selese. She tried to release her but was unable.

"Gina, I need your help. How do we get out of here?" Amanda pleaded.

Gina nodded, working as she did earlier to break Allison's restraints on Selese. Amanda worked to free Shrive and was startled to hear someone in the doorway, then relieved to see Ron standing there.

"We need to get them free," Amanda yelled.

Linda remarked as she entered, "Did you see the size of that hole in the wall?"

Amanda answered. "Yeah, the guy chasing me made it. He's down in the basement, I think."

Linda looked seriously toward Amanda. "Don't worry, he kept telling me he was immune to injury. I'm sure he's fine."

Ron rushed to help, seeing Gina working on releasing Selese. He went to help Amanda pull the bindings off Shrive. His eyes inspecting the wounds on the woman's side.

"Linda? We could use some healing over here," Ron said, his normal happy tone absent.

His wife rushed to check on Shrive's injuries. She looked at him shaking her head.

Amanda, concerned, asked what the problem was. Ron looked at her, "She's hurt bad. We're afraid that wound will open up if we pull her out of there, and she'll bleed to death. Amanda didn't know how to respond, but Ron looked at Linda. "You have any of those trauma packs left?"

Linda stood and worked to find the trauma pack to help Shrive. "Those are temporary, you know that."

Amanda asked, "What's a trauma pack?"

Ron looked at Amanda. "It stops bleeding. It's temporary. It also hurts like hell. I just want to stabilize her so we can move her."

Behind them, the witch's head twitched. And her eyes turned to face them.

Amanda was trying to understand why Ron knew what the pack felt like and didn't see the witch's eyes now full of rage. But as the witch opened her mouth, Gina stepped between them as the witch spoke.

The witch cast a sleep spell, and Gina took the brunt of it, falling to the ground, unconscious. Linda was ready nearby and punched the witch hard enough to make her head spin to the side.

"What the hell? I thought she was out cold from when I punched her," Amanda said.

Linda walked up to Amanda. "Next time, punch harder." Amanda could hear the warning in her friend's voice and watched as she knelt to check Gina.

She looked at Ron. "Sleep spell, she's out."

Ron looked to the door. "You said that the other one was immune to injury?"

Amanda confirmed what she said—making Ron look around. He

looked to see Selese in the bed. She was in bad shape, and Ron looked at Linda. "You grab her. Amanda, you grab your sleeping friend. I'll take Shrive."

Linda was about to argue but looked at him as he held out his hand. Then, she heard him say, "If that guy returns, there's no need for us all to get caught."

Linda agreed and handed him the trauma pack. "You stay right behind us, got it?"

Ron nodded as Linda lifted Selese from the bed and was amazed when Selese took a feeble step. Linda was shocked she was able to put some weight on her feet. Amanda had to sling Gina over her shoulder and groaned as she carried the woman toward the door.

Ron knelt. "Shrive, I'm going to remove your collar, but you're bleeding badly." He held up the trauma pack. "This'll stop it temporally. But it will hurt like hell when I put it on."

Ron pulled the collar apart and held onto her. He pulled her closer as he removed the covering on the pack exposing the material that made it effective. He held onto her telling her, "I know you're strong, but you can hold onto me, okay?"

Shrive's voice was a whisper as she put her arms around him. Ron quickly placed the pack over her wound, and his shoulder muffled Shrive's cry of pain. He felt her claws digging into his back. "Almost done. Stay with me, Shrive."

Shrive's muscles relaxed as she lost consciousness. Ron looked at her wound and saw the bleeding stopped, at least for the moment. He lifted her and quickly headed out the door.

* * *

Mack's eyes opened to see the dust on the floor. He shifted, feeling his shoulder behind him. He went to turn his head and noticed he was facing backward. He reached up, pulling his head around to face front again. He stood, his forearm bent in half and watched it again become straight, the knife held still in hand.

"Dammit! That girl got the best of me. Allison is going to kill me again," Mack muttered.

He then rushed up the stairs and saw the front door open and the witch's captives being carried away.

"No!" Mack yelled and rushed out after them.

241

He ran as fast as possible and caught up to the closest one. He lunged forward, knocking Ron and Shrive to the ground. The dust and black fur rolled away as Mack held the person he tackled. But he was surprised to feel the impact of Ron's elbow slamming across his jaw. He reeled back before placing it back from being dislocated.

He heard Ron complain, "Oh great, another immortal wannabe," before Ron's foot kicked him square in the chest. He watched the man look at the fur-covered creature and heard Ron yell, "Get up, Shrive, get out of here."

Mack watched as the woman struggled to her feet but couldn't stand and started crawling, blood dripping from her side. But Mack was ready for a fight and lunged forward with the knife he held aimed truly at Ron's throat. Ron held his own against the man and held the knife away, but the witch's assistant had the advantage. Then Ron noticed the gold chain on his wrist. *Immortality bracelet? I know how to kill this guy.* Ron used all of his strength and twisted the knife ever so slightly. Its tip digging into Mack's arm.

"You think that's going to kill me. I'm immune to injury," Mack growled with victory.

Ron grunted, pulling the blade as hard as he could under the gold chain, "I'm not aiming for your arm."

The blade sliced through Mack's wrist and the chain with one quick stroke. The pain caused the man to pull back, and Ron stood, running after Shrive, picking her up, and running as fast as he could toward the others waiting for them down the road.

Mack stood holding his wrist, the blood running from it. "It's not stopping?" He then looked to the ground and could see the gold bracelet, the link sliced through. He went to grab it, but his hand turned to dust as he was about to touch the gold. Mack's scream was nothing but wind as the rest of him followed.

Ron carried Shrive, and he felt relieved seeing the large group of hunters standing outside the shield. Amanda and Linda were almost to the barrier. He lifted Shrive from the ground, her feet no longer dragging behind him. "Hold on, Shrive, hold on."

Ron made it through the shield and handed Shrive to one of the hunters who worked to start healing her. Ron leaned forward, out of breath. He was relieved, feeling Linda's arms around him. They watched as Amanda helped the others with Selese and Shrive, even defending Gina as the witch's victim. He watched her look back to see them together. Amanda rushed over. "It's like old times."

Ron praised her before scolding her, "You did good, but next time wait for backup, like you're told. But, you still did good."

Amanda smiled as he pushed her shoulder. She looked to the house. "That witch is still up there. And they told me that they couldn't cross the barrier. Something about a covenant with her."

Cale approached after making sure Selese was stable. "She's right. We can't touch her. But she can't set foot near the Sanctuary or school either. And we can't bring her in as long as she's behind this barrier." He looked down. "I still don't know how you three got through."

Amanda held up her fairy ring. "Maybe this?"

Linda shook her head. "I don't think so."

Cale sighed. "I think Linda's right. I don't think it's your rings."

"Why?" Amanda asked.

Cale looked to Selese. "Selese stole the sphere of Lieben from her. That was the item taken from the Forge."

"So, this was a payback kidnapping?" Ron said.

Cale nodded.

Ron looked back, "And she's still alive back there. So, this isn't over yet."

He looked at Linda as Cale said, "We can't do a damn thing about her."

Amanda looked at the house. "We can. We can go in and get her. We're not Raven Hunters."

Ron smiled with pride but then looked to the house. "You said she can't step foot in the Sanctuary?"

Amanda spoke quickly, "Wait, the dungeons aren't part of the Sanctuary."

Ron turned, his brow raised in interest.

Amanda continued, "The Sanctuary surrounds the spot where the dungeons are. That's what Dr. Brentwood told me."

Cale nodded, then looked to Ron. He heard Ron say, "Amanda, why don't you make sure your friends are okay? We can wait to go back in there."

Amanda was going to protest, but she was worried about her friends. She looked back, and although she wanted to see the witch pay for her crimes, she decided to ensure her friends were safe first. Cale smiled, seeing Amanda rush over to help carry Shrive through the shadows. Then, he turned to Ron and Linda.

"Now what?"

Ron looked back to the house, then to Linda. "Looks like it's just us again."

Cale watched Linda nod. She held up her amethyst gate. "As long as she doesn't set foot in the Sanctuary? No one said anything about the dungeons."

Realizing what Amanda had said, Cale smiled before saying, "If you do this, we'll owe you."

Ron laughed. "We don't keep track. But you can do us a favor."

Cale yelled to them as they walked away, "What?"

Ron replied, "Have a cell ready and let us know where it is, would you?"

The leader of the Raven Hunters laughed as he entered the shadows, his voice tinted with a sense of satisfaction, "Give me a few minutes."

Chapter 35:
Her Real Name

Allison opened her eyes. The light dimmed and her vision blurred, causing her to reach out. Her hand caught a sliver of light. She shifted, her body ached, and she could see her hands now showing age. Out of habit, she reached up to touch the earrings she had worn. Her fingers suddenly searched for something that wasn't there. The witch's movements hadn't gone unnoticed, and the sliver of light suddenly darkened. She turned to see a shadow now covering the window of the iron door. Her eyes widened as she heard, "Are you looking for these?"

Suddenly there was light all around the witch, and she recognized the stone and metal that now surrounded her. She could see the dark eyes of Selese as she spoke, "I'm surprised you didn't look for a light switch, or maybe you like it in the dark."

"I'm in the Sanctuary dungeon? You can't hold me, the covenant—"

Selese's voice filled with resolve, "The Sanctuary is all around you. This area isn't a part of it. It never was."

The witch silently looked at the stone and steel walls. The small window was her only portal to the outside. She looked at her aging hands before lunging forward, grasping at the earrings that Selese held. The thief quickly stepped back as she tossed the stone earrings to the floor, stomping hard on them—the fragile stones fracturing to dust. All nearby heard the witch's gasp before she gripped the iron bars tightly. She looked up to see Gina standing next to another.

"Gina, my dear, get me out," Allison ordered.

Gina moved forward, her voice angry, "That's not my name." The witch caught the scent of the perfume Gina wore as she looked around. The witch focused on Shrive, who rushed forward, her hands covered in fur clutching over Allison's hands.

Her cat-like teeth were bared as she spoke, "You took away my freedom, causing them to take away what I was." Shrive extended a single claw, scraping it against the metal bar, its tip producing a fine, curled shaving as she drew it down toward Allison's hand. She stopped, releasing the woman, and allowing her to pull away from the door.

Allison moved forward after a moment. "The Raven Hunters couldn't have bought me here. So how did I get here?"

Selese looked to her right, where Linda, Ron, and Amanda stood. Her words filled with satisfaction, "Ask them. They brought you here."

Allison stared in disbelief. "You? The FOF's?"

Amanda stood tall. "Being a FOF isn't what you think. Hey, maybe—"

Ron interrupted. "No! We may not have a name for our little group, but we are not naming it that."

The group outside laughed, causing the witch to become angry. "When I get out of here, I'll hunt you all down."

Linda walked toward the door, "You keep excellent records of your spells and experiments. I don't think you have to worry about leaving here any time soon." Linda's voice became stern, "You are going to pay for the crimes you've committed, however long it takes."

As Linda walked away, the witch looked at Gina. "Gina, my dear release me."

Gina's voice was angry, "My name's Roslyn, Roslyn Elders. You took that name from me, made me forget."

Allison shifted back, hearing the anger in her former doll's words. She felt the sting as Roslyn said, "You left me everything. That servant of yours made sure things were filed in my real name." Roslyn moved closer. "I remember some of my past. I was homeless, a runaway. I broke in to find food and someplace warm. You did this to me." Roslyn paused. "I own everything that was yours. You gave it to me, remember?" Roslyn looked at the witch. "You were going to take my body, and where would that have left me?" Selese now moved beside her, reminding the witch that there was more than one way to steal a body from another. Roslyn stepped back, saying, "I'm going to give them access to the estate and use the money for good."

Allison stood in silence as they walked away from the door. But then Roslyn stopped, reaching into her pocket as she looked back at the witch. "Do you know that this is what helped release Shrive? The woman you had me torment and kidnap."

The witch looked at the small vial.

Roslyn walked closer, saying, "I will have to deal with what you did, what you made me do to them, to all the others before. But I can do one thing to make your life a little more pleasant." She then tossed the small vial of perfume through the cell door window. Its contents splattered across the floor as Roslyn turned and walked away.

The witch cursed and spoke magic words, but nothing happened. Ron stayed behind as the others walked down the hallway, his eyes steeled against the door. "I've run into some bad people since I started doing this. But most of them met the end of their run with me and her." Ron motioned toward Linda. "And I believe people should pay for crimes they commit, magic or otherwise. And it would be best if you spent the time thinking about what you've done. And if it was worth it."

The witch glared at him, but Ron smiled. "Without your powers and those cursed earrings, you may want to think about things quickly. It seems time may catch up with you sooner than later." Ron followed his wife as they walked off into the darkness of the hall, the sound of the witch's voice silenced by the dark as they exited the dungeon.

It was a few days later, as Roslyn sat at Allison's former desk, she groaned, seeing the mountain of papers that the lawyer placed before her.

"Your great aunt's lawyer was quite thorough. And I'm sorry for your loss. Especially after having someone so close be taken from you. And to have two in such a short time." The lawyer said as she sat in the chair across from Roslyn. The woman formerly known as Gina signed the papers as carefully as she could.

"I don't know why she started calling me Gina. She had the paperwork put in my real name. I think she may have had other problems," Roslyn said before looking up, causing the lawyer to turn and see Linda entering the room.

"It's good to see she had relatives able to help with this," the woman said.

Linda smiled. "We're not related. We were asked to come in to appraise some of the unusual artifacts Mrs. Thompson collected over the years. We were as surprised at her disappearance as her niece. That's why we contacted your firm, Ms. Estello."

"Call me Kara. We should have things finalized and filed in the next few weeks. I hope that doesn't interrupt your work."

Linda shook her head. "There's a lot to do. And now since, well, now our job has become much larger."

Kara looked around. "Yes, it seems Mrs. Thompson had some eclectic tastes."

Roslyn finished signing and handed the papers to Kara. She dutifully placed them in a binder and into her case. The professional manner of the woman was hard to ignore. She reached out her hand to Roslyn. "That should be everything. We'll notify you when everything is finalized." She looked to Linda, then back to Roslyn, "I'll be in touch."

Linda showed Kara out of the house while Roslyn walked over and stared out the window. It was only a minute before Linda returned, asking, "What do you plan to do with your new fortune?"

Roslyn was interrupted as the door to Allison's spell room opened. Ron exited holding some books and saying, "That place is huge. I think there's an entire city in there." They watched as Amanda nodded in agreement, and Selese followed but split away, looking at the Sphere of Lieben. She picked it up, placing it into a small cloth bag. Linda nodded in acknowledgment.

Ron placed the books on the witch's desk, "Do you know she kept records of all of the spells and her experiments?" He shook his head. "There is something seriously wrong with that woman." He looked to Roslyn, "I have no idea how to dispel that." He pointed to the door on the far wall of the former spell room.

They all watched as Roslyn returned to stare out the window, making Amanda ask, "Everything all right?"

Roslyn nodded. "There's a lake past those trees. I can feel it. It's deep and cold. It's like it's calling to me." She turned to look at Amanda with tears. "I'm so sorry for what I did to your friends. I didn't mean to. . . ."

Amanda hugged her. "We know. That was all that witch's doing."

Roslyn nodded. She looked at Linda. "You asked me what I was planning to do? Well. . ." she looked to the city within the small room's walls. "How big is that place?"

Ron shrugged. "No idea; we walked for a few hours. That place goes on for miles."

Roslyn was about to lean on the desk, but Amanda stopped her. She remembered that Allison had turned the drawer into a trap. She looked at Ron. "We may want to change the desk out, don't you think?"

Ron agreed. "After figuring out how to remove the barrier."

Roslyn leaned against the other end of the desk and heard Selese say, "What if we didn't?"

Linda looked curiously toward her. "You want to keep the barrier in place? Then the Raven hunters won't be able to come here."

Roslyn looked to Selese before saying, "You mean to keep the barrier, and what if we keep that city in there too?"

Selese nodded. "Some place like the Sanctuary, but not the Sanctuary. Someplace for those who aren't in school or want to hide from the world. Or, even from the Hunters because of what they are."

Roslyn walked to stand before the spell room door. "A city within these walls. A city for those like us. Hmm, I think that might be a good use of this place after all."

As she approached Roslyn, Linda looked on with approval. "That may be a lot of work."

Roslyn agreed, turning to Selese. "I could use some help."

Selese laughed. "I'll help some." She hugged Roslyn. "But I have some other exploits I want to pursue." Then, Selese seemed deep in thought, "But it would be nice to have a secret hideout, so people don't come after me so easily."

Roslyn laughed. "Well, you'll be welcome. You did face a lot of turmoil to help me."

Selese sighed. "Amanda is the one who figured out you were being controlled. But she had to convince everyone else that Shrive was innocent first."

Roslyn looked at Amanda. "I know you didn't want to accuse me. Shrive told me how difficult it was for you to find out I was the invisible thief."

Amanda shifted. "I was secretly hoping I was wrong, but when I figured out that you were probably being controlled, it became a little easier. And I'm glad I was right."

Roslyn smiled, then looked back at Selese. "You really think we could help people if we keep the city?"

Selese nodded. "From what I can tell, it's been there for quite some time. Some of those buildings are new, but there's a lot of older stuff in there. So it might work out for the best. And since neither myself nor Shrive are Raven Hunters, it might be a good place to crash once in a while. I mean, how many people know a twenty-four-year-old billionaire who owns a secret city in a closet?"

Amanda chimed in. "Speaking of which, we should probably find a better entrance. It would be awful to have everyone enter from this small room."

Selese laughed. "Did I just hear Amanda being practical?"

Ron followed, nodding with a smile.

Roslyn turned to see the smile on Selese's face. "I'm still not sure why you trusted me?"

Selese pointed to Amanda. "Because of her, she trusted you. And Amanda seems to find good people all around, magic or not."

Roslyn felt a little foolish. She didn't realize that Amanda had trusted her not to give her away while Allison hurt Shrive. And Selese knew that Roslyn helped release her, even willing to take the brunt of Allison's attack to save Amanda. But Roslyn looked at Selese. "You weren't always a thief, were you?"

Selese stepped forward. "I became a thief to survive, and so did you. I knew you were hiding something. And I knew because I had seen it before. You lost all of those memories, all of that time, all of that life you lived. I know what it's like to lose a part of yourself." Selese looked around, "We all have parts of ourselves that are hidden, some of us darker than others, but we still live life."

"Inspiring words," Linda said, placing her hand on Selese's shoulder.

Selese nodded. "You were the invisible thief that hurt Li Xiu and framed Shrive. But you also weren't that person. It was all that witch. You tried to help in the end. It's what you did when there were those harming others that matters."

Tears filled Roslyn's eyes, "You forgive me?"

Selese nodded.

Roslyn's words were studded with sobs as she said, "Anyone who can forgive like that after all of the things I did has to have a heart of gold."

Selese smiled, although a tear of happiness in her eye showed a glint of a devilish remark. Selese responded, "You're right, in more ways than one," before she lightly punched Roslyn's shoulder.

Amanda wiped her cheek, saying, "Too bad Shrive's not here."

Selese replied, "Well, she's getting a lot of apologies from the Silver and Raven Hunters. Let her get some payback in before we tell her about this place."

They all laughed, and when it quieted, Ron said, "Speaking of Shrive, I did find some information on her and other ailuranthropes. It seems that Thompson may have been the initial cause." He held up a tattered book. "There may even be enough in here to help undo it." Ron opened the book. "It may take a while. But we might be able to help." He held the pages away from his eyes. "It may take some time to figure out her codex, though. But, still, we might be able to help."

Selese looked at Ron. "You mean catgirl might not have to be a cat anymore?"

He nodded, then heard Selese say, "I'm not sure she's going to like that."

Ron smiled. "Well, we'll let her know about it anyway." He looked at Linda. "We should get these back and see what else we can find. Maybe figure out a better way to access that city in there. We'll get back to you as soon as we find something."

"You're going back to the Sanctuary?" Roslyn asked.

Ron shook his head. "Who said anything about the Sanctuary?"

Linda nodded, holding up the books he had taken from the witch's spell room. "Probably shouldn't tell anyone we have these yet."

Amanda nodded, looking at her friends. She sounded disappointed as she spoke. "Guess I have to go then."

Linda interjected, "Why don't you stay? You can always ask Selese to shadow walk you to our house." She leaned over, looking at Selese and

Roslyn. "Besides, I think someone should keep someone out of trouble."

Amanda stood proud. "I can do that."

Linda smiled as Ron grabbed Linda's hand, making them all laugh as he said, "She didn't say who needed to stay out of trouble."

The room lit a purple glow, and Ron and Linda faded from sight.

Chapter 36:
A City Within the Walls

A few hours later, Amanda and Selese could see the ornate door to Linda and Ron's home as they walked closer. Selese had shadow walked her to the closest tree, her complaint that her friends protected the house so well that even a darkling or thief couldn't get in. She chided Amanda and was going to join her when she heard her phone alert.

"It's Shrive. She's done with the formalities. She's asking what we found at the mansion," she told Amanda as she read the text.

"I wanted to see what they found first." Amanda sighed before she continued. "Why don't you show her the city? I'll see what Ron and Linda learned and meet up with you later."

Selese walked to the nearest shadow and vanished.

Amanda approached the door and stepped back as the mechanical bell that hung above rang as she was about to knock.

"That's new," Amanda said as the door opened on its own.

Inside, she turned to see Linda sitting at a desk in the office that was now attached.

"When did you remodel the house?" Amanda asked and was startled to hear Ron's voice on her right.

"Last year, guess you haven't been here in a while."

She looked around the room, the new furnishings and shelves full of books, old and new, behind glass doors. Amanda touched the glass of one of them, and the frame around it glowed. She turned to Linda, hoping to get an answer. Linda didn't disappoint her.

"They're all protected. You have to be given access to the cabinet." She walked over with a bit of pride in her voice. "Even skilled Raven Hunters couldn't get in."

Amanda nodded in approval, then said, "Like the Sanctuary."

Linda added, "In some ways, more so."

Ron proudly said, "With all of the enchantments that Roween and the others have done. If you're using magic, the house is impossible to find unless you know where it is."

Amanda looked around. "Hope no one figures out to look for everywhere but your house."

Ron looked to Linda. "Hmm, hadn't thought about that. It looks like we need to make another adjustment."

Amanda smiled at his remark, but that quickly faded. She looked around the room. The thoughts of her friends not including her in their other adventures still gnawed at her mind. She did understand that they were protecting her, but she wondered why they didn't trust her knowing.

Linda could almost feel the questions in Amanda's mind, and she said, "You feel a little left out, don't you?"

Amanda nodded. "I was with Selese and Roslyn, but they seemed to be able to use most of the things in that witch's office and the spell room. So not much happened when I picked something up."

Linda understood. She put her arm around Amanda. "That's just how things seem to work. It doesn't mean you are any less special." She paused. "I mean, you're friends with a fairy and pretty much all of the Raven Hunters, not to mention us. That's nothing to discount."

Amanda smiled. "Yeah, you're right. But it would be nice to have magic powers."

"Everything you've done so far has been without that luxury. And you've done some amazing things." Linda thought for a moment. "Although, it might make things interesting if you did."

Amanda seemed to look around, her eyes searching. "Speaking of fairies, where is she?"

Linda smiled. "You know her, many things to do. She'll probably show up later."

Amanda felt her words. It was good to have friends like these. She turned her head to see a fluffy gray cat run into the room. He jumped onto the desk and started meowing at Amanda, then looking at Linda and back to her. His tone something a mix of happiness and annoyance.

Amanda went to pick him up, but Jinx nudged her away and started meowing louder before he jumped on her to snuggle as she held him. She looked at Linda. "Why is Jinx acting like this?"

Linda said, "He's upset you didn't come to see him more. But he forgives you. He just wanted to tell you off a little."

Amanda chuckled. "You understand him. He seems to be more your cat now than mine."

Linda raised her brows, saying, "Oh, Jinx is your cat, alright. He never stopped."

Jinx made several meows and then snubbed Amanda. Linda took Jinx from her and stared into his eyes. Then, hearing him mew a few more times, she laughed.

"You are a naughty cat," Linda said as she handed him back to Amanda.

Amanda held him close, and he started to purr. "I wish I could understand him."

Linda smiled, "I thought you could. He's told me about your exploits since before I met Ron. Even one about when you and Gabs went to the neighbor's house to play video games when you told them you were studying. He remembered a boy named Jacob. I think he was there? Jinx helped you get in by opening the inside window?"

Amanda looked embarrassed, then looked at Linda. "Wait! You can talk to Jinx?"

Linda nodded. "I have been able for about a year now. I'm surprised you didn't know he could talk. He's always talking to you."

"Wait, when did you learn that?" Amanda asked.

Linda thought for a moment, "I learned it in London, near a place called Scrapply's. There was an enchanted rabbit statue eating people's gardens."

Amanda was dumbfounded. "I don't remember that. How come I wasn't there?

"You were in Hawaii with your family. We had to leave Jinx with Roween when we went. That was also where we found Tassam." Ron's voice became cold when he mentioned that name.

"Tassam?" Amanda asked.

Linda turned away, her gaze filled with sorrow. "Yes, it's how we knew what happened to Selese."

"What? Did you see them do it?" Amanda asked.

Ron shook his head, saying, "No, it was something, uh, similar. We, I had to intervene."

Amanda looked dejected. "You should have called. I could have helped. Why did you go on that adventure without me?"

Ron became stoic. "We've had several dozen, actually."

Amanda stood in disbelief.

"Amanda, there was a reason we haven't pushed you to join the Hunters. It's a lifelong commitment. "

Amanda retorted, "That's my choice."

Linda agreed. "Yes. But there are things we have seen that. . . ." Linda's voice faded as she thought. "You're too young to be burdened with things like that."

They could see Amanda was upset, and Ron stepped in. "Amanda, what I saw, I—" Ron hesitated as he fought back regret. "I wish I could have stopped what happened earlier. But, what I saw, that's something you shouldn't be burdened with."

"That's not fair. It's my life," Amanda protested.

"Yes, it is, but time gives temperance. You're too young, for the moment at least." Ron says, seeing Amanda about to speak, he interrupted her. "But, when the time is right, I know, we know, you'll face that burden head on." Ron sighed. "For now, enjoy things, Amanda. Trust us on this, okay?"

Linda continued, "I know you think we betrayed you, but we care about you. When we went without you, it was to protect you. Like we protected your family." Linda told Amanda about how her family's house and her parents are covered by enchantments and what they had done so far to dissuade the Feather from acting against her and them.

Several hours had passed, and Amanda finally understood that her friends had done what they thought was right. Even if she disagreed, their conversation eventually returned to the notebooks they had taken from Allison Thompson's spell room and the city.

"We did find an entrance on the lower level. The small carriage house was the entrance before the main house was built," Linda told her. "That witch kept detailed notes." She showed a copy of the page to Amanda on her phone. "We just have to find the other doors."

Amanda quickly pulled out her sketchbook and started drawing, making Linda laugh.

"I'll send you a copy. Maybe you could help the others figure out how to open it for everyone," she said as she tapped on her phone.

Amanda looked at her phone, saw the message, and looked at Ron seeing him holding the other book he mentioned. "What about Shrive?"

Ron was about to put the books onto the shelf, but he pulled back. "You know this witch's shorthand is hard to decipher." Then, he turned to Linda. "Maybe we should let the Circle handle this?"

Amanda looked at Ron. "You're giving up. It's only been a few hours."

Linda shook her head, showing Amanda her phone. "We made a copy. Honestly, we don't want the Circle knocking on our door when they figure out we have something from that mansion."

Linda looked to Amanda. "Maybe someone they trust should bring it back to them?"

Amanda snuggled Jinx before saying, "They trust you too, you know."

Ron smiled. "Yeah, but maybe it's better if you bring this in. It'll make you look like you convinced us to do the right thing."

Amanda glared, confused, at Ron. "But you do the right thing. Don't you?"

Ron smiled. "Most of the time, heh."

Linda smiled. Looking down, she said, "We do what we think is right. Mostly it works out."

Amanda held her cat, turning him to face her. "What ya think, Jinx? Should I take the books in?"

Jinx purred the gave a couple of meows, making her look at Ron, who responded, "Don't look at me. I can't understand a word he says." Then, he looked at Linda, "What'd he say?"

Linda looked embarrassed, then said, "Well, I won't repeat what he said exactly. And honestly, Jinx, you should clean up your language. He said, 'screw them'."

Amanda laughed, hearing a very satisfied purr from her cat, and she snuggled him, saying, "You are a naughty cat."

Jinx then started to wriggle out of her grasp and hopped to the desk, where he sat straight, looking at Amanda. He gave a few more meows and then looked at Linda.

Linda nodded. "Well, he thinks maybe you should give them the books." Jinx then meowed again, and Linda told them, "And he thinks you should complain that they don't allow pets. And they should do something about it. And if they don't, you should visit more often."

Amanda moved closer. "I should visit you more. I miss you too, you naughty cat."

Jinx nuzzled her back and then walked off the desk. He rounded the corner, seeming to chase something in the dark. Linda said, "I hope he's not after the brownies again. That was a misunderstanding that had to be cleared up."

Ron nodded. "Yeah, we had to bring in Roween and a bunch of other magical beings to settle things down." He then looked at Amanda holding the books up. "Maybe we should head back and drop these off."

Amanda agreed, and they all disappeared in a flash of purple light.

* * *

They arrived outside the administration office, appearing from the small door between buildings. Ron mentioned that it was good they could still use the shadows to cover any entrance they could provide. Although it did seem strange to some to see people appear from the darkness, it seemed only to be a concern to those new to campus.

They headed to Dr. Brentwood's office, and Amanda handed her the books Ron and Linda had taken from the witch's spell room. Ron apologized, telling her they had hoped to help Shrive if possible. The doctor understood, telling them that they would start working on things as soon as they had enough hunters well enough to do so. The doctor informed them that the attack had shown a weakness still within their ranks. And that after the first defeat at the hands of Dennon Fierst and the Feather, they still had things to secure.

"Do you think you can help Shrive?" Amanda asked.

Dr. Brentwood nodded. "Given time, perhaps. But that may be up to her." Linda noticed the doctor look at her palm after she spoke.

"Amanda, you helped Shrive and Gina, I mean Roslyn, a lot, not to mention my daughter. I never thanked you for that," the doctor said, her voice filled with subtle happiness.

"They're my friends. I'd do it for anyone who needed help. Especially them," Amanda told her.

The doctor looked at her, more disciplinary as she spoke, "Those two went through a lot. And you put yourself in danger without waiting for help. You should have waited."

Amanda was about to say something, then looked to her friends; she knew Dr. Brentwood was right. She was reckless and was beginning to understand why Ron and Linda had started some adventures without her. Nevertheless, she stayed silent, only lifting her head to acknowledge the doctor.

Dr. Brentwood took a breath and briefly glanced at her hand again before returning to Amanda. Her eyes were caring as she said, "Thank you for returning everyone, including yourself, alive."

Amanda felt the tears forming in her eyes as she looked at the doctor. She said nothing as she looked at her friends. Dr. Bentwood looked again at her palm and then to the desk. Her actions prompting Linda to say, "Hey Amanda, maybe you should go see Shrive and Selese. Have some fun celebrating. Maybe tell Shrive what we found."

Amanda nodded but was hesitant as she stood. She became concerned about her friends and the books she had just brought.

Ron allayed any fears she had. "It's okay, Amanda. We wanted to talk to the doctor about what we had found and about the city. We can do that while you're having fun."

She started toward the door. The doctor followed her, and Amanda looked back one last time. "I'll be back to see Jinx in a few days, okay?"

Linda nodded. "We'll expect you."

They all watched as Amanda left and the doctor closed her door.

Doctor Brentwood stood at the door and said, "I understand that

Roslyn is considering not removing the barrier."

Ron acknowledged, telling her, "It won't be a part of the Sanctuary, or the Circle for that matter."

As Ron spoke, the doctor remained silent. "We don't always have to agree with the Raven Hunters. This might be a good thing."

The doctor leaned against the door as if burdened. Ron spoke first. "We never did thank you properly for saving her and her family while they were in Hawaii. Or those other times."

The doctor walked graciously back to her chair. Her eyes were more concerned as she nodded. "It took over seventy hunters to take the Feather down in Hawaii. They would have killed her and her family." She looked relieved. "I take it the enchantments you and your little friend placed have been enacted effectively?"

"They're protected as are we when it comes to the Feather and most other threats. So you don't have to worry about that." Linda paused. "But I think there is something you should be telling us."

The doctor remained reserved, her eyes looking repentant.

Linda sighed, saying, "The Circle still wants her to join, doesn't it?"

Ron looked at Linda. "What?"

Linda leaned forward. "I watched you look at your hand. That's how the Circle communicates, isn't it?"

The doctor looked sternly toward Linda as she nodded. "Yes, it's always in contact with me."

Linda nodded. "It's part of the *Key of Spirit*?"

The doctor nodded.

"You still haven't answered my question. Does the Circle still want Amanda to become a part of it?" Linda asked.

Dr. Brentwood's voice was cold as she answered, "Yes." She paused. "With all of the recent happenings, it is concerned that Lord Cale and I can no longer protect this facility."

Linda looked to Ron. "The Circle knows all, does it?"

The doctor looked up, her eyes filled with fear as she heard the silent words of the Circle. Linda didn't need to know what it said. But she did know what to say.

"That's exactly why the mansion should be separate. We can help them make the barrier stronger. That way, the Feather or any others looking to harm anyone can't enter. It would be a safe place for everyone."

Dr. Brentwood looked at them both. "The Circle thinks that is a foolish decision. Adding the Mansion to the Sanctuary would increase its ability to protect."

Ron spoke, his voice carrying a warning. "That's exactly why it shouldn't be a part of the Circle. If Sanctuary were to fall, then where would anyone go?"

Dr. Brentwood sat straight, comprehending his remark, looked at her palm, and heard silence. Then, finally, she looked back at Ron to see a stare of victory.

"I bet it doesn't disagree with that logic. Does it?"

The doctor shook her head. "No, I don't think it does."

Ron leaned forward, "The Circle has been running things for thousands of years. And so far, it's done a good job protecting everyone. But The Feather and those like them have gained followers and are beginning to move more quickly. Regardless of if the Circle thinks it needs someone like Amanda or anyone."

Ron looked at Linda, seeing her agree.

"We don't always agree with the Circle. But what does it have to lose by allowing us, or for that matter, Amanda, the chance to do something other than what the Circle wants?"

Dr. Brentwood smiled, not hearing the voice of the Circle in her mind. But, in a way, she agreed with Ron and Linda. The Circle had warned her about allowing these two to roam free; so far, they had protected more than the Circle had predicted. But, there was one thing the Circle insisted on: Amanda needed to join the Raven Hunters.

The doctor understood the responsibilities of being a Hunter. But she never disclosed why it requested Amanda to be a part of it. There had been others, even younger, who joined. But why Amanda? That question stayed in her mind as she remembered. She never told anyone, even her husband, that the Circle had demanded Selese take over when she could. Dr. Brentwood disobeyed that order, worried about her daughter. The Circle even demanded her imprisonment because she refused to respond to its decree. Now, with the secret city on its own, the Circle would have no control over things there. That made the situation for her and the Raven Hunters uncertain.

"We have followed the orders of the Circle for centuries. It has been our voice and guiding principle. We cannot turn away from it," Dr. Brentwood said.

Linda nodded. "You don't have to follow orders blindly."

The doctor sighed heavily before saying, "I don't. I have disagreed with the Circle many times. But, unfortunately, it is becoming less tolerant of my doing so."

Linda's expression became concerned. "And what would Amanda have to do?"

Dr. Brentwood sighed, saying, "She would have to join the Raven Hunters and have access to the magic that the Circle offers."

"The same magic that the Feather and others use?" Ron asked.

The Doctor nodded. "She doesn't have any magic of her own."

"So, how would she gain access to that magic?" Linda asked.

Dr. Brentwood smiled. "The same way I did. She'd have to become a scroll witch."

Ron and Linda looked at each other. They knew one thing that the Circle didn't. Amanda had proven to have a strong will, it may not have been magic, but it was power. She walked alone during recent fights, with enough willpower to guide herself and save her friends. Amanda now also understood why they had excluded her from some of their encounters. Ron and Linda had hoped to protect her until she was ready. Now with the city within the walls kept separate from the Circle and the Raven hunters, there was one thing for sure. The Circle still wanted Amanda, but now they hoped she had a choice. She always wanted magic of her own, but would Amanda use the Circle, like the doctor, or would she find her own way and stand with the others?

Other Books in This Series

What happens when a former factory worker, turned ghost hunter saves a young girl injured in the forest? Something magical, what else? Enjoy the adventures that brought Amanda, Ron, and Linda together in the original story.

A Fairy's Light

What is a good deed worth? Well, maybe you should ask a fairy, what could go wrong?

Also check out

The Raven Hunters

It's seven years after their first adventure, and Amanda is about to discover that the world has more magic than she ever expected.

For more stories and books please visit:

www.wolfhammer.com

ABOUT THE AUTHOR

Stephen's career has taken him to many places allowing him to explore work in technology, engineering, and sales spanning over 30 years. He has been writing science fiction and fantasy for far longer—his work primarily for role-playing and personally, using his knowledge and imagination within his life. He is always known to have a story to tell and is usually sprinkled with a hint of adventure. Stephen decided to present his stories for all to see. And through his character's eyes, you find that life can be an adventure and that life can be better with a bit of magic.

www.ingramcontent.com/pod-product-compliance
Lightning Source LLC
Chambersburg PA
CBHW060535260626
47161CB00003B/913